Praise for Anyone But Ivy Pocket

'Miss Pocket was a maid at Midwinter Hall for eleven months,
three days and twenty-seven minutes. In that time we lost
five priceless vases, four cats, two butlers, a great aunt
and half a governess. Lock her up!'
Lady Patricia Midwinter

'A beast! If she tries to serve you soup, run for your life!'
Countess Carbunkle, Ivy's former mistress

'She said I wasn't half as stupid as I looked'
Mr Edmund Potts, train conductor who helped Ivy with her bags

'I had never seen a genuine countess drowning in a bowl of
fruit punch ... until Ivy Pocket came to stay at my hotel.
She is banned for life!'
Monsieur Gateau, manager of The Grand Hotel, Paris

'Who knew a twelve-year-old girl could cause
so much mayhem? She means well,
but I fear she's barking mad'
Mrs Vans, housekeeper

'My nerves are shot. I wake in the night screaming her name.
Please, do not tell her where I live!'
Ivy's guardian angel

'I think Ivy Pocket is perfectly lovely. And frightfully smart.
A girl without equal, really ...'
Ivy Pocket, junior lady's maid

ANYONE BUT IVY POCKET

Caleb Krisp

Illustrated by John Kelly

BLOOMSBURY

LONDON OXFORD NEW YORK NEW DELHI SYDNEY

Bloomsbury Publishing, London, Oxford, New York, New Delhi and Sydney

First published in Great Britain in April 2015 by Bloomsbury Publishing Plc
50 Bedford Square, London WC1B 3DP

This paperback edition published in January 2016

www.bloomsbury.com

Bloomsbury is a registered trademark of Bloomsbury Publishing Plc

A CIP catalogue record for this book is available from the British Library

ISBN 978 1 4088 5864 6

Typeset by RefineCatch Limited, Bungay, Suffolk
Printed and bound in Great Britain by CPI Group (UK) Ltd, Croydon CR0 4YY

1 3 5 7 9 10 8 6 4 2

For my housekeeper, Mrs Cuttlefish,
who I buried in the garden

Chapter 1

I found the note upon my lady's bed.

It read as follows:

Dear Miss Pocket,

As you can see, I have gone. Do not follow me. I repeat, DO NOT follow me!

I am sailing for South America for no other reason than it is far enough away from Paris to ensure that I never see you again. The hotel bill has been paid. As for your wages, after taking into account my pain and suffering, I have left you the sum of one pound. Which is generous, given your conduct. You are now on your own.

Good riddance,

Countess Carbunkle

I was stunned. Shocked. Appalled. Hadn't I been a loyal and kind maid to the Countess? *Hadn't I?* I thought long and hard about my conduct and I could find nothing wanting in it. If I needed further proof that Countess Carbunkle was unhinged, I now had it. The woman was bonkers.

Things had begun so promisingly. Countess Carbunkle had lured me away from a wonderful family in London. The Midwinters were delightfully eccentric and I had been very happy with them – until the Countess came to stay at Midwinter Hall. She spent a month at the mansion and saw me performing my duties, bringing order and cheer wherever I went. On the eve of her return to Paris she practically *begged* me to come and work for her.

In truth, I was reluctant to leave Lady Prudence and her six children. I admit they were an ugly bunch (Master Tobias had a head like a piglet and Miss Lucy was surely part bullfrog), but Midwinter Hall was the first real home I'd ever known.

Despite that, the chance to travel and see the world was impossible to resist.

Paris. We were in Paris. It was glorious and I was glorious in it. I was taller in Paris. Prettier too. And as I was a twelve-year-old lady's maid of the highest quality, Countess Carbunkle came to depend on me in all matters. I was always by her side, day and night, ready to be of service.

At times she was very difficult to find. One morning I found her crouching behind a chest of drawers with a sheet over her head. Another time she saw me coming and pretended to be a lamp. I put this odd behaviour down to the fact that Countess Carbunkle was an aristocrat and therefore barking mad.

Just how unhinged she was didn't become clear until the great disaster.

It was at the end of our first week in that magical city. Countess Carbunkle had been invited to a grand dinner party at our hotel. The cream of French society was to be in attendance. At first, Countess Carbunkle had been reluctant to let me attend.

'I don't want you at this dinner, do you hear?' she barked, trying to push me out of the lift. 'Good lord, how did I ever let Lady Prudence talk me into taking you? She knew I needed a new maid and like a devil, she saw her chance to be rid of you. Anyone, that's what I told her, *anyone* but Ivy Pocket. But she swore you weren't nearly as insufferable as you look. What a fool I am!'

'Well, of course you are,' I said, weaving around her and slipping back into the lift. 'But you must think clearly, Countess. This dinner party is a very great affair and you are as blind as a bat. Face it, dear – you *need* me.'

Countess Carbunkle huffed, but I could see the fight had gone out of her. 'Do not embarrass me or I will have your head.'

The dining room was aglow with silver candelabras and hundreds of fresh orchids. Dinner began in earnest. Countess

Carbunkle was seated between the president of France (fat, utterly bald) and a princess from Romania (short, hairy chin). But I was troubled. It was on account of the turtle soup. The Countess did not handle soup at all well. She tended to dribble.

I stepped forward as my lady took her first spoonful. She slurped like a blowhole, and a trail of soup tracked its way down her chin. With heartbreaking discretion, I hurried to Countess Carbunkle's side, gently tilted back her head, and used the hem of my apron to wipe her chin.

'Are you all right, Countess?' asked the president, with a mocking grin. 'You seem to be having some trouble with your servant.'

'All is well, Mr President,' cried the Countess, smiling madly. Then she turned to me, slapping my hands away. 'Go!' she whispered. 'Leave this instant!'

'Calm yourself, dear,' I said. 'Dribbling is no crime. I'm sure your mother was a dribbler and your father too.'

While Countess Carbunkle's watery green eyes glistened with rage, I could see the anguish behind them. My lady was in desperate need of help.

'Attention, please,' I said, placing a supportive arm around my mistress. 'Like many true aristocrats, the Countess has a drooping bottom lip and no real chin to speak of. This makes eating soup both difficult to achieve and unpleasant to behold.'

The Countess gasped. Her teeth clenched. Her nostrils flared like a charging bull. Then she started to growl at me. Surely not a good sign. 'I have had a great many maids in my long life, Ivy Pocket, but until now I have never wanted to stuff one in a cannon, point it towards the ocean and light the fuse! In short, I loathe you!'

The poor dear had lost her mind. Urgent action was required. With lightning speed – for I have all the natural instincts of a physician – I grabbed the Countess by the back of her neck and plunged her face into the fruit punch. It was the only remedy to relieve her brain fever.

As Countess Carbunkle came up for air, she shrieked like a donkey and started to sob. I took that as a good sign. Not wishing to make a spectacle of the Countess, I threw a napkin over her head and began to dry her face. In response, my lady called me a variety of unpleasant names and begged the princess from Romania to fetch a musket and shoot me.

In no time the entire dining room was ringing with mocking laughter. It was really rather awkward. The moment was saved by Countess Carbunkle, who decided that was the perfect time to run screaming from the room. Which allowed me to make a dignified exit, following swiftly after her.

When I got back to her suite, I found the Countess's door locked. I knocked, of course. Called out. Banged rather loudly.

But nothing. That night I slept out in the corridor. It was perfectly comfortable. So comfortable, in fact, that I did not wake until well after sunrise. Worse still, I awoke to find Countess Carbunkle had fled the hotel in the early hours of the morning. Her suite was empty. All that remained was the note upon the bed.

I collected my carpet bag from the wardrobe and sat down by the window. The situation was rather serious. My options, rather limited. I had one pound to my name. No job. No ticket back to England. No prospects.

I am remarkably good in a crisis – for I have all the natural instincts of a wartime prime minister – so in no time at all I knew what to do. I picked up my carpet bag and headed down to the lobby, replacing my anxiety with the flickering flame of hope. The streets of Paris were sure to lead to adventure and opportunity. No doubt I would stumble upon something utterly thrilling. Or I might end up a beggar, friendless and starving. Which would be terribly inconvenient. But on the bright side – how wonderfully tragic!

The lobby was a hive of activity. People coming and going and rushing about. I stopped for a moment to drink it all in.

Which is when it hit me. The answer to my problem was staring me in the face. A hotel like this was full of Englishmen and women – and who better to wait upon them than a genuine English maid? I would speak to the manager of the Grand and apply for a position.

He was sure to love me.

'We have no vacancies,' said Mr Gateau firmly, scratching at his thin moustache. 'Besides, you are too young.'

'I am twelve,' I declared with considerable pride, 'and you will not find a better maid in all of Paris. My talents are legendary.'

Mr Gateau smiled thinly. 'Yes, I have heard all about your *talents*. Countess Carbunkle had much to say about you before she left the hotel.'

'Well, there you go,' I said, slapping Mr Gateau on the arm to cement our budding friendship. 'When can I start?'

'Out!' he bellowed.

An ill-mannered doorman was escorting me from the hotel when a bellboy raced across the lobby and called me back. The poor chap was rather breathless. 'Are you Ivy Pocket?'

'Of course I am, dear.'

'The maid who was travelling with Countess Carbunkle?'

I was thrilled that he had heard of me. But not surprised. A good maid gets a reputation. 'That's right,' I said.

'She wants to see you,' said the boy gravely.

I gasped. 'Countess Carbunkle? Is she still here?'

The bellboy shook his head. 'The Duchess of Trinity. You've heard of her?'

Well, of *course* I had. My lady had called on the Duchess just the day before – slipping away from me rather sneakily – to pay a visit to her private apartment on the top floor. Countess Carbunkle said her old friend was the richest woman in England, though she had lived abroad for the past sixty years. Not sure why exactly. Something about a broken heart.

'What on earth does she want with me?' I said.

The bellboy looked alarmingly pale. 'She is dying. Please, just come.'

The next thing I knew we were hurrying up the grand staircase.

When I first set eyes on the Duchess of Trinity two things were immediately clear. One, she was gravely ill. Two, she was monumentally fat. A great big slug of a woman – part goddess, part hippopotamus. She was as magnificent as she was terrifying. The poor creature was lying in the centre of a large brass bed, her face a sickly shade of yellow, her enormous body spread out

8

on every side like an avalanche. The Duchess's eyes were shut, her head sunk deep into a pile of silk cushions. I might have thought her dead if it hadn't been for the wheezing breaths escaping from her grey lips.

I shivered. Which was shameful. Why was I feeling so spooked by a sick old lady? I was no coward. In fact, my bravery was celebrated across the land. Hadn't I saved that blind man from a runaway carriage by pushing him to safety? And wasn't I crushed under the wheels in the process, horrifically injured? Yet when I woke up in hospital my first thought was not about myself but rather the blind man I had saved. And wasn't I awarded a medal for bravery by Queen Victoria herself? Well ... no. Not exactly. Some of the particulars may be exaggerated. But I had certainly *thought* about doing such things. Which was practically the same thing.

The suite was enormous, filled with plump sofas, fine carpets, a grand piano and assorted antiques. But what did I care for any of that when England's richest – and possibly fattest – woman was lying right in front of me?

Yet, I must admit to a tiny pinch of fear – like icy water in my veins – as I stood there by the bed. Just the two of us. Me and the Duchess of Trinity. No witnesses. Nobody to help should the Duchess wake up, roll me in some sugar and have me for lunch.

The Duchess's heavy eyelids suddenly shot open. 'Close your mouth, child, you look like a bucket.'

I gulped. Like a frightened infant on a stormy night. Which was infuriating!

'You're a plain little thing, aren't you?' she said next.

'You poor deluded creature,' I replied, finding my voice. 'Dying has sapped the strength from your eyes. I'm remarkably beautiful and that's a genuine fact.'

The old woman shrugged. 'As you wish.'

A cool breeze blew in from the balcony outside, fluttering the Duchess's halo of white hair. For some reason it made me rather sad. I felt it was the right time to say something kind and reassuring to the invalid. I am skilled in such small talk.

'Your eyes are a fine shade of green,' I said softly. 'The rest of you is a nightmare, but your eyes are lovely.'

She smiled faintly. 'Are you hungry?'

I had helped myself to some crispy bacon from the silver breakfast tray sitting outside the Duchess's apartment door, so I wasn't at all hungry.

'Well then, down to business,' announced the Duchess. 'You've been travelling as Countess Carbunkle's maid?'

'More a companion than a maid,' I said. 'That half blind fossil loves me like a granddaughter. Or at the very least, a second cousin twice removed. In fact –'

'Hush!' The Duchess's green eyes fixed on mine. 'I know you have been abandoned. Left high and dry in this godless city. Did you *really* plunge the Countess's head into the fruit punch?'

'How else was I to relieve her brain fever?' I said crossly.

The Duchess looked rather pleased. 'Countess Carbunkle told me you were abandoned at the Harrington Home for Unwanted Children aged five – is that correct?'

'Highly doubtful,' I said. 'I'm certain I grew up in a violently loving family.'

'Bunkum,' muttered the old woman, though she appeared to grin. 'Before you came to Paris you worked for the Midwinters of London?'

'Oh, yes,' I said, 'I was with them for nearly a year. Delightful family. Monstrously unattractive, but delightful.'

'Then you are familiar with Lady Prudence's cousin – Lady Amelia Butterfield?'

'I met her once or twice,' I said, utterly baffled as to why she was asking me such things.

The Duchess of Trinity lifted her head from the pillow, her double chin swelling like a balloon. 'And her daughter Matilda?'

'Never met the girl,' I said. 'Why?'

'Go to the piano,' instructed the Duchess of Trinity, 'and open the lid.'

I did as she said.

'You know how to play?'

'Very well,' I said. 'Miss Lucy hated having to practise, but her mother insisted – so Miss Lucy would give me a toffee apple if I would go into the music room and pretend to be her. Turns out, I'm a natural.'

'You are familiar with "Row, Row, Row Your Boat"?' asked the Duchess.

I laughed. 'Everyone knows *that* one, dear.'

'Excellent. Play it.'

'Duchess, if you wish to hear a tune, let me play some Beethoven. You will be moved to tears.' I smiled proudly. 'Everyone cries when I play the piano.'

'Do as I ask,' she demanded. ' "Row, Row, Row Your Boat." Just once. From start to finish.'

The old bat was clearly off her rocker. But as I had nowhere else to go, and homelessness awaited me out on the streets of Paris, I sat down and played the tune. It sounded like a symphony. As I hit the last note I could feel the piano begin to vibrate beneath my fingers. Softly at first. Then more urgently. It was as if the ground were shaking. Then I heard a mechanism cranking from deep inside the instrument. *Click. Click. Click.* Without warning, a panel at the front of the keyboard began to move. Sliding back. *Click. Click. Click.* It only took a few moments, then there it was. A hidden chamber. A small cavity, cast in darkness.

Before I had a chance to ask, the Duchess of Trinity issued her next instruction. 'Reach inside.'

Now, I'm an adventurous sort of girl. Plucky. The courage of a lion. But the thought of sliding my hand into that dark recess – gaping at me like an open mouth – filled me with a small amount of trepidation. Still, I wasn't about to let that stop me. Carefully, I reached into the blackness. My fingers quickly hit upon an object. It felt soft and firm all at the same time.

'Pull it out,' the Duchess said.

It was a box. Roughly the size of a book. Covered in plush black velvet. An intricate silver keyhole carved in the top.

'Bring it to me' was the next instruction.

I placed the box in the Duchess's puffy hands. She held it like it was a sacred offering, her green eyes glistening in wonder as she stared at it. Then she set it down and her plump hand vanished inside the folds of the bed coverings and came out again holding a brass key.

She dropped it on the bed, her gaze never leaving the box. 'The key, child,' she whispered. 'Use it.'

Chapter 2

I slid the key into the lock and turned it. A crisp, heavy snap broke the silence. The velvet lid flew open. I felt a rush of anticipation. What on earth was I going to see? A severed finger with a signet ring still upon it? Or an eyeball frozen by the terror of a violent death? Or a human heart, still beating?

'Look,' cried the Duchess as she pulled out a perfectly ordinary necklace with a perfectly ordinary (if rather large) diamond hanging from it.

I was crushed. 'Is that it? Is that *all*?'

The old woman smiled grimly. 'You are not impressed?'

'Oh, I'm sure it's lovely,' I told her, sitting down on the bed. 'No doubt it's worth a fortune.'

'Priceless, in fact,' said the Duchess. She watched it hungrily. 'I haven't had the stone long, but I will be sad to part with it – though it has tormented me so.'

Tormented her? The old bat was bonkers. Dying does that to people, I supposed.

The Duchess huffed. 'You look at the necklace and all you see is a pretty jewel. But the Clock Diamond is so much more than that. It is a thing of withering power.'

I frowned. I may have even snorted (but in a dainty fashion).

'You doubt me?' said the Duchess, and now she looked rather delighted. 'Well, I don't blame you. But the fact remains, this diamond has several *fascinating* qualities. It keeps time, for one thing.' She thrust the necklace towards me and hissed, 'Look!'

If only to soothe this excitable creature, I did as she asked. The diamond was large, roughly the size and shape of an egg, but flatter. Above it, a tiny clock was set into the elegant silver mounting that connected the chain to the stone.

'Day or night, sunrise or starlight – you can set your watch by that necklace,' said the Duchess. 'And you will find no mechanism within the clock, nor can it be wound. Yet it has run for centuries.'

I frowned. 'But how?'

'The clock is powered by the stone,' said the Duchess with eager delight. 'No matter where you are in the world, the clock will adjust itself, right to the last second – as if by an unseen hand.'

I'd never heard of a diamond that could do such a thing. But I simply refused to lose my head over a silly clock. Beneath it, the stone sparkled and flared in the candlelight of the Duchess's dim bedroom, which was probably why I didn't see it. The *next* thing about the stone that made it different.

Inside, in the centre of the diamond, a grey mist billowed and churned. Then, without warning, it parted and I could see the sun rising over Paris – its shimmering glow bathing the rooftops in honey-coloured light. The whole city seemed to be captive inside that stone. It was remarkable, I suppose. Remarkable, but nothing to lose your head over.

'There is more,' said the Duchess eagerly. 'When the stone chooses, it can give the one who holds it a glimpse of the past, the present or the future. Not just their own, but others' too. These visions can delight.' Her eyes clouded over. 'And they can horrify.'

Now *that* was interesting. I didn't believe it, of course. But still, it was a delicious thought. 'Does the stone do anything else?' I asked.

The Duchess closed her eyes. 'Nothing that concerns you, child.'

I stared at the stone and began to sense an opportunity. The old woman was dying. She had sent for me. Showed me this precious necklace. Entrusted me with the key. There was only one possible explanation. 'You dear, sweet, sickly old windbag!' I cried, flinging myself at her. 'You are giving me the Clock

Diamond! Passing this mystical legacy from one generation to the next. Bless you, dear!'

Her laughter was weak and dry, but it filled the room. 'Don't be a fool. You are right in assuming I have business with you in connection with the stone. But as a messenger and nothing more.'

'Oh.' I cleared my throat and stood up. 'Of course, I didn't really think –'

'Your task is a simple one,' interrupted the Duchess of Trinity. 'I mentioned the Butterfields. I wish you to take the Clock Diamond to their estate in Suffolk – it is called Butterfield Park and will be easy enough to find – and present the necklace as a gift from me.'

'A gift?' I said.

The Duchess nodded. 'For Matilda Butterfield. She is about to turn twelve. You are to present the stone as a gift for her birthday. There is to be a ball in her honour – give it to her then, in front of all of her guests. Not a moment before, you understand? I wish the entire county to witness the moment. Do you think you're equal to the task?'

I shrugged. 'I'm sure I can manage to deliver a silly old diamond to Butterfield Park.'

'I am not finished,' snapped the Duchess. 'If you accept this commission, you must understand that it comes with conditions. Strict, unbreakable conditions.' She lifted a plump finger and called me closer. 'You are not to try on the necklace. Not once. Nobody is to see it before the ball, not even a glimpse. And absolutely *no one* is to wear the diamond except for Matilda Butterfield. Do you understand?'

Frankly, I was insulted. Did this half-crazed fatso *really* think that I was some sort of unprincipled street urchin who would try on her precious diamond the second I was alone? The nerve!

'You must get the stone to Matilda come what may.' The old woman's voice hissed like a rattlesnake. 'Do you *understand*, child?'

'Yes, yes, I understand perfectly. No offence, dear, but you seem rather overexcited by this whole business. That can't be good for your health. You know, being at death's door and whatnot.'

'Do not worry about my health,' said the Duchess of Trinity. She took a shallow breath. 'There is a ship leaving for England this afternoon. You will be on it.'

'That's a lovely idea,' I said, going to the window and staring out at the morning sun, 'but I haven't any money. A girl can't sail if she can't afford a ticket.'

'Stuff and nonsense,' said the Duchess with a wave of her hand. 'I will pay for your passage back to England and more besides.' She nodded at the table by the window. 'You will find everything you need over there.'

'Duchess,' I said casually, plonking myself back down on the bed, 'when you say *and more besides* – exactly how much more? I only ask because my savings are rather low at present.'

'Five hundred pounds,' said the Duchess. 'Fifty now. The rest payable through my lawyer, Horatio Banks, the day after the birthday ball.' She reached out and grabbed my hand (hers was astoundingly cold to the touch). 'Will you accept this task, Ivy? Will you swear to it? Will you give me your solemn word?'

'You have it,' I declared, looking grim as an undertaker. 'No one shall see the stone before the birthday ball and I will hang the Clock Diamond around Miss Matilda's neck myself.'

'You won't try it on, no matter how strong the temptation?' she said sternly.

'Never,' I promised. Then a frown creased my glorious forehead. 'Forgive me for asking, dear, I'm normally not one to stick my nose in where it doesn't belong – having all the natural instincts of a Highland hermit – but what is your connection to the Butterfields?'

The Duchess groaned softly, her eyelids fluttering. 'Matilda's grandmother, Lady Elizabeth, is an old friend. We grew up together as girls. I'm ashamed to say we had a falling out over a young gentleman many years ago. It seemed terribly important then, but rather foolish now. The necklace is a peace offering, I suppose. There is a letter inside the box for Lady Elizabeth – give it to her when you first arrive at the house.'

'It is a monstrously generous gift, dear,' I said with just a pinch of envy.

'Lady Elizabeth adores Matilda – all of her hopes and wishes reside in that child. You have no idea how it soothes me, as death draws near, just knowing that I can bestow this gift on her.' The old woman pointed to the box. 'Come, it is time to lock the necklace away.'

I was about to hand the stone back to the Duchess when it began to pulse in my hand. Faintly to begin with. Then with great intensity. Silvery light, soft and rippling, seemed to spill out from within it, illuminating every corner of the bedroom chamber. The necklace felt warm against my skin.

'It is happening!' hissed the Duchess, trying to lift her head from the pillow. 'Tell me, child, what can you see?'

At first I saw nothing; the light was too bright. Then it dimmed and, as before, a billowing grey mist churned and swirled, then parted. I stared closely. What I saw as the mist cleared was a wide hallway. It was long, dimly lit, panelled in dark wood, with red carpet upon the floor. The stone revealed a door; a silver tray stood on a trolley beside it. I recognised it immediately. It was the door to the very apartment I was sitting in.

I was about to tell the Duchess what I could see when it happened. Something moved. No, *someone* moved. Emerging from the shadows and stopping before the Duchess's door. It was a woman, though her face was shrouded in darkness. She wore a grey dress. Dark gloves. The woman dropped down, crouching before the door. Then her face pressed against the keyhole. She was peering inside!

'What is it, child?' snapped the Duchess impatiently. 'What do you see?'

I dropped the stone and raced from the bedroom. Bolting as fast as my legs would carry me – which was frightfully fast – I charged across the drawing room and threw open the door. My heart hammered in my chest as I prepared to confront the spy (for I have all the natural instincts of a five-star general). But the hallway was empty. The silver tray was there. The half-eaten bacon. But no sign of the devious woman. It was a crushing disappointment.

When I returned to the Duchess's bedroom the vision in the Clock Diamond had vanished. It now looked like a perfectly ordinary necklace. I told the Duchess what I had seen.

The blubbery old bat shivered, her eyes shifting about the room.

'A spy!' she whispered. 'I was warned … but I didn't believe it.'

'Warned about what?' I said.

'The Clock Diamond has its fierce admirers – and its enemies too. They have been after the stone since its discovery in the savage jungles of Budatta. I was told they would come for it before I die, but I didn't believe it. Superstitious claptrap, that's what I said.' She fixed her eyes upon me. 'It is possible someone may try to grab the stone before you reach Butterfield Park. That is why you are the perfect person to deliver the neck-lace. Who on earth would suspect a humble maid, orphaned and all alone in the world?'

That sounded vaguely insulting. Then I thought of the five hundred pounds and my desire to hit the Duchess on the head with a pillow fell away.

'Perhaps it was just a nosy maid,' I said helpfully. 'Or perhaps the vision was wrong.'

The old woman shook her head and when she spoke her voice trembled. 'The stone does not deal in fantasy, child – only facts: what was, what is and what will be.' Then the fear in her eyes seemed to fade. 'But perhaps you are right and it was merely a maid peering through the keyhole. They are always spying on me – hoping I will drop dead so they can steal my jewels.'

I looked down at the necklace and for the briefest moment I felt a kind of longing. A mad desire to stare into its heart again and see what it might reveal. Before I could, the Duchess had pulled it from my fingers, placed it in the velvet box and snapped it shut.

'Where on earth did you get such a diamond?' I said.

She paused. Licked her lips. 'An acquaintance.'

'Do you wish to write a note or a card for Matilda?' I asked.

'Give her the necklace at the ball,' she wheezed, each breath a struggle, 'and tell her it is sent with the kind regards of Winifred Farris. Her grandmother will understand. Now, lock it.'

I took the key from my pocket and did as she instructed. The Duchess handed me the box. 'Place it in your bag. Never let it leave your side from now until you reach Butterfield Park. My lawyer, Mr Banks, will meet you at the dock in London and see you on your way.' She looked me up and down. 'You can't go on board the ship looking like *that*. There is a dress for you in the wardrobe. You will find a dozen others in your cabin on the *Britannia*.'

I clapped my hands in delight. 'Duchess, you are barking mad, but wonderful!'

She huffed, yet seemed pleased.

The dress was lovely – a simple gown of white muslin with a pale blue sash – and I was lovely in it. Not like a maid at all. Like a princess. Or at the very least a postmaster's daughter.

With the box safely packed in my carpet bag and the envelope with my ticket and the fifty pounds in my pocket, the Duchess of Trinity appeared to have no further use for me. Her eyes were closed again. I assumed she was sleeping.

'Goodbye, Duchess,' I whispered, watching her plump cheeks billow with every laboured breath, her face masked by the shadow of death. 'Enjoy the journey which awaits you. It will be thrilling, I'm sure.'

As I closed the door to her suite I heard her voice for the last time, brittle and grim. 'Goodbye, child,' she whispered, 'and thank you.'

As I left the hotel, I was hoping that the ghastly manager would notice me taking my leave in a private carriage with two horses. But he was nowhere to be seen. The carriage took me to Le Havre and I quickly found myself amongst a great swell of people clamouring towards the *Britannia*. She was a fine ship and I was delighted to find that the Duchess had booked me passage in first class.

As the ship wasn't ready for boarding, I took a seat in the first class waiting room. The place was positively swarming with aristocrats – gentlemen in frock coats and top hats and ladies luxuriating in furs, feathered hats and jewels.

I had just checked my bag for the Clock Diamond (I found myself checking on the jewel every five minutes) when a short man wearing a white suit sat down beside me. He looked rather crotchety, muttering to himself with alarming frequency. Something about Paris going to the dogs.

'It's shameful,' he said, to no one in particular. 'I remember when you could sleep in this city with your window open. Your door unlocked. Now *this*. A crying shame, it is.'

'Is it?' I said, unable to resist. I have a fondness for lunatics.

'Yes indeed,' he said, shaking his head. 'Just be grateful you and your family are getting out of Paris, little miss.'

'I'm travelling alone,' I said proudly.

'A girl your age? Outrageous!' He was frowning. 'Main thing is, you're leaving this place. Shocking, it is. And at a fine hotel like the Grand.'

Suddenly I was very interested in the man's mad ravings. 'I was just there,' I said. 'What about the Grand?'

'That's where it happened. Terrible thing!'

'Stop babbling, you nitwit,' I snapped. 'Tell me what happened.'

'Murder, that's what. The body was found this morning,' said the man. 'A maid found her there, dead and all. A dagger plunged in her heart.'

A sliver of fear seemed to wake inside me, coiling its way up towards my chest. It slithered and curled. Twisting ever higher. Ever tighter. What I felt wasn't easy to explain. The only way to describe it is this: I knew before I *knew*.

'Who?' I said faintly. 'Who was murdered?'

'Nobody you'd have heard of,' said the man. 'She was old, she was.'

'Who?' I repeated, this time with more urgency.

The man smiled sadly. 'Very well. 'Twas the Duchess of Trinity.'

My heart began to pound in my chest.

'She was once a very great lady,' muttered the man.

'I knew her,' I said. 'I mean . . . I knew her name.'

'Don't look so grave, little miss,' said the man. 'You're not to trouble your mind with murder and mischief. Leave that to the grown-ups, you hear?'

He was right, of course. I was a junior lady's maid. Brilliant and beautiful. But still just a child. What did I know of murder and mischief? Of daggers plunged into hearts? Nothing, that's what. Until now. Until right now.

'Promise me you won't worry about this awful business.' He patted my arm, his eyes filled with fatherly concern. 'Do you promise, little miss?'

I tried my best to smile but it simply wasn't happening. 'I promise.'

Chapter 3

The ship had just set sail. I sat on a deckchair overlooking the sea and tried to think. Which I normally did stupendously well – for I have all the natural instincts of a philosophy professor. Or at the very least, an assistant librarian. But not now.

I was terribly anxious. My hands were trembling. My mind was a tangle. People were gathered like lemmings around the ship's railing, watching the final glimpses of the coast. Yet all I saw was the Duchess of Trinity lying in her bed with a knife in her chest. And while stabbing was a marvellously interesting cause of death, it was no way for a genuine duchess to kick the bucket. She deserved something far more dignified. Like choking on a lobster claw. Or being crushed beneath a falling chandelier.

The facts were as follows. A woman near death – she hardly expected to live out the week – had been killed in her bed. Why? And by whom? I thought of the vision in the stone – the woman crouched at the Duchess's door, peering through the keyhole.

Was she the killer? A shiver rattled my bones. There *must* be some connection between the Clock Diamond and the Duchess's gruesome death. Hadn't the old bat warned me that nefarious fatheads were after the one-of-a-kind stone?

It certainly made sense.

'Did you hear about the Duchess?' shrieked a woman with a glorious overbite and a neck like a giraffe, as she and her lump of a husband stopped at the railing in front of me. 'It's utterly shocking!'

'Too much money,' said the husband. 'Rich folks like that always meet a grisly end.'

The wife gasped (she sounded like a horse with a nail in its hoof). 'Don't be beastly, Angus! It's terrifying, that's what it is. I only pray they've caught the killer by now.'

'The murderer's still at large,' came the reply.

The wife gasped again. 'Angus, you don't suppose he's here on the ship?'

Angus said it was highly likely. His wife clutched her chest and declared an intention to faint.

'Don't be absurd,' I said, getting out of my chair. 'The killer is probably miles away by now. Of course, if he didn't find what he was looking for, he may be searching elsewhere, but as for him being on this ship – it's a violently stupid thought.'

The wife looked relieved. The husband frowned.

'You seem to know an awful lot about it,' he said, looking at me with interest. 'Where are your mother and father, young lady?'

'My parents fell into a volcano,' I said. 'My mother was blown deep into the Congo where she now lives with a tribe of vegetarian pygmies and my father had the good sense to explode on impact.'

The silly creatures looked positively bug-eyed. Which was the perfect moment for me to pick up my carpet bag and set off in search of my cabin.

I found it in no time. The room was small but perfectly comfortable. Though to be honest, first class wasn't nearly as luxurious as I had expected. I dropped my bag and lay down upon the narrow bed.

'Well, Ivy,' I said aloud, 'what on earth are you going to do?'

I could abort the mission. In the envelope the Duchess had given me was the business card of her lawyer in London. Mr Horatio Banks. I could take the necklace to him. Wash my hands of this murderous mess and walk away. Nobody would think me a coward. Of course, there were other options. I could throw the Clock Diamond overboard and pretend I never had it to begin with. But then I thought of the Duchess – and the five hundred pounds. I had accepted the mission, hadn't I? Sworn an oath and whatnot. It was probably the last promise anyone had ever made to the Duchess. Surely that meant something. To me. To her.

In the end, it was an easy decision. I would fulfil my promise. Come hell or high water, I would see the Clock Diamond hanging around Matilda Butterfield's neck.

I awoke a few hours later feeling remarkably fresh. The Duchess's grisly death still troubled me, but I would not let it deflate my spirits.

Before falling asleep, I had taken the necessary precautions to protect the Clock Diamond. I had pulled a small writing desk in front of my cabin door, thus blocking any intruder. And I slept with the precious stone under my pillow. I had dispensed with the black velvet box and the old key (but not before removing the Duchess's letter to Lady Elizabeth) – they were cumbersome and unnecessary and they practically shouted, *Please rob me!* Which wasn't helpful.

The second I woke up, I felt for the stone beneath my pillow. My sleepy body was flooded with relief to find it still there. I quickly decided to keep the stone in my pocket at all times during the day – the pocket sewn shut to eliminate the possibility of theft.

Before I slipped the diamond into my pocket and stitched it up, I held the stone up to the light. Through the porthole I could see the shimmering sun across the rippling blue horizon, casting the cabin in a bronze haze. In the heart of the diamond, the sun loomed in miniature above the ship, the stone glowing like an iridescent egg yolk. It was beautiful. And all I know is, I got lost in that stone. Lost in its wonder.

And then it happened. The longing bloomed inside me again, just like in the Duchess's bedroom chamber. A mad desire. A desperate need. And it had a single focus: to wear the necklace. To put it on. To see myself with the Clock Diamond around my neck. Yes, yes, I promised the Duchess I wouldn't. But how could it hurt? I could try the necklace on – just for a second. A minute or two. Then take it off. No one would know.

I walked over to the mirror, the silver necklace pooled in the palm of my hand like a puddle. I looked splendid in my new dress. My dark hair was tied back in a braid and looked very fetching. I placed the chain around my neck and pulled the clasp back. I glanced in the mirror. The Clock Diamond hung before my chest, the heavy stone swinging like a pendulum. My hands trembled. My mouth was dry. A feeling of lightness rushed through my head.

With new determination I steadied my fingers and fixed the clasp together. The necklace dropped to my neck and hung there. Its warmth radiated through my dress.

The Clock Diamond glowed a silvery white. Then the stone began to pulse. I could feel it beat against my chest. At first it was irregular. Throbbing out of rhythm. Then the pulse steadied. I cannot say for sure, but it seemed to have synchronised with the beating of my heart.

The stone dimmed, glowing faintly now.

Thump. Thump. Thump.

It felt awfully hot in the cabin. Stuffy. I took a breath. It took more effort than normal. My head was positively spinning. Or was it the cabin? The stone pulsed, its orb filled with a billowing black mist.

The dark fog churned like a thunderstorm, then cleared.

In its place I saw something move.

A baby. Looking up and laughing.

In an instant the infant was older. A girl now. Dark hair in two braids. Gorgeous blue eyes. But pale. Plain. She was crying. Sitting by the window. Wondering why she had been left in that awful place. Then older. Eleven or twelve. Dressed as a maid. Serving tea. In a fine house.

Then a glittering white mist bloomed, filling the stone. And the girl was gone.

The girl who was me.

A glow burst from the diamond like a searchlight. It seemed to reach for me.

Swallowing me up.

Then the world fell away.

All was black.

Tap. Tap. Tap.

The door.

Someone was knocking at the door. I opened my eyes and blinked. My head ached. I was lying on the floor of my cabin, the afternoon sun filling the tiny room. I squinted, shielded my eyes and slowly got to my feet.

Tap. Tap. Tap.

'Just a moment!' I called out.

My brain felt like it had been taken out of my head, kicked around like a football, then shoved back in. I had over-excited myself. Such things were always happening to girls in novels.

Tap. Tap. Tap.

I quickly straightened my dress and took a deep breath. My hand was gripping the door handle when I remembered. The necklace! I was still wearing it. I unfastened the clasp and slipped it into the pocket of my dress.

Then opened the door.

'I'm Geraldine Always,' said a rather prim-looking woman in a brown dress and matching gloves. 'My cabin is right next to yours. I heard a thump coming from this direction and I was concerned. Are you all right?'

She had unremarkable brown hair pulled back from her face. Round spectacles. Excellent teeth. And I liked her from the start.

'I'm perfectly fine,' I said. 'I dropped . . . my bag. Yes, my bag. That must have been the noise you heard.'

Geraldine Always sprang up on her tiptoes (she was short, but not shockingly so) and looked over my shoulder. 'You are travelling with family?'

'Heavens no,' I said. 'My parents are currently on an expedition in Mongolia. Hunting aardvarks. I am returning to England to spend the summer with my grandmother. She's beastly.'

'You must think me awfully nosy, knocking on your door and interrogating you,' said Miss Always rather meekly.

'Yes, dear, that is *just* what I was thinking.'

Miss Always laughed. Which was odd. She said, 'You see, like you, I am travelling alone – which is very dull. What is your name?'

'Ivy Pocket.'

'Well, Ivy Pocket, we shall have to be companions for the length of our voyage. There is no other option.'

And so we were.

The poor woman was a writer. Her first book – *Famous Ghosts of Scotland and Wales* – had sold just sixty-three copies. For the last year she had been travelling the world on a frightfully unsuccessful lecture tour and writing a new book on lost myths and legends – cursed relics, hidden worlds, vengeful gods and whatnot. Now Miss Always was heading back home to England to care for her sick mother. My new friend was sweet-natured and monstrously dull. But being a generous sort of girl – for I have all the natural instincts of a missionary – I did my best to ensure she had a jolly good time.

That first evening, Miss Always and I were taking a moonlight walk along the upper deck after a heartbreakingly light supper (following my fainting spell, I had the appetite of a small army). We were discussing my parents' many adventures. They were map-makers by profession. Travelling to the darkest corners of the globe, recording its uncharted valleys and gorges and mountains. They had been everywhere. Done everything. Dug up mummies in Egypt. Carved tracks through the Amazon. Miss Always was utterly fascinated by their adventures. As was I. After all, I was hearing them for the first time.

Yes, yes, it is wrong to tell lies. But I couldn't help it. I knew nothing of my real parents. The only information I had was that someone – a lady of grim countenance – had brought me to the Harrington Home for Unwanted Children in London and left me there. I was five. My memories don't really begin until after I arrived at the orphanage – the years before it are a blur. But I am certain my early life was filled with amazing adventures.

'You must treasure your parents, Ivy,' said Miss Always gravely. 'That is why I am so keen to get back to England, to see my poor mother. She is terribly ill.' She came to a stop, resting her hands on the railing. Beyond us the milky moonlight played upon the black sea. 'Shall I tell you a secret, Ivy?'

'I insist that you do,' I said.

'In Paris, I bought a very special gift for my mother,' she whispered. 'A diamond ring. My father couldn't afford one when they first married. But Mummy has always wanted one.'

'Was it stupendously expensive?' I asked.

'Shockingly,' said Miss Always. She leaned close to me. 'Perhaps you could help me, Ivy. For I haven't been able to think of a place to hide the diamond while we are at sea. You know, somewhere no one would ever think to look. I'm *terrible* at such things.'

I looked around to make sure we were quite alone. 'I shouldn't be telling you this, Miss Always,' I said softly, 'but I'm travelling with a diamond myself. Very rare. One of a kind.'

'You are?' The writer looked stunned.

'Nobody knows about it,' I said. 'Not even the captain.'

Now perhaps it was unwise of me to speak of the stone. But I am an excellent judge of character and I knew I could trust Miss Always. She wrote *books* – how dangerous could she be?

'Where did you get it?' asked my friend eagerly.

'From a fat old duchess,' I said. 'We were monstrously close. It was her dying wish that I deliver the diamond *personally* to Matilda Butterfield of Butterfield Park. The Duchess trusted no one but me with the mission.'

'Then you know how nervous I feel about carrying something so valuable,' said Miss Always. She licked her lips (clearly chafed by the sea breeze). 'How on earth did you figure out where to hide the Duchess's necklace?'

'It was easy, dear,' I said brightly. 'I always carry the stone with me.'

Miss Always' innocent eyes bloomed. 'You have the Cl–' She coughed all of a sudden (I assume she was choking on a wasp or some beastly sea bug). 'You have the diamond on you right now?'

'I do.'

She looked at me eagerly. 'May I ask where?'

What a simple-minded nincompoop she was.

I giggled. 'I keep it in my pocket and sew it shut,' I explained. 'So you see, it's perfectly safe. Nobody could get at the stone without my knowing about it.'

'And at night?' asked Miss Always. 'What do you do at night?'

'Under my pillow, dear,' I answered. 'I'm a very light sleeper. If anyone tried to steal it I would wake up and thrash them brutally. Plus, I barricade the door.'

I thought Miss Always looked slightly disappointed. But I'm sure I was mistaken. She swiftly took me further into her confidence (that dear, trusting, dim-witted creature). 'My mother's ring,' she whispered, 'would you like to see it?'

Now I must confess, apart from the Clock Diamond I have little interest in jewels as a general rule. But the bonds of friendship demanded that I at least try to look excited.

'I would love to,' I said.

Miss Always' cabin was just like my own. Only darker – lit by a single candle on the bedside table. With the door safely locked, my friend patted down her mousy brown hair, pushed up her spectacles and took a deep breath. Then she opened her travel bag and pulled out a large book on Ancient Greece. For a moment I feared she was going to read to me. Fortunately, it had a far more interesting function – carved inside was a chamber and in it a small red box. Miss Always pulled it out and with great care opened the lid.

'Here it is,' she said dreamily.

'Oh, it's beautiful!' I cried.

It wasn't. It was small. And dull. A thin gold band. A tiny diamond. I'd seen dust with more sparkle. Still, it was my job as a bosom friend to lie. I *oohed* and *ahhed*. Was suitably complimentary. Declared that her mother would be so delighted she would probably die of shock. Which was unfortunate given the poor woman's perilous health. But Miss Always seemed pleased by my reaction.

The smile soon faded from her lips. 'The ring must appear very insignificant when compared to *your* diamond, Ivy. Could I – ?' She shook her head. 'No, I shouldn't ask. It's terribly rude of me.'

'What is?' I said.

'I was going to ask if I might take a look at it,' she said shyly. 'But please forgive me. I shouldn't ask such a thing.'

Now of course I had vowed to show no one the stone. Not until the birthday ball. But Miss Always was a sweet-natured blockhead. What could be the harm in giving her a glimpse? 'Come closer and I will show you,' I said quietly.

Miss Always edged towards me, hands behind her back. 'Only if you are sure,' she said with heartbreaking intensity.

She was close to me now. As I turned, searching the bedside table for a pair of scissors to cut open the stitching of my pocket, I could feel her breath upon the back of my neck.

'You don't know how much this means to me, Ivy,' I heard her say. 'You will never know how much.'

'Calm yourself, dear,' I said, opening a series of small drawers. 'It's only a silly diamond. Though I will admit, it *did* look rather glorious when I tried it on.'

As I turned to face Miss Always, her arm was swinging towards me. Something in her hand flared in the candlelight, blinding me for a moment. It sliced through the air. Coming right at me. There wasn't time to react. I didn't even flinch. Just as quickly, Miss Always froze. Her hand was steady. She had the scissors poised right in front of my chest. Which was rather troubling.

'Miss Always?'

The poor creature looked horribly bewildered. A small gasp escaped her lips. The scissors slackened in her hand. 'What . . . what did you say?'

'Be careful with those scissors, dear,' I said with a furrowed brow.

Miss Always blushed. Looked down at the scissors. 'Goodness. Yes, of course. I found them on the desk. I was so eager to hand them to you, I nearly . . . oh, Ivy, I'm awfully sorry. It's all the excitement, I suppose.'

I took the scissors from her. 'Yes, dear, you're monstrously excitable.'

'Ivy, did you say you tried on the necklace?'

I nodded and began to cut the stitching of my pocket. 'Only for a moment. I didn't see any harm in it. Of course, then I fainted and the next thing I knew, you were knocking at my door.'

'I . . . I don't believe it,' she muttered.

'Oh, it's perfectly all right,' I said brightly. 'The stone wasn't damaged and as I said, it was only for a minute or two.'

Miss Always smiled tightly. 'You really are full of surprises, Ivy.'

With the stitching cut away, I slipped my hand in to retrieve the necklace. Suddenly Miss Always' fingers snaked around my wrist. Her grip was rather tight. 'Stop,' she commanded.

'Whatever's the matter, dear?' I said.

'I hear voices outside,' said Miss Always, glancing towards the door.

'I'm sure it's just passengers walking by.' I was now rather eager to show Miss Always the stone, hopeful she might actually explode with excitement (which would be frightfully tragic, but violently entertaining). 'Don't worry, dear. We are perfectly safe.'

But Miss Always did not believe it. Only moments ago she had been drooling with anticipation at seeing the stone, and now she refused to even look at it. Said she would see it some other time. Then hurried me from her cabin, suggesting I get a good night's sleep.

'Oh, and Ivy,' she said, pushing me out into the hallway, 'do be sure to lock your door. With a diamond so rare and valuable, you must be terribly careful. There are thieves around every corner. You will be careful, won't you, Ivy?'

Before I could answer, Miss Always had closed the door.

The next evening, before dinner, I went hunting for food. I was hungrier than I had ever been in my entire life. Some of my cravings were really very odd. I had a newfound appetite for potatoes. Raw ones. Also, cabbages. Unfortunately, all I found in the empty tea room was half a strawberry cream cake and two stale scones. Still, they were rather scrumptious.

When I returned below deck to freshen up, a peculiar thing happened – and it stopped me in my tracks. As I rounded the narrow corridor leading to my cabin, I spotted Miss Always at the far end. She had her back to me. Her head was bowed. She appeared to be talking. And in front of her was a small hooded figure, dressed in some sort of brown cassock. The figure was partly obscured by Miss Always, but from where I stood, it looked as if the two of them were deep in conversation. Miss Always and a monk. A very *short* monk.

'Miss Always?' I called out.

She lifted her head, then turned around with a sweeping gesture – and as she did, the hooded figure seemed to vanish with the swish of her skirt. As if into thin air. Which was frightfully odd.

Miss Always hurried towards me. 'You look pale, Ivy,' she said. 'Whatever is the matter?'

'Who were you talking to, dear?'

'Talking to?' Miss Always smiled and waved her hand. 'Oh, *that*. Just some passenger who had lost his way. I was telling him how to get back to his cabin.'

'He was dressed very strangely,' I said.

'Was he?' Miss Always looped her arm through mine and began to walk with me. 'One passenger is much the same as the next to me, Ivy.'

'But his robes were positively medieval,' I said, 'and he was terribly short.'

Miss Always stopped. Put her hand on my forehead. Frowned a great deal. 'You don't look well at all and you are making very little sense. The man I spoke with was dressed in a dinner suit.' She nodded grimly. 'I'm afraid you have a bad case of seasickness, Ivy. The most common symptoms are hallucinations – which you are clearly suffering from – and sudden changes in appetite. Have you noticed anything unusual in your eating habits?'

Well, of course I had. Ravenous hunger and whatnot. 'Not really, dear.'

'You looked flushed and your forehead is terribly hot,' said Miss Always.

Was it? It seemed all the signs were there. I was monstrously hungry *and* I had conjured up a hooded dwarf from thin air! 'Perhaps you are right, dear,' I said, as we mounted the stairs towards the dining room.

At dinner, Miss Always' interest in my plans knew no bounds. Not just about my mission to deliver the Clock Diamond to Matilda Butterfield. But about where my grand-mother lived in London (I had told Miss Always I would be staying with Grandma Pocket until I left for Butterfield Park). Which was rather difficult to explain, as I didn't exactly have a grandmother.

Naturally, I made something up.

'Grandma has several homes in town,' I said helpfully. 'One never knows *exactly* where she will choose to sleep. Grandma's something of a halfwit, but we love her dearly.'

Miss Always looked bothered. Just for a moment. She said, 'I only ask because I will be staying in London for a few hours to meet with my publisher. I would love to pay you a visit.'

'Sounds delightful, dear,' I said, 'but quite impossible. Grandma hates company.'

Miss Always gave me the address of her publisher. She practically begged me to write to her the moment I was settled with the address where I would be staying. I promised that I would.

The next morning, just after sunrise, the great ship sailed through a blanket of heavy fog towards land. The Britannia was to anchor at the Royal Albert Dock and Miss Always seemed to dread our parting. She looked smart in her best scarlet dress, but her washed-out face looked gaunt and depressed. To my surprise, she said I looked tired, urging me to stay in London for a few days to rest. Made mention *again* of me writing to her with my address in town.

We stood together on the deck and watched the city drift into view.

'Perhaps we could take tea in the saloon before we get off?' I said, certain that Miss Always would leap at the chance. To my surprise she declined.

'I am meeting my publisher the moment we berth,' she explained. 'He is anxious to hear all about my new book on lost myths and legends.'

We parted then and there. Miss Always cried. I pretended to. It was touching. An hour later I had my carpet bag in my hand, the Clock Diamond in my pocket and London in my sights. Just before I departed, I glanced around for one final look at the ship. She was splendid. There was a line of passengers mounting the gangway. I took my place but it was a painfully slow business. Looking down, I noticed a black carriage with four horses carving a path through the bustling crowd. It turned sharply, pulling up around the side of the terminal. The windows were covered in dark drapes. The driver wore a hat, pulled low. All very interesting. I waited for a moment to see who would get out. No one did.

When the line started to move again, I followed the stream of excitable passengers who were alighting. I would never have given the black carriage a second thought, were it not for the streak of scarlet that caught my eye and drew me back. A dress. A scarlet dress. Moving swiftly towards the large black carriage. The lady in the scarlet dress had a companion. I stopped and stared at them, utterly captivated. As they reached the carriage, the door swung open. The tiny figure I had seen on the ship wearing the hooded brown cassock was the first to climb in.

Followed swiftly by Miss Always.

Chapter 4

London was just as I had left it. Grim. Filthy. Miserable. But my mind was elsewhere. What on earth was Miss Always doing getting into a carriage with that strange little monk? A strange little monk Miss Always claimed I had hallucinated due to seasickness! It made no sense. And didn't she say that her publisher would be meeting her at the dock? I stopped outside the terminal to wait for the Duchess of Trinity's lawyer, putting down my carpet bag. A cyclone of thoughts spinning through my mind. That hooded dwarf had forced Miss Always into the carriage at knifepoint. Yes, that must be it! No, wait. Miss Always had climbed into the carriage *after* the strange little fellow.

'You're a brilliant girl, Ivy,' I said aloud. 'Just *think*.'

For a fleeting moment the Clock Diamond came into my mind. Which was odd. There was no connection between the stone and Miss Always. Instinctively my hand flew to the pocket of my royal blue dress. I felt for the precious jewel. It was there. Safely sewn in. How stupid of me! Yes, Miss Always had taken an interest in the Duchess's one-of-a-kind diamond. But only because I told her about it. And in the end, she hadn't wished to see it at all.

I thought a little harder. Only took a moment. Perhaps two. By way of my natural instincts (which would rival a Scotland Yard detective), I quickly solved the puzzle of Miss Always and the hooded stranger. The black carriage did indeed belong to Miss Always' publisher. And her mysterious travelling companion was the publisher's long lost *son*. I'm certain the young man was a pitiful creature – monstrously short, face like a chimpanzee, heartbreakingly stupid – banished from England after a scandal and forced to live in France with a brutish uncle. The poor chap had sneaked on to the ship, desperate to return to his family but terrified of being rejected. The kind-hearted Miss Always befriended the stowaway and learned his tragic tale. Delighted to be of help, she arranged the ship-side reunion I had just witnessed. A father and son, separated by an ocean, now reunited. It made perfect sense!

Nothing gets past Ivy Pocket.

It was late morning. Most of the passengers had left the dock and still I waited for the Duchess's lawyer to come. Which was infuriating! Eager to get on with my adventure, I took a rickshaw into the city, intending to spend the night in a suitably upmarket hotel. I had ten pounds left from the voyage and – as I was soon to deliver the Clock Diamond to Matilda Butterfield and collect the bulk of my reward – I figured I could certainly afford a little luxury.

Unfortunately there was some trouble at the hotel. The Grosvenor was suitably grand, but *apparently* twelve-year-old girls aren't supposed to stay in a deluxe suite all on their own. Ridiculous! I told the manager (who had teeth like a walrus) that I was in London to meet my neglectful parents – self-absorbed mathematicians helping the British government decode a Russian cable concealed in a circus elephant's left hoof. All very top secret. Thousands of lives at stake and whatnot. The manager didn't believe a word and I was just about to tell him what I thought of him when –

'Miss Pocket?'

I turned around to find a tall man standing right behind me. Grey hair. Stern eyes. Long face. Dark suit. Top hat. He regarded me coolly. 'Miss Pocket?' he said again.

I nodded. 'Who are you?'

'That can wait,' he said firmly. 'Come, let us take a walk.'

Now I am not one to go strolling with strange men. But the remarkable thing was, I felt I didn't have a choice. Top Hat walked out of the hotel without another word and like a lemming, I followed after him. Extraordinary!

We walked to St James's Park and took a seat under a maple tree. He told me his name was Horatio Banks – he was the Duchess of Trinity's lawyer. He explained that he had been delayed at his office and by the time he arrived at the dock to collect me, I had already departed. How Mr Banks had tracked me down was a mystery that he was unwilling to shed any light on.

But on other matters he had much to say.

'Tell me about your voyage,' he said, looking at me with his fierce green eyes. 'Any strange occurrences? Anything unusual?'

'Nothing. I was on my guard.'

'Did anyone befriend you?' he asked.

'Hundreds of people, dear. I'm the sort of maid who attracts a crowd.'

Horatio Banks cleared his throat. 'Did anyone show an interest in the Clock Diamond? Did anyone know you were travelling with it?'

'Mr Banks, do I look like the sort of girl who would go blabbing to strangers about the Clock Diamond?'

I *could* have told him about Miss Always, but what was the use? She was a penniless writer. An innocent spinster. Terribly fascinated by me. But delightfully clueless.

The lawyer got up from the bench and began to pace back and forth. He pressed his finger to his lip and frowned a great deal. Then he stopped, turning to face me.

'You've heard about the Duchess of Trinity's murder?'

'Oh, yes. Terribly sad. Monstrously tragic. I can't imagine who would do such a thing.'

'I can,' said the lawyer grimly. 'Miss Pocket, did you see anything suspicious, *anything* at all, when you were in the Duchess's hotel suite in Paris?'

'Nothing, dear.' I didn't see the point in telling Mr Banks about the vision of the mysterious woman at the keyhole. It proved nothing. And besides, I suspected the lawyer would gladly try to separate me from the diamond. And without the diamond there would be no five hundred pounds.

'What did the Duchess tell you about the stone?' asked the lawyer.

'Only that it's rare and valuable and it was her dying wish that I should present it to Miss Butterfield at her birthday ball.'

'I don't like it,' he muttered. 'The Duchess refused to tell me how she came to possess this mysterious diamond – I just know that it cost a sizeable chunk of her fortune. When are you leaving for Suffolk?'

'Tomorrow morning,' I said, tightening the bow of my braid (it seemed the right moment).

'Very good,' said the lawyer. 'There is a deeper mystery here, Miss Pocket, and I intend to find out what it is. I am still baffled as to why the Duchess would wish to give a priceless jewel to Matilda Butterfield – a girl she had never met before.'

'There is no great mystery there, dear,' I said matter-of-factly. 'The Duchess had a falling out with Matilda's grandmother decades ago. The necklace is a peace offering. Old people are awfully keen on such things.'

'Miss Pocket, I believe there is a direct connection between the Duchess's murder and the Clock Diamond. I also believe you were probably followed from Paris.'

Poor man. He was shockingly melodramatic. I suspect he had a fondness for the theatre. 'Mr Banks, wake up. If someone were stalking me on the boat they would certainly have struck by now.'

Horatio Banks looked stumped. Which I found rather thrilling.

'There is a bigger picture,' he said at last. 'But I cannot see it as yet.'

'Well, I can,' I told him. 'I will leave in the morning, stay a few days at Butterfield Park, then give the necklace to Matilda at her party. Then you will pay me my money and this whole thing will be at an end. Agreed?'

He did not.

'The Duchess has a town house in Belgravia. I've arranged for the housekeeper to open a few of the rooms for your use.' He handed me a card. 'The address is on there. Collect your things and be at the house by three o'clock. I will meet you there.'

I protested. Stomped my feet. Poked out my tongue. Nothing worked. Which was infuriating!

'If you want your payment, Miss Pocket,' said the lawyer, 'you will do as I say. I have an important meeting in the city, otherwise I would escort you myself. Talk to no one. Do not tell a soul where you will be staying. Are we clear?'

'Perfectly,' I said in my most sullen voice (which is astoundingly sullen).

Then the beastly man turned on his heels and stalked away without so much as a goodbye. He stopped suddenly and looked back. 'I worked for the Duchess of Trinity for forty years and in all that time I never knew her to trust a single person,' he said. His eyes narrowed and fixed on me. 'Why did she pick you to deliver the Clock Diamond? Why *you*, Miss Pocket?'

I smiled sweetly. 'Oh, I just assumed you knew, dear – I'm one of a kind.'

Mr Banks may have smiled then. Just for a flash. Then he tipped his hat and walked away.

My journey to Belgravia was unremarkable. Except for one thing. I bumped into Miss Always. Quite by accident, of course. She was taking a walk in the park just as I was leaving. The poor creature was thrilled to see me. Hugged me several times. I was curious why she was still in London. She explained that her publisher had asked her to stay on and discuss her new book – the one on myths and legends. Apparently it was shockingly dull. Needed more *colour* and *excitement*. Miss Always seemed bitterly disappointed. She talked a great deal about the changes she had in mind. But I stopped her. For I had questions.

'Miss Always,' I said gravely, 'I saw you leaving the ship. You got into a carriage with that little hooded man from the ship. The one you said I had *imagined*. What is going on, dear?'

Poor Miss Always looked stunned. Her mouth dropped open. Her eyelids blinked rapidly. She adjusted her glasses. 'Well, Ivy, that is a very good question.' She looked at me keenly. 'Nothing escapes your notice, does it? Tell me – what do *you* think I was doing with that little man?'

What a clever woman! She knew that I was full of startling insights. I told her my theory. About her publisher and the hooded dwarf being long-lost father and son. About the poor little man being exiled to France following a scandal. About Miss Always' role in reuniting them.

My friend gasped. 'Ivy Pocket,' she cried, 'you are a wonder! Everything you have said is true. How do you do it?'

I spent the next several minutes explaining my brilliance to the baffled writer.

'Where are you staying in London?' asked Miss Always casually. 'On the ship, you were not sure which one of your grandmother's *many* houses you would be lodging at. I am sure the matter is now settled.'

'Oh yes, thoroughly settled,' I said, pushing a lock of hair behind my ear. 'Grandma has a fine house in Belgravia. I am staying there.'

'How grand.' Miss Always leaned closer. 'Where exactly? I only ask because I am leaving London after my meeting and I would like to write to you while you are in town.'

Of course I remembered Mr Banks's warning – Do *not tell a soul where you will be staying*. But that hardly applied to dear Miss Always. Besides, the Duchess's London home was sure to be terrifically impressive. Just the place for Grandma Pocket to live. I gave Miss Always the address. She wrote it down rather furiously in her pocketbook. Closed the pocketbook. Opened it again. Read the address out to me so as to confirm it.

Questioned me again about my plans. Was I *sure* I would stay in Belgravia tonight?

Poor Miss Always. I was touched that she found me so fascinating. But I was anxious to get moving. We parted with a hug. Miss Always promised to write to me that very night and I promised to read her letters when I could find the time.

I reached the Duchess's town house in Belgravia just before three o'clock and was ushered inside by Mrs Vans, the housekeeper (a toothless, red-faced butterball of no importance), who quickly vanished into the kitchen to smoke her pipe. Horatio Banks was waiting for me in the drawing room, still in his dark suit and top hat. He quizzed me about my activities and seemed rather fixated on my meeting with Miss Always.

'I would like to meet this friend of yours,' he said sternly.

I shrugged. 'I can't think why, dear. She would find you a terrible bore.'

Then Mr Banks forbade me from leaving the house. Said it was much too dangerous. So dangerous, in fact, that he had decided to chaperone me until I was safely on the train to Suffolk.

Even worse, the crusty old lawyer insisted I write a note to Lady Amelia Butterfield (Matilda's mother), informing her that I had a birthday gift for her daughter from the Duchess of Trinity. He said it was the *proper* thing to do. As if I needed a lesson in manners! With the note written, Mr Banks vanished into the Duchess's study to attend to some legal matters, issuing me with strict instructions to stay in the drawing room and read a book. Naturally, I promised to do just that.

Alone at last, I set about exploring the Duchess's house.

It was old. Dusty. Full of outdated furniture. Faded carpets. Vulgar antiques. Even the paintings on the walls were dull and lifeless. The Duchess had appalling taste.

I wandered through a series of tragic rooms on the upper floors. Furniture covered by sheets. Windows shuttered up. There was only one chamber of interest amongst the dozen I passed through. The music room. It was as stuffy and dark as the rest, but a sliver of light from the late afternoon sun washed in through a break in the shutters.

It hit like a spotlight upon a grand piano.

I sat at it. Opened the lid. My mind flew back to the Duchess's hotel suite in Paris. Something stirred in me. A kind of fluttering in my stomach. Which is probably why I played 'Row, Row, Row Your Boat'. Or perhaps I had a hunch. Either way, I wasn't completely shocked when I played the final note and a familiar cranking sound sprang to life deep within the piano. A panel drew back, revealing a darkened cavity. I reached in. Felt around.

Nothing there.

I admit, I was rather disappointed. I suppose I was secretly hoping that the Duchess might have other hidden treasures. Still, it was as good a place as any to hide the necklace. I unpicked the thread of my pocket, pulled out the Clock Diamond and placed it inside the hidden chamber. Much safer than carrying it with me all the time.

There was another reason to hide the stone. I'd become rather preoccupied with it. Thinking about it. Remembering how it felt to wear it. Picturing what I saw when I looked into it. The girl who was me. And about the glorious, blinding light. And the darkness.

'Stuff and nonsense,' I said aloud. I closed the piano lid. The panel slid back, vanishing into the woodwork. Then I went off in search of food.

The evening was devastatingly dull. Horatio Banks was buried in his papers. Mrs Vans stayed holed up in the kitchen smoking her pipe. I read a little. Wandered about looking at the Duchess's odd collection of art – she had a fondness for marble statues of animals dressed in evening wear.

It was almost a relief when Mr Banks ordered me to bed.

The mattress was gloriously soft. The pillow a delight. Sleep came quickly.

I'm not sure what woke me. The snap of a floorboard? The low murmur of a window being pushed up? Something, anyway. My eyes shot open. My nerves were afire. The bedroom was a patchwork of shadows – a splash of moonlight slipping in through the parted curtains. Then something. Movement. On either side of my bed. Two small figures scurrying away. I leapt up. At least, I tried to. But I couldn't move. Not an inch. I was strapped down – the bedsheets pulled tightly across my body with the sort of enthusiasm usually reserved for mummified pharaohs. I struggled to free myself. Squirmed and kicked. But it did little good. I was utterly trapped!

A pair of shadows flew across the room and out of the door.

A current, urgent and hot, surged through my body. The Clock Diamond! I gritted my teeth and pushed hard against the impossibly tight bedsheets. I pushed and kicked with all my strength. Did a large amount of grunting. Wiggled my shoulders. At last, the restraints began to give a little. Showing heartbreaking strength and perseverance, I managed to loosen the top of the sheets enough to wriggle my way up and out. Not unlike a caterpillar.

Once on my feet, I could see that my bedchamber had been ransacked – drawers opened, clothes scattered. Had they come for the Clock Diamond, just as Mr Banks predicted? I was sure they had. Luckily the stone was hidden away in the Duchess's piano. It would be impossible to find.

Flying out of my room, I crossed the landing and hurried down the curved staircase. I wasn't afraid. Not a bit. In fact, I was wondrously calm – having all the natural instincts of a sedated cow. Taking two steps at a time, I had reached the entrance hall, unsure where to begin my search.

'Shhhh!' A woman's voice. Coming from the drawing room. Then hurried footsteps. They grew louder. Indeed, they seemed to be coming right towards me! I stepped back against the wall, vanishing into the shadows. Two figures dashed across the darkened entrance hall and disappeared into the kitchen. As villains went, they were remarkable short. A cauldron of anger bubbled up in me. Monstrous thieves! I stepped out of the shadows and hurried after them, fully prepared for battle.

The kitchen was gloomy and still. A candle flickered on a bench. Copper pots and pans hung from an iron rack above the table. Mrs Vans was sound asleep in a rocking chair, a spent pipe dangling from her lips (apparently she could sleep through a hurricane). A fire burned in the large open hearth. No sign of the intruders.

I walked around the table. Looked under it. Nobody there. Perhaps they had fled through the back door? I was about to check when a plucked chicken came flying out of the larder. Followed by a side of beef. Then a sack of potatoes. Then footsteps. I ducked behind the table just as the two little intruders came scurrying out of the larder. They wore dark cassocks, their faces concealed by hoods. I thought immediately of the strange little man getting into the carriage with Miss Always. The resemblance was striking. Which was odd. One of the devious dwarfs had a large bag of flour in his hand – he tore it open as if it were made of tissue, and emptied the contents on to the floor.

Filthy beast!

The villains stopped suddenly. Then turned their heads in perfect unison. They appeared to be staring straight at me! Then the blackguards split up, taking rapid little steps as they rounded the kitchen table from either side. In moments they would be upon me. I shot up and grabbed a pot from the rack above. Just then, I felt something coil around my left wrist. With no time to spare, I swung the pot as forcefully as I could – hitting the hooded cretin in the head. He tumbled to the floor.

The second intruder made a beastly hissing sound. His face was shrouded by the hood, but I was certain he was an ugly

64

little wretch! I reached for another pot, but too late. The four-foot fathead grabbed my arm and flung me across the table as if I were a rag doll. The nerve! I slid across the table, flew off the other side and rolled across the stone floor. Remarkably, I was unhurt, jumping quickly to my feet.

In moments both my attackers were upon me again. The one to my left struck first, his hideous talons grasping for my throat. With no suitable weapon in sight, I reached down to the mountain of flour at my feet and threw a large handful in his face. The tiny brute reacted badly. Hissing. Shaking his head. Stumbling back.

His accomplice lunged for me. I ran at speed across the kitchen, jumped on a chair and leapt on to the table. A shadow flew past me, while from behind, I felt a hand grasping for my ankle. My options were rather limited. They had me surrounded. The only way to go was up. With momentum on my side, I reached up for a hook hanging from the iron pot rack above my head and swung at great speed just as the hooded thief appeared before me. I let go of the rack. Flew through the air. My foot connected wonderfully with the villain's head, knocking the stuffing out of him. I felt like whooping with delight. Unfortunately there was no time. For I was still rocketing through the air. With no way of stopping myself, I flew over Mrs Vans' head with gusto.

Then crashed right into the fireplace.

Which wasn't at all good.

My body landed in a tangle. A burning log crumbled beneath me. The flames raged – licking my legs and my arms. Smoke billowed. I heard Mrs Vans scream.

Once again, darkness.

The housekeeper pulled me out. She was hollering a great deal. Crying and praying and whatnot. It only took a moment or two and I was wide awake. I blinked several times. The fire in the hearth had been doused. My arms and legs (and no doubt my face) were covered in soot and ash. But my skin was unhurt. Not even a slight burn or red mark, Mrs Vans informed me. She looked thoroughly befuddled. Said the flames had swarmed around me. Said it was a miracle. I very much doubted that. I was certain my nightdress had snuffed out the fire.

Then I remembered.

'The intruders,' I said, getting to my feet. 'Where did they go, Mrs Vans?'

The housekeeper had no idea what I was talking about. Indeed, she seemed to doubt my story about a pair of hooded dwarfs ransacking the house. Then we heard it. A crash – probably a vase breaking. It came from the drawing room. Mrs Vans looked terrified.

'You must wake Mr Banks,' she whispered frantically. 'And I will call for the constable!'

'No time, dear,' I said.

Mrs Vans tried to stop me as I ran from the kitchen – but she was no match for Ivy Pocket.

I charged majestically into the drawing room and I was met with a scene of utter destruction. The whole room had been turned upside down. Moonlight pooled in the middle of the floor like a milky pond, while shadows clung to the corners and walls. I saw movement in the darkness. One of the tiny hoodlums was rifling through a bookcase by the window. The other was busy pulling out drawers from a writing table. Both had their backs to me. I searched amongst the wreckage for a suitable weapon.

Near my feet was a marble statue of a bear dressed as a footman in a frock coat and bow tie. Perfect. I picked it up and lunged at the nearest villain. He seemed to sense me, turning around as I swung the statue at his head. But *turning* is not really the correct word. The tiny blackguard spun on the spot. At great speed. Rather like a spinning top. So fast and so furiously that it created a violent gust of wind. It lifted me from my feet and sent me flying back. Which was shameful. I wasn't the kind of girl to blow away in a breeze!

I landed with a thump against the wall – my head and back

bearing most of the impact. The statue broke in my hand, gouging a large hole in the plaster. I fully expected a broken bone or two. Perhaps a crack in the skull. But no, nothing. I felt slightly sore, but everything else seemed to be in full working order as I got to my feet.

My quick recovery seemed to fascinate the hooded duo. They looked at me. Their heads tilted to one side in unison. Then I heard a dry laugh from the shadows behind them.

'Remarkable,' hissed a voice. A woman's, I think. It was faint. But cold as ice.

'Who are you?' I shouted, unable to see this third intruder. 'Show your face!'

Stepping forward, I reached for the closest weapon – which unfortunately was a bowl of fruit. With arms raised – and a pear grasped in each hand – I walked towards the curtain of shadows concealing the woman. The tiny villains stepped in unison towards me, blocking my path.

'I must warn you,' I said firmly, 'at Midwinter Hall I once felled a runaway chimney sweep with only half an apple. So just imagine how lethal I could be with two pears!'

At that moment Mr Banks thundered into the room, brandishing a pistol and making all sorts of declarations about policemen and putting hands into the air and whatnot. There was sudden movement in the gloomy half-light. I saw a shadow bolt along the wall. The edge of a dark skirt flaring in the moonlight. The woman jumped through the open window, followed by the two hooded henchmen – who seemed to dive into the thick swarm of dusk right behind her.

Chapter 5

'Miss Pocket, explain yourself!'

Horatio Banks wasn't at all happy. He was pacing back and forth in the drawing room as the police scurried about. His endless forehead bulged with purple veins. His steely eyes looked me over as if I were a regular halfwit. The nerve!

'Why would you attempt to take on the thieves by yourself?' he barked. 'Have you any idea what might have happened to you?'

I was magnificently composed. 'I am perfectly capable of dealing with a few hooded dwarfs, dear. As you can see, I had the situation under control.'

Mr Banks pointed to the hole in the wall. Which was terribly unfair. 'It doesn't look like it, Miss Pocket!' he thundered. 'And from what Mrs Vans has told me, you very nearly burned to death.'

'And not even a mark on her,' said Mrs Vans, clutching her rosary beads.

'Miss Pocket, the deal is off,' said the lawyer gravely. 'The situation is far too dangerous. As the executor of the Duchess's estate, any decision concerning her property can be made by me. That is the law.'

I was stunned. I hadn't expected this. Call off the deal? Could he *do* that? I could see the five hundred pounds slipping from my grasp. But I hadn't just fallen off the turnip truck. I knew precisely what to do. Which is why I began to sob. Rather hysterically.

'I've had an awful night!' I wailed. 'Horrible! Treacherous!'

Mr Banks regarded me coolly. Before he had a chance to speak, I launched my offensive. Leaving no detail unsaid, I recounted the events of the evening. Being strapped to my bed. Attacked in the kitchen. Flung about the drawing room. Mr Banks listened to every word. He said nothing for a moment or two. And then ... 'This woman, the one who stayed in the shadows, did she speak at all?'

'Only once,' I said, rather disappointed that of all the questions he might have asked me, *that* was the one he chose. 'She said *remarkable*.'

'What do you think she meant?'

I shrugged. 'Perhaps she noticed my naturally silky hair.'

'Thieves in the night!' cried Mrs Vans. 'Roaming about looking for treasure!'

The lawyer huffed. 'This was no random robbery, Mrs Vans. They came for Miss Pocket as much as for ... a certain necklace in her possession.'

'Stuff and nonsense!' I said with a frown.

'Do not be foolish, Miss Pocket,' said the lawyer. 'Why did the intruders seek to immobilise you in your bed, but not Mrs Vans or me?'

I hadn't an answer for that.

Mr Banks continued, 'I believe they intended to find the Clock Diamond, then come back upstairs and take you.'

'But why?' I said. 'For what purpose?'

Now it was Mr Banks who had no answer. He looked about at the wreckage of overturned furniture and scattered books. 'All I know is this – you are in grave danger.'

I shook my head. 'Fear not, Mr Banks. I'm terribly good in a fight. Stupendously violent. But your concern is understandable – as I possess all the delicate beauty of a princess in a tower.'

Mrs Vans snorted. '*You* a princess.'

'You're not the first to notice, dear.' I smiled regally at the bloated dingbat. 'My mother is from a noble family. *Tragically* noble. Enchanted castles, wicked stepsisters, poisoned apples and whatnot.'

'Enough of this foolishness, Miss Pocket,' said Mr Banks gruffly. 'The necklace, is it safe?'

'I think so.'

His voice softened. 'It might be an idea if you checked.'

'I will.' It was curious he never asked me where the diamond was hidden.

Mrs Vans went out into the hall and began berating the night constable. Mr Banks followed after her, trying his best to calm her down. I decided to return to bed, but not before paying a visit to the music room to make sure the Clock Diamond was still there. It was.

'Who knew that a silly stone could cause so much fuss?' I heard myself say.

The hidden panel slid back into place, swallowing the priceless jewel into darkness.

They searched the house. The police and Mr Banks. Looked everywhere. It was no great shock to find a window broken at the back of the house. Clearly that was the thieves' point of entry.

By lunchtime the next day a letter had arrived from Lady Amelia Butterfield. I read it with interest, Mr Banks looking on.

'Well?' he said at last.

'It's as I expected,' I said, folding the note. 'Lady Amelia was delighted to hear from me. I'm invited to bring the necklace down to Butterfield Park on this afternoon's train. She claims not to remember me from her visit to Midwinter Hall – which I put down to a slight case of stupidity – but she says I am very welcome. So you see, Mr Banks, our business is nearly at an end.'

The grumpy lawyer didn't look at all happy. 'I think you should wait before making the journey to Butterfield Park – see if the police have any luck locating the thieves. Then we can decide what to do next.'

'Wait for what?' I demanded to know.

'Miss Pocket, I am worried about you.' Then he looked at me with something like tenderness. 'I had a sister once upon a time. She was a force of nature, rather like you, I suppose. I was very fond of her and . . . well, you remind me of her.' He cleared his throat. 'We must keep you safe, Miss Pocket, that is all there is to it.'

This caught me off guard. Just a little. While people loved me as a general rule, I hadn't much experience of them *worrying* about me. That's the sort of thing a parent might do.

Or so I am told.

I smiled brightly. 'I have a job to do, Mr Banks, and I intend to do it. I shall catch the train to Suffolk at four o'clock.'

'Then I am coming with you,' he said quickly. 'You can't do this on your own. It's too dangerous.'

'I won't be on my own,' I said, feeling rather pleased with myself. 'Lady Amelia writes that her niece Rebecca is in London and will be travelling on the same train. We will make the journey together.'

The lawyer had no comeback to this. But he had a stipulation.

'I will escort you to the station and see you safely on board.'

I sniffed. 'As you wish. Silly man.'

Mrs Vans had packed me a hamper for the train, but I confess I ate most of it on the carriage ride to the station. Mr Banks barked at me the whole way there – giving me a list of dos and don'ts that stretched on for days. I nodded in most of the right places.

While the lawyer was seeing to my ticket, I busied myself at the news stand, selecting a novel or two for the journey ahead. Imagine my surprise when I ran into Miss Always – who was due to catch a train to her mother's village in the north. The pitiful creature explained that she had been delayed in London overnight due to the monstrous demands of her publisher. The brute loathed her new book – said it had all the excitement of watching tomatoes grow – and was demanding a great many changes. But dear Miss Always was far more troubled by the events of the night before in Belgravia.

'When I read of the break-in in the newspaper and I saw that it was the *very* house where you were staying ...' Miss Always was overcome with the sort of emotion only a terrified spinster can summon. '... I was filled with horror! Ivy, are you all right? Are you hurt?'

'Monstrously hurt, dear,' I said bravely. 'The whole ordeal was thrillingly dangerous. I came close to death on at least two occasions. Flung about. Burned to a crisp. I won't go into detail about how greatly I suffered – it's plain bad manners – but rest assured, it would make even a hardened pirate shudder in agony.'

'You poor girl!' cried Miss Always, pushing her spectacles up her nose. 'I trust the police have caught the villains who harmed you?'

I shook my head. 'Still at large, dear. Probably planning their next attack.'

Miss Always gasped. 'Heavens!'

Which seemed like the perfect moment for me to mention the startling similarities between my pint-sized attackers and the hooded stranger I had seen talking to Miss Always on the ship. 'It was uncanny,' I said, as I paid a shilling for two novels.

'How *peculiar*,' said Miss Always. Then she looked terribly grave. 'Goodness, Ivy, you cannot suspect my acquaintance from the boat? Walter was reunited with his father and is now in Bristol for a family reunion – so you see, it simply *couldn't* be him.'

Which made perfect sense. Not that I ever suspected him. Well, not *really*. It was just that, well, how many hooded dwarfs does one come across in two days?

'Of course if you have any doubts, then you must report poor Walter to the authorities,' said Miss Always, watching me carefully. 'Unless . . . unless you already have?'

I assured her I had not. Which seemed to please her. What a kind soul she was!

'I'm dreadfully worried for you, Ivy,' she said, linking her arm in mine as we began to walk. Her voice dropped to a whisper. 'Travelling with the Clock Diamond. Keeping it safe until Matilda Butterfield's birthday ball. It's a grave responsibility for a young girl. I wish . . . I wish I could come with you to Suffolk – so you wouldn't be all alone.' Miss Always was suddenly bug-eyed. 'Oh, Ivy, I've just had the most wonderful idea! What if I change my ticket and come with you to Butterfield Park? Wouldn't that be thrilling?'

'How can you, dear?' I said, rather startled. 'Your mother being at death's door and whatnot.'

Miss Always looked slightly vexed. But it quickly passed. 'Yes, of course. Poor Mummy.'

I saw Mr Banks coming towards us from across the platform and pointed him out to Miss Always – keen to make an introduction. Unfortunately, it was at that *exact* moment that Miss Always realised she was going to miss her train if she didn't hurry away. Which she did. At great speed.

Mr Banks was terrifically interested in my friend. Asked a dozen questions. Looked about, this way and that. Then he walked me to my carriage (I had a first class ticket, as you would expect) and waited on the platform until the train had left the station. He looked as if he expected an attack at any moment, poor man. I waved, but he didn't wave back.

I was glad to be leaving London and all its calamities behind. I had the Clock Diamond sewn into the pocket of my dress and my carpet bag at my feet. I looked breathtaking. Just like a banker's daughter. Or at the very least a cheese-maker's niece.

Rebecca Butterfield was already on the train when I boarded. Dear Mr Banks arranged for me to have the seat next to hers (*in first class!*). Rebecca was thirteen and pretty, in a plain sort of way – though her freckles were deeply unfortunate. She had wavy blonde hair worn loose around her shoulders, dull brown eyes and unremarkable lips. The girl seemed rather glum – which caused her to stoop, giving her the posture of a washerwoman. A small box wrapped in brown paper and tied with string sat on her lap. She seemed rather fixated on it.

'Is this your first visit to Suffolk?' she asked not long into our journey.

'Well . . .' I looked out of the window, then back at Rebecca. 'I was recently in Paris. You see, I travel the world a great deal. So many places, it's hard to keep track.'

'How lucky you are, Ivy.' She looked positively dazzled. 'I would love to see the world. To travel across exotic lands. To go far away.'

'Oh yes, it's violently interesting.' I sighed winningly. 'Though sometimes I wish my life were slightly less thrilling, a little less astounding. It might be rather nice to be an utterly unremarkable lump like yourself, dear.'

The girl looked stunned. Clearly, she hadn't expected a junior lady's maid to have such fine manners!

I said, 'Do you live at Butterfield Park?'

Rebecca nodded her head gravely. 'I have nowhere else to go.'

'You mustn't look so glum,' I told her. 'I've only known you a short time but already I can tell your skin gets awfully blotchy when you're glum.'

She gasped. 'What did you say?'

The poor creature was obviously hard of hearing.

'Blotchy, dear,' I said, this time louder. 'When you think gloomy thoughts, which I imagine is terribly often, your cheeks flare up like you've been hit in the face with a cricket ball.'

Remarkably, this seemed to please the strange girl. She grinned for the first time and said, 'Where are you from, Ivy?' She shifted in her seat to face me, her hands clasped around the box in her lap. 'Who are your parents?'

'My parents?' I fixed the ribbon in my hair, which gave me a moment to think. 'My father is Polish. A painter. Mainly fruit. Occasionally flowers. Poor, but hauntingly gifted. My mother is defective. Has an obsession with the pan flute. She ran away to join an orchestra in Berlin when I was eight. She sends money when she can and writes every week. Her letters are in German so I have no idea what she's saying – but I'm certain they're full of longing and heartbreak.'

Rebecca Butterfield looked at me with a mixture of shock and envy. 'But who takes care of you?'

'I do,' I said brightly. 'I've been in service for a year and a half and it suits me very well. And just between you and me, I'm soon to come into a small fortune – on account of the diamond necklace I'm delivering to your cousin, Matilda.'

The girl paled at the name. 'Oh. Yes, of course. I suppose it is a gift for her birthday?'

I nodded. 'A special, one-of-a-kind present from the Duchess of Trinity. The Duchess is dead – stabbed through the heart, poor dear – but it was her dying wish that Matilda should have the necklace.'

'Matilda has a great many jewels.' Rebecca was smiling but looked rather like she had swallowed a dung beetle. 'Too many to count. Do you know why I was in London, Ivy?'

'Nerves, dear?'

Rebecca shook her head. 'To be fitted for a new dress. Do I need a new dress? Do I want one? It doesn't matter. Grandmother said I *must* have one for the birthday ball. No one will be looking at me, but everything must be perfect for Matilda.'

'Is she a horrid sort of girl?' I said.

'Matilda is very pretty,' came the meek reply. And then she said no more.

A lengthy silence settled in and I was nearly lulled into sleep by the train's gentle rhythm when Rebecca offered me a slice of cherry cake. Which I took gladly. I asked if she was travelling with any potatoes. Or perhaps a pumpkin. Unfortunately, she wasn't.

'I'm the eldest,' she said between mouthfuls. 'A full three hundred and seventy-six days older than Matilda.' She looked intently at me. 'That's nine thousand and twenty-four hours. You understand, Ivy?'

I had no clue. 'Perfectly, dear.'

'Butterfield Park should go to me, being the eldest. But Grandmother says that Matilda will be her heir.'

'But surely there are rules about these things,' I said. 'Laws and whatnot.'

'When Grandmother first married, the estate was in ruin and had to be sold,' explained Rebecca. 'Her father bought it for her as a wedding gift. So Butterfield Park is Grandmother's to do with as she pleases.' She looked down at the parcel in her lap. 'Mother wanted the estate to be mine – she loved it dearly, the gardens best of all. If she were here, she would never let Grandmother do such a thing.'

'Your mother is dead?'

Rebecca nodded her head. 'Last year. Her heart.'

'I'm awfully sorry, dear.'

'Father has a new family in Italy,' said the girl faintly. 'So it was just the two of us – Mother and I.'

'Now that she is gone, are the rest of your family shockingly cruel?' I said rather hopefully. 'Do they beat you and lock you in the cellar and starve you half to death?'

She didn't answer for a long while. Then she glanced out of the window and said, 'They do not notice me most of the time. And when they do, it makes them uncomfortable. They think that I am strange.' She looked at me earnestly. 'What do *you* think, Ivy?'

'You're not the prettiest of girls,' I said with heartbreaking tact, 'and you seem slightly odd – but I like you very much. Besides, you seem awfully tortured, which is *terribly* interesting.'

Rebecca was looking down again at the box she was clutching.

As such, I pointed to it. 'What's inside?'

The question seemed to stun her. She gulped. 'Nothing. What I mean is – nothing special.'

'Why don't you let me be the judge of that? Come now, dear, I am *dying* to know.'

Rebecca frowned. Looked slightly terrified. Then said, 'Honestly, Ivy, you would be very disappointed. It's just a little something I picked up in London. Very boring.'

I sighed. 'I won't stop asking, dear. I will drive you batty.'

A great wave of defeat washed over the girl's freckly face. She placed her hands around the package, holding it tenderly.

'Very well, Ivy,' she said. 'It is a present for Matilda's birthday. Yes, that's all – just a little present. A few ribbons for her hair and a sash. Matilda will think it very dull. So you see – it's really not very interesting at all.'

But I didn't believe her for a moment.

Chapter 6

We stood outside the station, bags at our feet, and waited for the carriage to come and whisk us away to Butterfield Park. I'm usually an excellent waiter. I once waited for a miracle. It took seven and a half weeks. Yet I never gave up.

But right now I was tired. And it was getting late.

'Lady Amelia didn't say she would send a carriage in her letter,' I said, swatting away an insufferable moth. 'I just assumed on account of me being a *welcomed* guest . . .'

'Don't be shocked, Ivy,' said Rebecca, still gazing with alarming fondness at the mysterious box in her hands. 'I'm sure my aunt *meant* to send the carriage, but it's easy to be forgotten at Butterfield Park – unless your name happens to be Matilda.'

'Do you have any more cake, dear? I'm positively starving.'

'You ate the last piece twenty minutes ago.' Rebecca sighed. 'We'll have to go on foot, so I hope you're a good walker.'

'Stupendous,' I told her, picking up my bag. 'When I was

four I walked across India with my father. He wanted to paint ashrams and elephants. I hardly broke a sweat.'

Rebecca frowned. 'You're lying.'

'Who can say?' I pointed to her suitcase. 'Shall we get started?'

We mounted the crest of a small hill which led to an avenue of lime trees, through which Butterfield Park was revealed in all its glory. It was a fine building with marble columns, magnificent turrets and chimneys reaching towards the heavens. A clock tower crowned the east wing. Surrounding the main house were a tapestry of formal gardens, full of roses and tulips, a wild-flower meadow, an apple orchard and a pretty summer house. The entire estate was surrounded by woodlands.

'It's perfectly lovely,' I declared.

'Wickam took care of the gardens,' said Rebecca softly. 'He loved them so. I think he was the only person around here Grandmother actually *liked* – well, apart from Matilda.'

I didn't need her to spell it out. 'Has he been gone long?'

'He died last winter. We have a new gardener now.' Rebecca scratched her nose. 'He's young and clever and full of new ideas for the wild-flower meadow. Everybody hates him.'

'Quite right too,' I said.

Rebecca giggled.

We ambled up the gravel drive and the girl looked glum again. 'They are probably still packing up from the theatrical last night. My aunt fancies herself a writer. She loves to put on plays and recitals.' She noticed the ravishing smile upon my face. 'Do you act, Ivy?'

'Brilliantly,' I said. 'I toured America in a production of *The Secret Garden*. I played Mary Lennox, of course. The critics raved about me. Said I lit up the stage like a midsized house fire.'

Rebecca was frowning. 'You did no such thing.'

'I certainly did.' I shrugged. 'I'm practically positive.'

We reached the large oak doors and were ushered into the great hall. I spun around, taking in my surroundings. The hall had dark panelled walls, a massive carved staircase, a large coat of arms above the marble fireplace and a stupendous chandelier suspended from the vaulted ceiling. The house had over ninety rooms. A west and east wing. Servants' quarters. A majestic library. Staircases everywhere you looked. Banks of leaded-light windows. More hallways and corridors than a hospital.

'Where is my aunt?' Rebecca asked the butler.

'She's in the library waiting for little Miss Pocket,' came a voice from behind us.

'Blast!' hissed Rebecca. Before I could turn around, she

pushed the small box she had been carrying into my arms. 'Pretend it's yours,' she whispered. '*Please.*'

Of course, I played along – for I have all the natural instincts of a professional trickster. I turned and was rewarded with my first glimpse of Matilda Butterfield. She was a contrast to her fair cousin – dark hair, hazel eyes, the reddest lips I ever saw, and an olive complexion. She looked like a doll. Lovely, but somehow unreal.

Rebecca introduced us and we exchanged a polite greeting, but the whole time Matilda's eyes were fixed on the package I was holding.

'Is that it?' she said eagerly. 'Is that my diamond?'

I looked down. 'This? Of course not, dear.'

'Then what is it?' asked Matilda.

Rebecca gulped and looked at me with pleading eyes. I had no idea what was going on. But I knew she needed me. 'Nothing. Just something I picked up in London.'

Matilda smiled coolly. 'Is it nothing or something?' she said. 'You seem confused, Pocket.'

I sighed. 'It is really rather personal, dear. My Aunt Agnes is a fruitcake. Barking mad. She's been locked away for years on account of her blowing up Mrs Digby's prizewinning dairy cow. Naturally, Aunt Agnes spends most of her time in a straitjacket. But once a week, for one precious hour, she is freed from her restraints. And in that one hour, my insane aunt likes to bake. Fairy cakes. For a lunatic she's very talented.' I looked down at the box in my hand with suitable affection. 'I receive a package like this every week containing a single fairy cake with vanilla icing. It's really very sweet, don't you think?'

The girl didn't say anything at first, her eyes moving back and forth between Rebecca and me. At last she said, 'Can I try it?'

'Try what, dear?' I said.

'Your insane aunt's fairy cake, of course,' said Matilda, flicking her dark locks.

Before I could answer, Matilda Butterfield snatched the box from my grasp. Then she did the strangest thing – she put the box up to her ear. I looked to Rebecca for an explanation. But she just groaned wearily and stared down at her feet.

Matilda pulled the box from her ear. 'I knew it!' she declared. 'You've done it again, haven't you, cousin?'

'Done what?' I said.

Now it was Rebecca's turn to snatch the box away. 'Mind your own business!' she hissed. Then she hurried away, practically running up the staircase.

I looked back to Matilda for an explanation. But she offered none.

'Come on, Pocket,' she said, turning on her heels and walking from the hall, 'my grandmother wants to see you.'

'Where is Rebecca?' That was Lady Amelia's first question after I set down my carpet bag and introduced myself with a breath-taking curtsy.

'She's gone to her room, Mother,' said Matilda sweetly. 'Same as always.'

Lady Amelia was a regal and rather pudgy creature, in a yellow gown of the finest silk, perched before a writing table, a black cat at her feet. She had Matilda's dark hair and features (apparently she descended from Italian royalty). 'Did she ... did she do it again?' asked Lady Amelia anxiously.

Matilda nodded. 'I'm afraid so, Mother.'

'I don't know what to do,' said Lady Amelia wearily. 'We have tried everything to make her stop – but she will not.'

I could only assume they were talking about the mysterious box that Rebecca had brought home. Now, while I had no idea what *that* was about, I was certain I could help. 'Forgive me, Lady Amelia,' I said, pushing a bowl of grapes out of the way and sitting down on the edge of her writing table, 'but I got to know Rebecca rather well on our train journey from London. It's clear the poor girl is unhappy. *Why* is she unhappy? Well, I can't say for sure, but I'm almost certain it's all your fault. Not just you, dear, the whole family.'

Lady Amelia was smiling now (strange woman). 'I see. Go on...'

I jumped off the writing table and picked a grape from the bowl. 'Well, if melancholia is her problem, I have an excellent remedy. All I need is a glass of cranberry juice and a hammer. It's remarkably effective.'

Lady Amelia's laugh was rather musical. Why she was laughing, I hadn't a clue.

'She's mental,' said Matilda with a huff. 'She makes no sense at all.'

I assumed she was talking about her cousin – which was *very* rude. But before I could slap some sense into her, Rebecca appeared in the doorway. Rather sheepishly she entered the library.

'Welcome home, Rebecca,' said Lady Amelia. 'Was London a success?'

'If you mean did I get fitted for the dress, the answer is yes,' said Rebecca.

Lady Amelia regarded her niece carefully. 'And did you keep your promise?'

Rebecca immediately looked to Matilda. Who was smiling wickedly.

'Of course she didn't keep her promise,' came a brittle voice from somewhere across the room. I looked over but could see no one. That corner of the library overlooked the rose garden and in front of the windows stood a single winged-back chair. An elderly woman dressed all in black began to rise up from behind it. She walked slowly, with the aid of a cane.

'Foolish girl,' she hissed at Rebecca.

'Lady Elizabeth, do not be too harsh,' said Lady Amelia. 'I am sure Rebecca tried her very hardest. This is a complicated matter.'

'Claptrap!' spat the old geezer. 'She must stop and she will. Or *else*. Is it any wonder I will not make her my heir?'

Lady Elizabeth was not at all what I had expected. While she spoke with all the regality of Queen Victoria, she had a head like a walnut. Hands like claws. A body withered and thin as a rake. Her skin had seen more bad weather than a lighthouse. She was also rather mean.

Rebecca mumbled something about being sorry and promising she would try harder and whatnot. I was on the point of asking for a snack when Lady Elizabeth turned her icy gaze on me.

'Where is the necklace?' she said coldly. 'That is why you are in this house, is it not?'

'The diamond is somewhere safe,' I said, smiling at the old woman. 'Now be a dear and fetch me a dozen uncooked potatoes.'

'Fetch you *what?*' she spat.

'You must be famished after your journey, Ivy,' said Lady Amelia, hastily ringing the bell.

'Starving,' I said. 'Haven't eaten in days.'

'The necklace, Miss Pocket,' said Old Walnut Head, eyeing me fiercely, 'bring it here this instant.'

'Not possible, dear,' I said, shaking my head. 'The Duchess of Trinity gave me very strict instructions about the Clock Diamond. No one can see it until the birthday ball and it must be given to Matilda in front of all of her guests.'

Just then a pale woman with startling red hair pulled back in a tight bun entered the library.

'Please excuse the interruption,' she said crisply. The poor creature had an accent. American, I think. 'I am after a book of French poetry for my next lesson.'

'Where are the smelling salts?' muttered Matilda. 'I won't survive another of her *dreary* lessons!'

'Matilda, what an awful thing to say,' whispered Lady Amelia. 'Miss Frost has only been here a few days. You must give your new governess a chance.'

Miss Frost hurried over to the shelves by the spiral stairs and busied herself sorting through the books. All the while she kept stealing glances at me. There was something vaguely familiar about her but I couldn't think what. Which was odd.

'I demand you show me the diamond, Pocket,' snarled Matilda, turning her beastly gaze back on me. 'I have a right to see it – how else can I be certain it will complement my dress for the birthday ball?'

'Fear not, Matilda,' I said brightly. 'You are blessed with such a naturally pasty complexion, I am certain the necklace will do wonders for your appearance.'

A bitter smile creased the awful girl's mouth as she glared at me. 'I pity you, Pocket. You'll never know what it's like to wear a priceless jewel. To have every girl in England just *wishing* they were you.'

'Don't be so sure,' I said, unable to help myself. 'Not the part about having every girl in England wishing they were me, of course. Although I *was* voted "Girl Most Likely to Burn at the Stake" two years running. But as for the Clock Diamond – I hate to burst your balloon, dear, but I've already worn it and I looked heartbreakingly pretty.'

A loud bang echoed through the great library. All eyes shifted to Miss Frost, whose book had tumbled to the floor. She looked violently pale as she bent down to pick it up.

'You had no right to wear what doesn't belong to you,' hissed Matilda.

I felt the moment was right for some serious lying. 'The Duchess of Trinity said that I could. In fact, that dear, sweet, pot-bellied dingbat positively insisted. She was very particular when it came to the Clock Diamond.'

'I am rather stunned that she wished to give Matilda such a valuable gift,' said Lady Elizabeth shrewdly. 'We were not exactly *friends* these past sixty years. It is most unexpected.'

I retrieved the Duchess's letter from my bag and handed it to Lady Elizabeth. 'I have a feeling she wished to make peace with you.'

'Hush,' snapped Walnut Head. She read the note and I saw the fire in her eyes dim just slightly. She muttered softly, 'Well, well, old friend . . .'

'It's just so tragic,' said Lady Amelia gravely, 'what happened to the Duchess.'

Matilda's pretty face clouded over. 'I'm not sure I want a necklace from a dead woman.'

'Claptrap!' barked Lady Elizabeth. 'The Duchess was rich and friendless; it's no wonder someone put a knife in her chest.'

'Do you have any idea who killed her, Miss Pocket?' said Miss Frost rather suddenly. She had the book of poetry open in front of her and was running her eyes over some verse or other. 'She was murdered very soon after giving you the necklace, was she not?'

'Yes, dear,' I said, rather thrilled by all the attention. 'The whole business is terribly mysterious. Lunatics left, right and centre. And as the Duchess's messenger, I feel a great sense of responsibility to her memory.' I sighed mournfully. 'I was the last person to see her alive.'

Miss Frost slammed the book shut. 'I would imagine the *killer* was the last person to see her alive.'

Then she excused herself and walked from the library.

'Well I don't think it's fair,' muttered Matilda, throwing a cushion at the cat. 'Why should I have to wait until my birthday to get the necklace? That's not for four whole days!'

'Because it was the Duchess's dying wish, you nincompoop,' I said helpfully. 'You will get the Clock Diamond at the ball and not a moment sooner.'

'That is not the worst part,' said her grandmother. 'We are to be stuck with Miss Pocket for four whole days.' She looked at me hopefully. 'Unless you have somewhere else to be?'

'Heavens no,' I said. 'I'm soon to come into a fortune. Until then, I'm free as a bird.'

Rebecca picked up my carpet bag and said, 'Ivy must be exhausted and I'm sure she wishes to freshen up. I'll show her to the guest bedroom.'

Which was thrilling.

'Certainly not!' cried Old Walnut Head in outrage. 'Put her in the attic. Miss Pocket may be our guest but she is not one of *us*. She is a maid and maids do not sleep in guest bedrooms.'

And with that she turned her back and returned to her chair by the window.

Beastly bag of bones!

The attic was tucked away in the east wing – up the main stairs, across a landing, down a long hallway and up three flights of rickety back stairs. I was led into a dimly lit corridor. Frightfully narrow. A door on either side. A narrow staircase at the far end leading up to the roof.

My bedroom was plain. Wood floors. Sloping ceilings. Whitewashed walls. Jug and basin. Little window overlooking the summer house. Which was a blessing. I had no tolerance for comfy chairs, pretty curtains or comfortable beds.

I washed my face, changed my dress and went to explore the house. But not before sewing the Clock Diamond into my new dress. I felt it was probably best that I keep the stone with me at all times. Much safer that way.

The first floor landing overlooked the great hall. I stood at the banister and looked down – a maid or two hurried past carrying brooms and mops. Then my eyes were drawn by the radiant chandelier suspended above the great hall. Could that be just the place to hide the necklace? If only I had a ladder.

Footsteps clicked rapidly down the hall to my left. I heard a door open. Being naturally curious, I tilted my head and peered down the vast corridor – just as a girl slipped into a doorway at the far end. The door shut quietly. I *thought* it was Rebecca.

Only one way to find out.

'Rebecca?' I knocked gently on the door.

Nothing. Except for a constant banging sound (probably someone tenderising a side of beef in the kitchen).

'Anybody there?' I said next.

Then I heard movement on the other side. Shuffling of feet. The door opened. Just a crack.

'Yes?' It was Rebecca. She looked guilty. Or scared. Or something.

'Is this your bedroom, dear?' I asked.

She nodded. It was clear she had no intention of inviting me in.

'I have a dreadful problem,' I said. 'As you know, I'm soon to have five hundred pounds. Which means I will need to smarten up my bedroom. And I was very much hoping you would let me see yours, dear. You know, as inspiration and whatnot.'

'It's awfully messy, Ivy,' she said. 'Perhaps some other time.'

'Oh, don't worry about the mess,' I said brightly, putting my hand on the door and pushing just a little. Well, I tried to.

Rebecca had her foot wedged against the other side. 'If you like, I'll help you clean up. I'm an excellent duster.'

Rebecca shook her head. Then she opened the door just enough to squeeze herself through and slipped out into the corridor. The door closed behind her before I could catch more than a glimpse inside. She then took a key – threaded on a ribbon around her wrist – and locked the door. Which I thought was rather excessive.

'It's such a lovely evening,' she said, 'why don't I take you outside and show you the summer house? It used to be Lady Elizabeth's summer house, but now it's the schoolhouse where Matilda and I have our lessons. It's really very pretty.'

Before I had a chance to protest, Rebecca led me quickly down the hallway.

We ambled through a blooming avenue of yellow tulips which led directly to the summer house. It was white, with a thatched roof and lattice windows. Terribly fetching. Miss Frost passed us, carrying a large dictionary and hurrying in the same direction. She stopped and turned her attention to Rebecca.

'Class commences in ten minutes,' she said crisply. 'You have completed your book report?'

'It is *nearly* done, Miss Frost,' said Rebecca rather meekly. 'If you just give me a little more time . . .'

'Oh, Rebecca,' said Miss Frost with a sigh, 'you have only been my pupil for a few days and already you are behind. I am certain you are a bright girl with great potential, but I cannot think what you do all day locked up in your room.' Miss Frost's gaze softened. 'Will you promise to try harder?'

'Yes, Miss Frost,' came the faint reply.

'It's my fault, dear,' I said, giving the governess a congenial slap on the arm. 'Rebecca was hunched over her report when I found her. I practically begged her to show me the gardens. I cried. Hit my head against the wall. All sorts of madness. So you see, it's really my fault, not hers.'

To my surprise Miss Frost didn't bite my head off. In fact, her freckled frown faded and she laughed lightly. 'You have a way with words, Miss Pocket. I don't know that I believe any of it, but it is most entertaining.'

I huffed. The nerve!

The governess turned her attention to Rebecca. 'You have exactly eight minutes to finish your report,' she said, pointing to the summer house. 'I suggest you hurry along.'

'Yes, Miss Frost,' said Rebecca, making a hasty retreat.

When we were alone, Miss Frost quickly turned her attention to more serious matters.

'I have no business saying this,' she said, her eyes falling intently on to mine, 'but I am worried, Miss Pocket.'

'What about, dear?' I said.

'The diamond,' was her answer. 'I read a great deal – it is rather a habit of mine – and I have learned something of the Clock Diamond's history. It is dark, indeed. Have you ... has there been any trouble since the stone came into your care?'

'Not really,' I said brightly. 'The odd break-in and whatnot. A darling old lawyer in London thinks differently – he sees danger around every corner – but the necklace is perfectly safe. I keep it with me at all times.'

'That is very unwise,' declared Miss Frost, her face hardening. 'In the last few weeks there have been several brazen robberies in the county. Lady Francesca's daughter was hit on the head and had her gold watch stolen as she walked home from church. Furthermore, people in possession of the Clock Diamond have a habit of dying rather violently. You would do well to remember that and to hide the diamond somewhere safe.'

I sighed. 'I suppose you think the stone is cursed?'

'There are no such things as curses,' said the governess tersely. 'Where the stone originated from, no one knows. Few people have even laid eyes on it. But I have read that once they do, they find the stone *very* hard to resist.' She looked monstrously grim. 'Do you agree, Miss Pocket?'

'Not at all, dear. The stone didn't tempt me for a moment. And as for someone stealing it, fear not – I will take your advice and find a suitable hiding spot.'

'I am glad to hear it.' Funny though, she didn't look terribly pleased – and I knew why. This wasn't about some silly diamond.

'Forgive me,' I said, taking Miss Frost's hand in mine, 'but I can see from the pinched look upon your face that you have a heavy heart.'

She looked startled. Just for a moment. Then it passed and the governess smiled as if she hadn't a care in the world. 'Do I?'

'You mustn't be embarrassed,' I told her. 'Spinsterhood is no great crime.'

She frowned. Pulled her hand away. 'I *beg* your pardon?'

'Spinsterhood.' I said it slowly so she would understand my meaning. 'You find yourself without prospects – heartbreakingly ginger and monstrously unattached. This sort of thing is terribly common amongst grim, sour-faced governesses, so you are *not* alone. And do not give up hope! I feel certain there is a hunchbacked footman or a toothless blacksmith just waiting to sweep you off your feet.'

Miss Frost looked as if she had been sucking on a particularly sour grapefruit. Which was thrilling. Then the governess tucked the dictionary under her arm and stalked off towards the summer house. She may have muttered something about washing my mouth out with soap.

But I can't be sure.

Filled with the warm glow that comes when you have helped a fellow traveller in need, I set off to find the perfect hiding spot for the Clock Diamond.

Chapter 7

I had dinner in my room that first night, then retired to bed. Rebecca insisted that I should dine with the family downstairs. Lady Elizabeth insisted that I shouldn't. I didn't press the point. After all, I was dead tired. Or so I thought. But instead I just lay there. Looking up at the grey moonlight playing upon the eaves. Trying not to think about anything remotely troubling.

Normally I'm an excellent sleeper. But not tonight. For as much as I didn't want to admit it, Miss Frost had unnerved me with her grisly warnings about the Clock Diamond. I'd spent all evening roaming about the great house looking for a suitable hiding place for the stone. There were so many rooms. So many nooks and crannies. In the end, none felt right. The stone was now tucked under my pillow, but my bedroom door had no lock. Anyone at all could come in. See me sleeping like some sort of heavenly angel. Slip their devious hand under the pillow.

And take the stone.

Eventually I drifted off to sleep. I must have. After all, you have to be asleep to wake up. And that's what happened. I woke up. Suddenly. Flew up in my bed. Wide awake.

Something had startled me. I just didn't know what.

The room was thick with silvery shadows. All was still. Silent, save for the snapping and creaking of an old house. I looked about in the darkness. Nothing. Nothing . . . but *something*. I didn't feel alone. Which was foolish. Of *course* I was alone. And yet . . . it wouldn't hurt just to make sure. I felt around on the side table for a match and lit a tallow candle.

The flame bloomed inside the darkened room like a bubble of honey-coloured light.

'Pull yourself together, Ivy,' I said, leaning over to blow out the candle. 'There's no one here.'

'Look closer, child.'

I screamed. Jumped. Grabbed the candle. Thrust it forward – its flickering light swallowing the darkness. The tattered armchair in the corner of the room was shrouded in shadow. But I heard something move. Or wheeze. I crawled to the end of the bed, the candle trembling in my hand.

'Who's there?' I hissed.

'Don't you know?' A blue glow bloomed in the far corner of the attic. And there she was. The Duchess of Trinity. Her body spilling over the armchair like a ginormous mollusc. Her face ashen. Blood drenched the front of her nightdress. She was just how I remembered her. Only dead.

'What do you want?'

'The truth,' she said softly.

Instinctively, I backed away. Creeping up the bed until my arm hit the wall behind.

'I know why you're here,' I whispered.

The ghost seemed to find this amusing. 'Do tell . . .'

'It's about the necklace,' I said. 'You're upset because I tried it on.'

The Duchess of Trinity smiled darkly. 'You broke your promise, child.'

'It was only for a moment, dear. I just wanted to see what it felt like. And no harm was done.'

She seemed to find that amusing. 'Are you sure?'

'Perfectly sure. And it wasn't pleasant at all – in fact, I fainted – and I won't be doing that again. So you see, there's really no need for you to haunt me. In fact, I'd be terribly grateful if you'd shuffle off.'

The dead woman closed her eyes. Perhaps she was taking a nap.

'A great deal has happened since last we met,' said the Duchess slowly. 'I would hate for you to be distracted from your task. No matter what, the Clock Diamond *must* be given to

Matilda Butterfield at her birthday ball. Not a moment before. You won't disappoint me, will you?'

'Of course not.' Then I heard myself sigh disagreeably. 'Though I can't think *why* you'd want her to have it. She's violently unpleasant.'

The ghost purred softly. 'Lady Elizabeth adores her. Every hope and dream she has for the future of this great house is wrapped up in that girl.'

'If you say so.'

'The view from here is marvellous,' said the Duchess playfully. 'I can see *everything*. When the stone was around your neck, you looked into it. What did you see?'

'Nothing,' I said quickly. 'Nothing at all.'

The ghost shook her head and as she did starlight seemed to fall from her white curls. 'What did you see, child? The *truth*.'

She was rather stubborn for a dead woman.

'I *may* have seen a girl,' I said.

'Who was she?'

I shrugged. 'I don't remember.'

'Lies,' she spat. 'The girl was plain. Friendless. Alone in the world. Sound familiar?'

I huffed (I may have rolled my eyes). It was perfectly clear what the Duchess of Ghostville was getting at. 'She looked a *little* like me, I suppose.'

'The stone has much to show you,' sang the ghost, 'but it will bring you no joy. Only suffering. Do not be tempted. Leave it alone, child – for your own good.'

'Really, dear, you've picked the wrong girl for this sort of thing. I don't scare easily and to be frank, you are giving off a revolting odour. Now if you don't mind, I'd like to get back to sleep.'

All at once the distance between us fell away. I can't say if I flew to her or she to me. All I know is, I lifted from the bed. Moving rapidly. My nightdress billowing. Legs kicking. There wasn't time to scream. Then there was a buzzing sound. Loud and urgent. Right in my ear. I looked up. Her face loomed before me. Her whole body seemed to vibrate, the radiant blue of her skin blinding my eyes.

'Remember your promise, child,' hissed the dead woman. 'Do not disappoint me.'

Then I fell. In a tangle. Landed on the bed. The candle blew out and dropped from my hand. Darkness and moonlight filled the attic. I groped around the bedsheets. Found the candle. Struck another match. The flame shook in my hand as I searched the room. She was gone. I jumped up and began walking about madly, my mind a jumble of ghostly thoughts.

Finally, exhausted, I returned to bed. Pulled up the sheets.

But I didn't blow out the candle. I didn't dare.

Pancakes. Pancakes and sweet tea. Perhaps an omelette. A raw potato or three. That's what I needed. A hearty breakfast. I smoothed the creases of my white muslin dress (the diamond was safely sewn into the pocket) and gazed at my reflection in the mirror. I didn't look tired. My skin was glowing. Outside, the morning light with all its promise seemed a million miles away from last night. A nightmare. That's all it had been. Murdered duchesses didn't come back from the dead. Maybe in books. But not real life.

Not to me.

That's when I heard them. The noises. Coming from the room opposite. A fluttering sound. Like something moving. Then silence. Then more fluttering. The blubbery ghost was back! The blood ran cold in my veins.

With breathtaking courage, I opened the door and crossed the narrow hall. The room next to mine was used as a storeroom for the costumes and backdrops of Lady Amelia's theatricals – filled with crates, boxes, trunks, spears, shields and swords.

I stepped inside, looking up as two swallows glided between the rafters. The soft light sliced through the beams of wood, illuminating the creatures' arched wings and casting majestic shadows upon the sloping ceiling. The birds landed with ease on a high beam.

It was really rather wondrous. So wondrous that I stayed in that dusty attic for the longest time. Wandering about, looking in trunks and chests full of faded costumes, wooden swords, drooping hats, rusted tiaras and worthless costume jewellery all tangled in a cluster. I had never seen so much tattered rubbish in all of my life. Which was when it hit me. The most brilliant idea.

'Of course!' I said aloud. For I knew *exactly* where to hide the Clock Diamond.

Just at that moment, I heard approaching footsteps in the hall outside. No doubt a maid coming to tidy up my bedroom. I closed the lid of the trunk and hurried from the room.

My first breakfast at Butterfield Park was heartbreaking. Not a pancake or raw potato in sight. Lady Elizabeth suggested I would be more comfortable eating in the kitchen – with the help. I told her I was completely comfortable eating in the dining room – with the aristocrats.

She nearly choked on her boiled egg.

The morning passed swiftly. I received a letter from Miss

Always. Terribly depressing. While her mother was feeling better, her family's cottage was small and crowded. It was impossible for her to get any writing done. And the changes to her book were due at the publisher's in less than a month. Her most cherished dream was of a quiet country house where she could write in peace. But alas, she hadn't the money. *Oh, Ivy,* she wrote, *whatever will I do?*

Poor, wretched Miss Always!

I went out for a walk in the wild-flower meadow. Tried my best to think happy thoughts. Only three days until the birth-day ball. Soon I would begin my new life. I wasn't about to let a silly nightmare spoil my sunny horizons. And that was all it had been. Just a dream. I felt guilty for breaking my promise to the Duchess, so I had conjured her up in my sleep. Made her say a lot of gibberish about the stone. That I mustn't be tempted by what it had to show me. That it would bring me suffering. Stuff and nonsense!

I wandered back towards the house and found Rebecca sitting in the conservatory working on her French. She glanced up when I entered the room, a curious look in her eyes. She said, 'Did she scare you?'

I gasped. How could she know about the ghost?

'I'm sure I don't know what you mean,' I said brightly.

Rebecca closed her book. 'I don't believe you,' she said.

'As I was walking to the summer house yesterday, I heard Miss Frost warning you about the diamond.'

Oh, Miss Frost. The gloomy governess. I felt a wave of relief. 'Well, yes,' I said, 'perhaps she did bother me a little. She seemed rather fixated on the stone.'

'I don't think she likes you,' said Rebecca.

'Miss Frost is a terrible governess,' I said, in my most disapproving voice. 'Why would Lady Amelia employ an American? Strict, humourless, fat, lonely and British. *That's* what a governess should be!'

'Our last governess was from Wales,' said Rebecca softly. 'Miss Rochester. She was lovely.'

'What a coincidence,' I said, falling into an armchair. 'My last governess was a Miss Rochester. Jolly good sport, she was. Only one arm, but a gifted knitter.'

Rebecca looked baffled. 'Is that true, Ivy?'

'I certainly hope so. But back to *your* Miss Rochester – where did she go? Did she marry? The good ones always do.'

Rebecca shook her head. 'She vanished.'

'Vanished?' Suddenly I was very interested. 'What do you mean, dear?'

'We woke up last Friday and she was gone,' said Rebecca, her voice ripe with sadness. 'No note. No forwarding address. No explanation.'

'Goodness,' I said. 'How deliciously mysterious! My god-father vanished once. In a puff of smoke. Didn't reappear until the following spring.'

Rebecca said nothing. Her fingers were knotted together. Her gaze far away.

I said, 'And you have heard nothing from Miss Rochester since?'

'Not a word,' said Rebecca flatly. 'She lived with us for two years. That's over seven hundred days. Seventeen thousand five hundred and twenty hours. Then she was gone.' She looked at me. 'People do that, don't they?'

'Vanish?' I asked.

'Run out of time,' she whispered.

The poor girl was positively bonkers. Who could keep track of all those silly numbers? I did my best to get back to the matter at hand. There was a puzzle here. I could feel it. 'So Miss Rochester vanished last Friday?'

The girl nodded sombrely.

I frowned. 'How on earth did you find a new governess so quickly?'

'Aunt Amelia met Miss Frost on a train the very day Miss Rochester vanished,' answered Rebecca. 'Turns out Miss Frost had come all the way from America to take up a position with a family in London. But they had to sail for Australia all of a sudden. Miss Frost was reading Aunt Amelia's novel – that's what got them talking.'

'Lady Amelia wrote a novel?' I said.

'*Summer Tempest*. Nobody bought it – well, apart from Miss Frost. Anyway, they started talking and by the time the train reached London, Aunt Amelia had hired Miss Frost to be our new governess.'

'How lucky for Miss Frost,' I said, my mind spinning with dark thoughts about the vanished Miss Rochester. 'It must have been the hand of fate.'

Rebecca shook her head. 'I'm not so sure.'

After lunch that same day, I decided to spend a few hours in the library reading Lady Amelia's book. I was on my way there when a maid came rushing out of the morning room carrying a bowl of water, a damp cloth and a grimace – she looked on the verge of tears. The tormented creature explained that Lady Elizabeth was having one of her headaches. As such, she was making everybody's life a misery.

Naturally, I knew just what to do.

I found Lady Elizabeth in the morning room, resplendent in a black silk gown, lying back on a couch. Her withered head was propped up by a pillow. She was muttering about her life of suffering.

'You look terrible,' I said brightly, setting my basket of supplies on the table. 'Do you get headaches often?'

'Constantly,' she snapped. 'My suffering is monstrous. The future weighs heavily upon me. Thank heavens for Matilda. Without her, I would give in to complete despair.'

'What about Rebecca?' I said firmly. 'She is your grand-daughter too.'

Lady Elizabeth huffed. 'That girl is as deluded as she is bumbling! No, Matilda is the future of Butterfield Park.' The old bat thrust a bony finger into the air. 'She will be my legacy!'

'I think you should worry less about your legacy and more about your nose.' I wiped Lady Elizabeth's dripping nose with my handkerchief. 'Big blow, dear – get it all out.'

The old woman slapped my hand away and gasped. 'How dare you!'

I looked into her fierce eyes and suddenly felt a wave of pity for her. It must be monstrous, being so old and so unhappy. 'Lady Elizabeth, there is no great crime in being a dried-up bag of wrinkles. In fact, I'm not even sure it would be kinder to drag you outside and shoot you.'

Walnut Head gasped and the cat leapt from the couch. 'Help! Somebody help!'

'But I believe it is the headaches that are making you such a miserable old bat.' I climbed on to the couch, kneeling beside the old woman. 'Luckily, I have an excellent remedy. I have a gift for such things.'

Before she could protest, I dipped my handkerchief into a cup of beef tea and began blotting Lady Elizabeth's forehead with it.

'What are you doing?' she hissed.

'Be a dear and shut your cakehole.' I picked up a sliced onion from my basket of supplies. 'Now for best results I normally require a butter knife and a corkscrew – but we will make do with what we have.' I held out the halved onion. 'Take one in each hand.'

'What for?' she barked. 'Get off this couch!'

'For once in your life, do as you're told.'

With a huff, she took the onion. I grabbed her hands, pressing the flesh of the onion against her skin. 'This will ease pain in the temples.'

'Claptrap!'

I picked a stalk of lavender from the basket, broke off the flower, cut it into two pieces, then wedged each one into the old woman's nostrils. Before she could protest, I let my fingers do their work, massaging Lady Elizabeth's forehead with small circular motions. At regular intervals I told her to breathe the lavender in deeply. And from time to time I blew gently on her face.

In a minute or two, five at the most, Walnut Head was quiet, her breathing slow and even. I pulled the lavender from her nose and took the onions from her hands.

'Job well done,' I said.

'Claptrap,' said the old woman faintly.

Then Walnut Head drifted off to sleep.

Summer Tempest was a terrible book. Frightfully bad. Full of breathless maidens trapped by dark secrets and hideous villains obsessed with revenge. In short, I loved it!

The library at Butterfield Park was a two-storey wonderland – just the place to spend the hour before afternoon tea. I had come to find Lady Amelia's book, which took pride of place in a glass cabinet by the spiral staircase. Then I settled down in Lady Elizabeth's chair to read. The view of the rose garden – shimmering in the soft light – was so splendid, I was torn between Lady Amelia's book and the tapestry of red and white flowers outside.

A warm glow seemed to wash over me. I wasn't tired. I *never* got tired. I have the energy of a large rabbit. Or at the very least a field mouse. But I hadn't slept at all well last night. That silly dream. I didn't drift off to sleep. Just dozed.

The murmur of voices roused me. Whispers echoing through the vaulted library. I opened my eyes. Peered around the side of the chair. Miss Frost and Rebecca were standing up on the library's first-floor landing. They seemed deep in conversation. Voices low. Rebecca looked distressed. It seemed as if Miss Frost were doing all of the talking.

'I don't believe you!' Rebecca's voice shattered the quiet.

'Shhh!' was Miss Frost's reply.

What on earth were they discussing? Something passed between them. A book. The governess slipped it into Rebecca's hand. It was red. Small. Rebecca didn't want it. Shook her head. Miss Frost pushed it at her. Her manner was most insistent.

'Read it,' ordered the governess. 'It will explain a great deal.'

'What you're saying isn't true,' said Rebecca. 'It *can't* be!'

'And yet it is.' Miss Frost sounded tired. 'I will endeavour to bring you more proof, but there isn't much time. The matter is urgent. Believe me, I wouldn't involve you if I didn't have to. She must be watched and I cannot keep an eye on her day and night. As such, I need your help. I need it and I will have it.'

Rebecca began to cry. 'How ... how could she not know? It's *impossible*.'

'Crying will not alter the facts.' The governess grabbed the girl's chin with her fingers and pushed it up. Her voice was cold. 'Read the book. Do as I ask. If you don't, this house will see a great deal of suffering. I promise you that.'

Rebecca's head dropped in surrender. She took the book then rushed down the spiral stairs and fled from the library. Poor creature!

Miss Frost seemed to struggle for breath. She shuddered. Reached out and grabbed the iron banister. Then she straightened herself up. Patted her red hair into place. Came quickly down the stairs. She was clearly in a hurry. In fact, she was almost at the threshold of the library when she stopped and looked back across the vast library, her eyes hungry. I edged quickly behind the chair. Held my breath.

'Hello?' Miss Frost's voice was urgent. 'Is someone there?'

How slowly the seconds passed! I couldn't see her any longer. Had no idea if she was roaming the library looking for a spy. I prayed. Yes, *prayed*. I don't know why I feared Miss Frost so completely at that moment. But I did.

All was quiet. Then, the rustling of a skirt. Then silence again. I dared to peek around the side of my chair.

The doorway was empty.

Miss Frost had gone.

Chapter 8

'You really liked it?'

'Liked it? Loved it, dear. *Summer Tempest* should be required reading in every finishing school. Young ladies must be warned about the dangers of accidentally marrying a villainous cheesemaker. I still have a few chapters to go, but so far it's a triumph. A monstrous triumph!'

Lady Amelia clapped her hands (not unlike a seal). 'Oh, Ivy, I *am* pleased!'

After the curious incident in the library, I had searched the house for Rebecca – there was no sign of her. I had hoped she would be at afternoon tea in the rose garden. She was not. But the delicate sandwiches, fresh pastries and chocolate cake were delicious. Lady Amelia was thrilled to hear that I had read her novel. Old Walnut Head was seated in the arbour, the cat curled up on her lap. Fortunately, she was asleep again.

'The critics were rather unkind,' said Lady Amelia meekly. 'I fear they didn't appreciate my little tale.'

'Writing a book is a fine achievement,' I said, taking another slice of cake. 'Who cares if it was terrifically bad?'

Lady Amelia paled slightly. Indigestion, I expect. Fortunately Matilda was on hand to take her mind off it. She spent the next half hour complaining that she had to wait three whole days until her birthday ball. She felt it a grave injustice. I helpfully pointed out that there were children in the world who had never had a birthday party in their lives and that she was a hideous ingrate. Matilda responded by suggesting I drown myself in a bucket. Which was most unhelpful.

'Luckily, I have enjoyed some wondrous birthdays,' I said, taking a sip of tea. 'One year my parents rented a theatre in New York and had a troupe of Romanian puppeteers re-enact the most thrilling episodes from my life – my heart-stopping duel with a double-crossing juggler was a high point. Another year we travelled across India in a hot-air balloon. Took hours. We landed on a mountain somewhere south-east of whatsit. Delightful village – populated entirely by panda bears. Wonderfully friendly, but *terrible* cooks.'

When I finished my tale the whole family was staring at me (except for Lady Elizabeth, who was still fast asleep). 'Nothing you say is true, Pocket,' sneered Matilda, 'not one word of it. You're even crazier than Rebecca.'

'I do love a birthday ball,' said Lady Amelia dreamily.

'Although masquerade balls are my favourite. I wanted Matilda to have one, but she says her face is far too pretty to hide behind a mask. Ivy, I hope our little party compares well to some of the others you have been to.'

'She's not invited!' barked Matilda.

'I know you two are not great friends,' said Lady Amelia, looking hopefully at her daughter, 'but as Ivy will be there to present your special gift, she simply *must* come as your guest.'

Adorable creature!

Matilda looked violently unhappy. Which was delightful. It seemed the perfect time to gloat shamelessly. And I would have, but for two things. The first was that Lady Elizabeth woke up with a start. The second was that Miss Frost came across from the summer house to collect Matilda for her French lesson.

'If I could have a brief word, Lady Amelia,' said Miss Frost. 'It is about the birthday ball. I assume Matilda is to give a speech?'

'Only if she wishes to,' said Lady Amelia. 'Matilda isn't terribly fond of –'

'Of course she will give a speech,' said Lady Elizabeth, interrupting gruffly. 'It is a Butterfield tradition.'

Miss Frost frowned. 'The trouble is . . .'

Lady Elizabeth slapped her bony hand on her knee. 'What is the trouble? Matilda, is there a problem I should know about?'

Matilda stole a glance at her grandmother but said nothing.

'Only this, Lady Elizabeth,' said the governess. 'My talents are rather wanting in the speech-writing department. I think Matilda will need help. Professional help.'

'To write a birthday speech?' huffed Lady Elizabeth. 'Claptrap!'

'Oh dear,' said Lady Amelia. 'Perhaps I could help her. After all, my book –'

'I've read shopping lists with more flair than your ghastly book!' snapped Lady Elizabeth.

The poor woman looked crestfallen.

'Matilda doesn't want to disappoint anyone,' said Miss Frost with a sigh. 'She is a Butterfield and the whole county will be at the ball.' She sighed again rather loudly. 'If *only* there was someone who could help.'

Then it hit me. The most wonderful idea!

'I think I may have just the answer,' I announced.

'Heaven help us!' barked Lady Elizabeth.

'My dear friend Miss Geraldine Always is in desperate need of a quiet place to work on her new book and she would be a great help to Matilda,' I said, smiling winningly. 'I shall write to her this very minute and invite her to stay. It's a perfect solution, don't you agree?'

Lady Elizabeth glared at me. 'You think it is your place to invite guests to *my* home?'

I nodded. 'Just the one, dear.'

'Miss Pocket, the fact that *you* are a guest at Butterfield Park gives me constant heartburn. If you think I would welcome another ghastly interloper, you are even more deluded than I thought.'

Which wasn't very nice. I put this down to the fact that Lady Elizabeth was shockingly old. And slightly evil. Amazingly, Miss Frost saved the day.

'I think it is an excellent idea,' she declared.

I jumped in. 'Miss Always is terribly plain but *very* gifted, Lady Elizabeth. She has just completed a lecture tour and could help Matilda craft a brilliant speech – thrilling, funny, moving. One that would have the whole county talking.' I took a large bite of chocolate cake. (I felt I had earned it.) 'And in her spare time, Miss Always could work on her book.'

'Not the *worst* idea I've ever heard,' muttered the old woman. 'A compelling speech would honour the Butterfield name.' She nodded her shrivelled head. 'Yes, I like it.'

Lady Amelia looked thrilled. 'Well done, Ivy!'

Miss Frost did not. 'The ball is in three days. We haven't much time.'

'Time enough,' I declared. 'I will write to Miss Always at once – the letter should reach her by nightfall. I will explain everything and beg Miss Always to come to us immediately.'

And with that, the matter was settled.

With the letter written and sent, I wandered down to the summer house looking for Rebecca. I wanted to lure her away and speak with her about Miss Frost before dinner. Their whispered conversation in the library would not leave my mind. *Something* was afoot. I found the summer house empty, the blackboard covered in Miss Frost's ornate handwriting. Some nonsense about the cycles of the moon.

I sat down at Matilda's desk to wait and drummed my fingers in a dainty fashion. A sketchbook was open before me containing a woeful drawing of a bower bird. Glancing out of the window, I spotted an old man – no doubt a gardener – bending over a rose bush with a pair of clippers in his hand. He had white hair. A tatty straw hat. Whiskers that went on for miles. I took up a pencil and began to draw him. And I became so engrossed in the sketch that I didn't even hear Miss Frost return to the summer house. Her pupils were in the orchard learning about bugs and she had come back to fetch a magnifying glass.

'I am surprised to find you here, Miss Pocket,' she said crisply.

'Can't think why,' I said. 'I'm terrifically studious.'

'Tell me, have you had any formal education?'

'Certainly. My father is a professor of criminal history – pirates, highwaymen, that sort of thing. My mother teaches Latin and armed combat.'

The governess picked up the magnifying glass from the bookcase and turned back to me. I glanced up at the blackboard. Just for a moment. But it was enough to catch Miss Frost's attention. 'Do you know much about astronomy, Miss Pocket?'

'Only what I learned at Cambridge, dear.'

She laughed. Which was unhelpful. 'The moon's four cycles are rather fascinating, don't you agree?' she said.

I shrugged. 'Not really. Of course, I have a soft spot for the full moon – murderous rampages, werewolves and whatnot.'

'Superstitious nonsense,' she declared. Miss Frost walked to the front of the room and pointed to the blackboard as if she were teaching a class. 'The *real* power lies in the first half-moon. When it is both revealed and hidden all at once – half there, half not. Great things are possible at such a time.' She let out a sharp breath. Smiled a little. 'Matilda's birthday ball falls on the half-moon. I feel it will make for a most *interesting* evening.'

I sighed and went back to my drawing. 'If you say so.'

Miss Frost sniffed. Shook her head as if I were a nitwit. Then she began to walk briskly from the room, but stopped suddenly at my desk. 'What are you drawing, Miss Pocket?'

I pointed out the window to the ancient gardener. 'Him.'

'Him?' The governess looked at my sketch. Then out of the window. Then back at my sketch. Clearly it was better than I thought. Then she muttered, 'How fascinating.'

I put down the pencil and admired my picture. The roses weren't a great success. But it was a good enough likeness of the old man.

'Miss Pocket, may I have this drawing?'

I shrugged. 'If you wish.'

The governess took the sketch, walked to her desk and placed it in a drawer. Then locked the drawer with a key. No doubt she planned to have it framed. People do that with marvellous drawings.

Then Miss Frost hurried from the summer house without another word.

Nightfall. It had been a day of brilliant ideas. First, inviting Miss Always to stay. Second, finding the perfect hiding place for the Clock Diamond. I had known right away that it was just the spot to conceal the stone. So I had waited until the household was fast asleep, then grabbed a candle and made my move.

After all, I didn't want any prying eyes.

The room across from mine in the attic contained all the relics from Lady Amelia's theatricals. All worthless and discarded. What better place to hide a mystical necklace?

I sat down upon a crate. Plucked the stitching from my pocket with a small pair of scissors and pulled the Clock Diamond out. Somewhere in the back of my mind I heard the Duchess's ghostly warning. To not be tempted by the stone. Foolish dingbat!

I held the silver chain up to the candlelight and looked into the diamond. Outside, a blanket of stars and a near half-moon filled the sky. Inside the stone, a twinkling of stars and a near half-moon rose high above Butterfield Park.

Behind me a bird fluttered its wings. I turned and saw it take off and glide under the rafters, landing in the shadows at the far end of the roof. When I looked back at the stone a snowstorm was swirling within it, each flake sparkling like a gemstone. Behind this curtain of snow I could see a house. It was grey and grim. No lights flickered in the frosted windows.

Suddenly the front door of the house flew open. A woman came out. A woman carrying a sleeping child. She wore a heavy dark coat and a yellow bonnet obscured her face. The child was small with long black hair. The woman hurried away, stealing backward glances at the house. The child in her arms . . . I knew her. Was it me? I knew it was. But younger.

I watched as the woman passed through a rusted gate and crossed a dirt road. Then she began to run – trudging through a field thick with sludge and sleet. She was running away. Holding me and running away. Where to? Where from? There were no answers. Just questions.

Questions. And footprints in the snow.

A dark mist whirled madly, eating the light. The vision was gone. Replaced by the stars and near half-moon of the night sky. I dropped the necklace and stood up. Began to walk in circles. My mind was crowded with thoughts. My stomach in knots. Perhaps it was just a trick of the stone. A cruel trick. Just as quickly, I recalled the Duchess's words about the diamond – it did not offer fantasies. Only visions of what was, what is and what will be.

If that was true, what had I just seen? Who was that woman? My mother?

The stone. The stone had the answers. I raced back and scooped up the necklace, holding the diamond to the flickering candle. Praying it would show me more.

It did. But not a field in a snowstorm. Nor the woman in the yellow bonnet carrying me away. Instead, I saw the summer house at Butterfield Park glowing in the soft light of a crescent moon. A figure holding a lantern was moving along the garden path towards the darkened schoolhouse.

It was Miss Frost. What on earth was she doing?

The Clock Diamond offered glimpses of events past, present and future – so which was I seeing now? There was only one way to find out. I returned the stone to its hiding place, raced across the hallway and ran to the small window in my bedroom. I got there just as Miss Frost, holding a lantern, vanished inside the schoolhouse. I watched as she walked to each window and drew the curtains. Minutes ticked by. Then, as the clock in the great hall struck midnight, another figure stole down the avenue of moonlit tulips and headed for the schoolhouse. This person was clutching a small book and when she reached the schoolhouse she stopped and looked back the way she had come. Her face a ghostly white.

Next, Rebecca Butterfield stepped inside, closing the door behind her.

Early morning. The sun was yet to rise on my third day at Butterfield Park. A blanket of fog hovered above the flower beds. The grey mist parted as I hurried down the path towards the summer house. I hadn't slept a wink. Well, perhaps a wink. Maybe two. In fact, I had fallen asleep at the window waiting for Miss Frost and Rebecca to come out. When I awoke, hours had passed.

That's when I decided to solve this curious mystery. All the while questions bubbled and popped in my mind. About the vision in the stone. About the mysterious woman in the yellow bonnet. About Miss Frost and Rebecca.

What was the stone trying to tell me?

The door was unlocked. The schoolhouse, a chamber of shadows. I struck a match, lit a candle. I searched the room thoroughly – for I have all the natural instincts of a lighthouse keeper. Arithmetic books, history books, paper, ink, pencils: it was a symphony of disappointment. There was nothing that could offer a clue as to why Rebecca and Miss Frost might be conducting a secret midnight meeting.

Walking to the back of the classroom, I glanced out of the window. The sun was just breaching the woodlands behind the summer house. Time to go. I had to get back to the house before anyone noticed I was gone.

I blew out the candle.

'You are making a grave mistake, child.'

I didn't turn around. No need. I knew who it was. I could see her reflected in the window. 'You're not real,' I said softly.

'I am as real as you and that is a fact.' Her voice was practically singing.

I turned around. The Duchess sat at the teacher's desk before the blackboard, her magnificent blubber swallowing the chair beneath her. Fingers, fat like sausages, drumming on the desk. Blood soaked the front of her nightdress. Her head was a radiant blue. She looked very pleased with herself.

'What do you want?' I said, hands on my hips.

'I cannot rest.' Her fiery eyes fixed on me. 'Since I put the Clock Diamond in your care you have become rather attached to it. That is a mistake.'

I shrugged. 'You're wrong, dear. I barely even *think* of the stone.'

The Duchess smiled darkly. She didn't speak. She didn't have to. Thick ribbons of dark smoke coiled from her nose, twisting into the air like serpents. The threads of billowing mist curled this way and that, and in moments had arranged themselves into a series of letters. This was what they said:

Deliver the necklace to Matilda at the birthday ball
Collect five hundred pounds
Begin a new life

The ghost cackled madly and the message began to crumble and fall like sand, each word dropping to the desk in a pile of ash.

'Stop looking into the stone,' said the dead woman. 'No good can come of it. You are seeking answers to questions that will bring you nothing but suffering, child.'

'You're dead,' I said. 'Why don't you float away or cross over or whatever it is murdered fatheads do?'

'I am in waiting,' came the reply.

'For what?'

The Duchess smiled again. 'The birthday ball. I must ensure you carry out my orders.'

I looked at the hideous bloodstain on her chest and asked the question that had haunted me since Paris. 'Who killed you?'

'Excellent question!' cried the ghost. 'Alas, I was dozing at the time.'

'Why were you killed?' I said with some urgency. 'You must know why.'

'You *know* why, child,' she purred.

'To get the Clock Diamond?'

'Very good,' hissed the ghost. 'But think only of your promise to me. Forget what you have seen in the stone. You are no longer that little girl.'

I felt a deep sadness reach for me like a grasping hand. Pulling me down. I shook my head. 'I don't understand. Who was that woman in the yellow bonnet? Was she my mother?'

'You have no mother,' said the ghost, her hair suddenly alive with stardust. 'Only I can offer you a new beginning. Trust no one in this house of shadows. Keep the stone safe. Watch over it. But do not look to the diamond for answers. Do not look, child!'

I was shaking. Trembling like a rabbit in a snowstorm. And I hated it. I hated *her*. I shut my eyes. 'Why shouldn't I look? I want answers, you ghoulish fatso, and I will have them!' I suddenly felt rather brave. Which is why I added, 'Perhaps I will keep the necklace until it tells me what I want to know. It's not like you can stop me. You're dead!'

I heard it then. The vibration charging the air. I opened my eyes just as the Duchess, this creature of death, lifted up. It wasn't graceful. It was a rampage. The desk toppled over. The chair shot back against the wall. And she flew at me, glowing like a winter dawn, her bloodstained nightdress billowing, an instrument of rage and thunder.

And I knew she would devour me in seconds.

I don't recall running, but I must have, for my hand was on the door handle and I was flinging it open. I didn't look back. I just ran. Until I hit it. Not it, *her*. We collided like trains. I screamed. She didn't. I blinked. Looked up into her face.

She looked baffled. 'Good heavens, Ivy, whatever's the matter?'

I gasped. 'Miss Always?'

The formal introductions happened at breakfast. Miss Always met the whole family. She was asked many questions about her travels and her books – and she answered them all admirably. Lady Amelia asked the writer what time she had arrived. Miss Always explained she caught the night train from her mother's and waited in the station house until dawn. She made no mention of the summer house. And finding me running out of it like a lunatic. Nor did she mention walking me back inside and helping me put the desk to rights and straightening the place up.

'My speech will be the highlight of the ball,' said Matilda, her gaze far away.

'Goodness,' said Miss Always rather meekly. 'I shall do my best.'

Rebecca didn't come to breakfast. In fact, I didn't see her at all until I was giving Miss Always a tour of the house. We were passing through the great hall, talking of our voyage from Paris and her mother's miraculous recovery, when Rebecca hurried down the stairs and into the sitting room – where I saw her exchange words with Miss Frost, who was waiting by the window.

'Ivy?'

I looked back at Miss Always. 'Sorry, dear?'

'I said, are you well?'

'Never better,' I answered. But I was unable to get the vengeful ghost from my mind. 'As it happens, I have a great deal of time on my hands at Butterfield Park and the books in the library are of little interest. I was thinking I might give your last book a try.' I smiled as if I hadn't a care in the world. 'Wasn't it about ghosts?'

Miss Always nodded. 'The great ghosts of Scotland and Wales.' She was looking at me rather curiously. 'Ivy, you know that as my bosom friend you can ask me anything. *Anything* at all.'

'You would be shocked, dear,' I heard myself say.

A smile creased her thin lips. 'I very much doubt that, Ivy.'

Without going into all the grisly details, I briefly explained to Miss Always what had been happening with the dead Duchess.

Miss Always stared at me with great intensity. For a moment her dark eyes seemed to crackle and flare, like coals in a furnace. No doubt, I had stunned the poor creature. 'That is most interesting,' she said softly. But she didn't look at *all* shocked. 'There are very few rules with regard to ghosts, Ivy, but there are two which are most important. The first is that only earthbound ghosts can haunt the living.'

I frowned. 'Earthbound ghosts?'

The writer nodded. 'Ghosts who remain tethered to this world because they have unfinished business here. Most of these ghosts are perfectly harmless – they are messengers and soothsayers. But some are very wicked indeed, seeking vengeance for past crimes.'

'Can they . . . can they hurt the living?'

'Oh yes. Dreadfully so. Rage generates great power, Ivy.'

Which was rather unsettling. 'What is the second rule?' I asked.

'When a person dies, their spirit is given a very short time to decide whether to stay earthbound or to pass into the afterlife. It is possible they may make a fleeting visit to a loved one. But only for a short time. Then they must depart, never to return.' Miss Always clasped my hands in hers. 'You can be sure the Duchess haunts you for a reason, Ivy. Can you think what it might be?'

'Her dying wish was that I give Matilda the Clock Diamond at her birthday ball. I'm certain the blubbery phantom will haunt me until I do as she asks.'

Miss Always' cheeks coloured at the mention of the stone. 'Matilda must have been delighted when she saw the necklace. Tell me, did she try it on?'

'She hasn't seen it,' I explained. 'No one has.'

'Very sensible,' said Miss Always. She reached out and grasped my arm. 'Do you still carry the diamond sewn into your pocket?'

'Heavens no,' I said, as if it were the silliest thing I ever heard. 'I have hidden it away.'

The dear creature seemed delighted. 'I'm sure it's somewhere utterly ingenious.'

'You are right, Miss Always,' I said proudly.

'Wait.' She giggled shyly. 'I will try to guess. You mustn't give me any hints now. Not even a little one. Oh dear, this house is so vast it could be *anywhere*.'

'You must let me tease you with a clue or two,' I said playfully.

'Well, if you insist.' Miss Always' smile faded. 'Go on then.'

'Think of a place where –'

'Excuse me, Miss Pocket.' It was Miss Frost. She was striding across the hall towards us. 'Forgive me for interrupting, but I wanted to give Miss Always directions to the summer house. She is to begin work on Matilda's speech this morning.'

Miss Always regarded the governess rather coldly. 'No need, Miss Frost, I know exactly where it is. I met Ivy coming out of the summer house when I arrived this morning.'

I very much wanted to die. Poor Miss Always had no idea she had betrayed me. I kept my eyes on my hands (they were fascinating). I could feel the governess's glare upon me. But to my surprise she said, 'Well then, Miss Always, you will have no trouble finding us.'

Miss Frost departed and as she did, I saw Rebecca slip out of the sitting room and steal away up the stairs. Miss Always was keen to see the library, so I pointed her in the right direction and said a hasty farewell. For I was on a mission.

Taking two steps at a time, I mounted the stairs and hurried after Rebecca.

'Wait!'

She was pulling the key from the lock. About to vanish into her bedroom. She looked rather startled. 'Ivy,' she said nervously. 'I don't mean to be rude, but I cannot stop to chat. I have some work to do before my history class.'

I pulled up outside her door, rather puffed. Rebecca was already inside. Beginning to close the door. 'Surely you can spare a moment or two,' I said, catching my breath. 'I fear that you are avoiding me, though I cannot think why.'

'We spoke yesterday,' said Rebecca faintly.

'Yes, dear, but it's not the same, is it?' I put my hand on the door. 'If anything is the matter, you can tell me. I am a fount of wisdom and bright ideas.'

'Nothing is the matter.'

'You look tired,' I told her.

The girl made no answer. It was then that I noticed the strange rhythmic sound again – only this time I was certain it was coming from inside Rebecca's bedroom. I frowned. 'What on earth is that noise?'

The girl pushed on the door, trying to shut it. 'I have to go, Ivy.'

'I saw you in the library with Miss Frost yesterday,' I said hastily. 'You looked awfully upset. Then last night you stole into the summer house under cover of darkness. We both know who you were meeting there.'

Rebecca gulped. I saw it clearly. 'Miss Frost has been helping me with my work,' she said.

It might have made sense, if not for the fact that she and the governess had met in the dead of night. Whatever their business, it was of a secret kind.

'You can trust me, dear,' I told her, in my most trustworthy voice. 'In the library, you seemed to doubt what Miss Frost was telling you – she said something about getting proof. Proof of what, Rebecca?'

The girl's gaze travelled over my face for the longest time. She looked at me as if she were seeing me for the first time. Then her eyes pooled with tears. 'Miss Frost thinks that . . . she is worried. She is worried about *you*, Ivy.'

'Me?' I sighed wearily. 'She's not *still* fretting about the Clock Diamond, is she?'

Rebecca nodded gravely.

'Well, she needn't worry,' I said brightly. 'I have the stone safely hidden away.'

Strangely, this did not seem to reassure the peculiar girl.

'You are good . . .' she said next, tears trailing down her face. 'You are good, aren't you, Ivy?'

'Good? Of course I'm good. Wonderfully good. Everyone says so.' I pushed on the door but it wouldn't budge. 'Let me come in, dear. We can discuss what is troubling you.'

'Be careful, Ivy,' Rebecca whispered. 'Things are not as they seem.'

Then she shut the door in my face.

I heard the key turn in the lock.

Chapter 9

'May I speak with you?'

She came before lunch. I had only just finished checking on the Clock Diamond and was changing the sash on my dress. Without waiting to be invited, Miss Frost walked into my bedroom.

'I was hoping to have a word,' she said, stopping at the window.

'How odd.' I smiled brightly. 'I was just thinking the exact same thing.'

'Oh?'

'Yes,' I said, 'I thought we might talk about Rebecca.'

That seemed to startle Miss Frost. Her eyes left mine and she looked around. 'What about her?'

I fixed my gaze upon the grim governess. 'She said you had been speaking to her about me. She warned me to be careful. That things are not as they seem.'

'She might be right,' said Miss Frost. 'Turn around.'

Before I could argue, the governess had taken the sash from

my hand and was fixing it around my waist. She said, 'Perhaps Rebecca is slightly upset at present, but it will pass. You see, I have asked her to help me with a project I am working on.'

'Is that why you met her in the schoolhouse last night?'

If the governess was shocked she hid it well. 'I am teaching Rebecca about the history of a faraway place. A hidden place with a secret history.' Her eyes clouded over. 'I told her the facts as I know them. But she had doubts.'

'I should think so,' I declared. 'Sounds bonkers.'

'Fortunately I was able to show her compelling proof,' said Miss Frost crisply. 'My methods may be unorthodox, Miss Pocket, but our lesson was a great success.'

I was frowning with tremendous enthusiasm. 'Have you spent any time in a madhouse, dear? I'm almost certain you must have.'

The governess walked back to the window, her rusty locks flaring in the light. 'Are you seeing ghosts, Miss Pocket?'

'Perhaps,' I said with a shrug.

'The Duchess of Trinity?'

I gasped. 'How did you know?'

She made no reply.

So I said, 'She only comes because of that silly stone. I'm certain that is why I can see her – because I have the Clock Diamond.'

The governess shook her head. 'The stone does not allow one to see ghosts, Miss Pocket.'

She sounded terribly sure.

I didn't want to ask. But I simply *had* to. 'Then why can I see her?'

'I haven't an answer that would satisfy you. I only know that the stone has no such power. At least, none that I have ever heard of.'

'How do you know so much about the necklace?' I asked doubtfully.

'I confess, the Clock Diamond intrigues me. It has a dark but fascinating history.'

I sighed. 'I do hope you are not going to babble on about it, dear.'

'The stone was first discovered in Budatta,' continued Miss Frost, as if I hadn't spoken. 'It was found quite by accident. A local tribe was cutting down whipple trees to build a canoe. The stone was found embedded in one of the logs. There it was, perfectly formed, in the middle of a tree trunk. Its origins are a mystery. It couldn't possibly have been created in there. Diamonds are not forged from wood.

'Once the local people saw its power – that it controlled the clock and offered visions of the past, present and future – they took it as some sort of divine totem. But that was not all. It is rumoured that the tribe discovered the stone had *another* great power. They turned the diamond into a kind of god, and built a temple to display it. The diamond was stolen from Budatta a century ago. Nobody knows how or by whom. After that, its history is unknown.'

'You said the stone has *another* great power,' I said, sitting down on the bed. 'What is it?'

'I don't know,' she said quickly. 'Nobody does.'

I wasn't sure I believed her. In truth, I didn't like Miss Frost. Perhaps it was her freckles or her pointed nose. Yet I suspect it was her manner. She was polite. But cold.

I stood up. 'Well, whatever the history of the diamond, it doesn't matter to me. The day after tomorrow it will be Matilda's problem, not mine.'

The governess headed towards the door. She paused and regarded me doubtfully. 'If you say so, Miss Pocket.'

'How nice it is to see a familiar face!'

I found Miss Always in the library. She was in the mythology section (holding a book on ancient curses) – though when she saw me coming, she closed the book and put it back on the shelf. Naturally, she was thrilled to see me. But I was rather confused when she looked past me and frowned into the distance.

'Looking for something, dear?' I asked.

'Not really,' said Miss Always, shaking her head. 'It's just that every time I turn around, Rebecca seems to be peering at me from afar. Which is most puzzling.'

I shrugged. 'She's frightfully shy. I'm sure she just wishes to know you better.'

'Yes, you are probably right.' Then my friend sighed wearily. 'I am taking a break from speech-writing.' She threaded her arm through mine and walked with me towards the row of large windows overlooking the terrace. 'Miss Matilda is a *special* girl.'

'She is a fathead and a tyrant.'

Miss Always laughed. 'I confess, Ivy, I don't know why the Duchess of Trinity wished to reward her with the Clock Diamond.'

'You are right – I can't think of a girl less deserving than Matilda Butterfield.'

'Ivy . . .' Miss Always looked suddenly very grave. 'Matilda told me something rather shocking this morning. She said that you have no family. That you are an orphan.'

I thought back on all that I had told Miss Always during the voyage from France – about my map-making parents and my frightfully rich grandma. I was certain that now was the right moment to speak the truth. Get it all out in the open and whatnot. As such, I said, 'How monstrous! Don't believe a word of it, dear!'

Miss Always smiled at me tenderly. 'I quite agree. In fact, I told Matilda that she was *quite* wrong about you. For I know a member of your family *most* intimately.'

I tried hard not to look stunned. 'You do?'

She nodded. 'I should think so. After all, we may not share blood, but are we not sisters?'

I felt a mad impulse to hug Miss Always most violently. And so I did.

I may have even whispered, 'Bless you, dear.'

We sat down on a red velvet sofa, the warm sun pouring in through the windows.

'I have unearthed a thrilling legend for my new book that is sure to delight my readers,' said Miss Always, grinning madly. 'It is long forgotten, dating back centuries. Would you like to hear it, Ivy?'

'Heavens no. Hearing about holy grails and Greek gods bores me silly.'

Miss Always took off her spectacles. Gave them a polish. 'But this one is different, Ivy. It has tragedy and hope. Death and salvation. And the hero is a girl about your age.' She popped her glasses back on. 'It is called The Legend of the Dual.'

I realised the pitiful creature was going to inflict her tale upon me whether I liked it or not. So, being a bosom friend, I said, 'Get on with it, dear.'

'It concerns a land cursed by a plague,' said Miss Always. 'They called this plague The Shadow – because when a person became infected their skin would colour as if a shadow were passing over them. Death was always swift. Millions died. The queen and her entire family were wiped out in a single year.'

'Sounds beastly,' I said. 'Was there no cure?'

'None,' said Miss Always gravely. 'The entire kingdom was filled with despair. Then a story began to circulate through the villages and towns. It was said that on his deathbed, the queen's mystic, who had a gift for prophecy, whispered to his son: *There will come a girl child. She is not from our world, but she will come. A child who is ignorant of the power she possesses and walks the earth unnoticed. She is the Dual – a girl who can pass freely between our two worlds. Only she can heal the plague cursing our land. Only she can save us.*'

The story had me intrigued. 'Did they find her?'

'Not yet,' whispered Miss Always. Then she blinked and shook her head. 'What I mean is, as far as the legend goes, the Dual was never found. A few were chosen to leave the kingdom and search for the child. But it was like looking for a needle in haystack. The plague continued to kill across the land. The legend goes that if the Dual was ever found, she would bring healing to this cursed world and ascend the throne.' Miss Always blushed slightly. 'In the interest of my book, I am filling this particular legend with a great deal of murder and treachery. Much of it my own invention. Is that terribly dishonest of me?'

'It's shameful, dear, but perfectly reasonable. These stories are all nonsense, after all.'

Miss Always smiled. 'Ivy, are you happy here at Butterfield Park?'

I nodded but said nothing. Part of me wished to confide in my bosom friend. About Rebecca and Miss Frost. About the vision in the stone. And I might have, if Matilda hadn't stormed into the library waving around a sheet of paper.

'The speech is awful!' she spat. 'This will not astound my guests or make them laugh or move them to tears! Where is the excitement, Miss Always? Where is the humour? Stop loafing about and fix it!'

'Oh dear,' said poor Miss Always. 'Well . . . perhaps we could include a thrilling episode from Butterfield family history. Something sure to excite your guests.'

'Impossible,' I said with certainly. 'Nothing interesting or thrilling or scandalous *ever* happens to aristocrats. It's scientifically proven.'

'What would you know, Pocket?' snapped Matilda. 'There's plenty of scandal in my family. You would be shocked.'

I was hoping to learn something about Rebecca's troubles. So I said, 'I doubt that, dear. But if you think you can shock us, go ahead.'

Then Matilda did something I had never seen her do before. She laughed. 'Grandmother would *kill* me for telling you this.' Then she frowned, but her eyes were dancing. 'She was married before. He was a local man who worked in the village as a clerk. I think he was engaged to someone else, but Grandmother *had* to have him. His name was –'

'That's not really what I had in mind, Matilda,' Miss Always interrupted, looking flustered. 'Come now, let us go to the summer house and work on something more appropriate.'

Miss Always got up and began to hurry Matilda from the library.

'Wait!' I said, calling to Matilda. 'Your grandmother and the clerk – how did it end?'

'They married,' she said. 'He died – struck by lightning. Grandmother *never* talks about him.' She grinned wickedly at me. 'Is your little heart stunned, Pocket?'

'Not at all,' I said casually. 'My first governess was struck by lightning. Nothing left of her but a pile of ash, poor dear.'

'You had a governess?' said Matilda doubtfully.

'I certainly hope so,' I said.

Miss Always practically dragged Matilda from the library. As they hurried off, a frightfully handsome footman came in carrying a silver tray. He walked up to me silently and held it out. The tray contained an envelope with my name scrawled upon it. I tore open the letter. It was from Mr Banks.

Dear Miss Pocket,

I write to you on a most urgent matter. It concerns the gift you are set to deliver at the ball. Some information has come to light that is most troubling and makes me fear for your safety and that of those around you. If my letter alarms you, I am glad of it. Be alarmed, Miss Pocket, and be on your guard. The Clock Diamond is not what it seems. I believe you are ensnared in a wicked scheme. Keep your nerve and trust no one. I will come to Suffolk the day after tomorrow by the morning train and I will explain myself then. I have the money owed to you and more besides. There is a way out of this mess.

Hold tight, help is at hand.
Your friend,
Horatio Banks

What could it mean? Only this – Mr Banks was deluded! The poor man had been full of conspiracies when I was in London and now . . . now his imagination had run away with him. What proof did he offer? None. Yes, it was true, ever since I had taken possession of the Clock Diamond, strange events seemed to shadow me. But I was perfectly safe. After all, I was amongst friends here at Butterfield Park. No harm could come to me.

Yet, as I slipped the lawyer's letter in my pocket and left the library, I could no longer deny one simple truth.

I had doubts.

By lunchtime it was raining heavily. Storm clouds gathered over the park, low and menacing. Inside, the house seemed to surrender to the gloom. Candles burned in all the public rooms and thunder shook the sky. I had taken Horatio Banks's note up to my room and hidden it in the pages of Lady Amelia's novel. I didn't want anyone reading it by accident. There was sure to be a fuss when the lawyer turned up at the house in two days – he was a stubborn old goat – but for now I would act as if nothing were afoot.

How did things get so terribly muddled? It was such a simple task – deliver a diamond for a miserable brat's twelfth birthday and collect five hundred pounds. Where was the harm in that? What could go wrong? Nothing. Or a very great deal.

Perhaps it was the house's fault. It was big and old and full of gloom. Or maybe it was my mind. Which was big and young and full of ghosts.

I came down the narrow back stairs from the attic and walked along the dim corridor, past Matilda's and Rebecca's bedchambers. When I got to the landing, I saw Miss Always crossing the hall below with a lamp, on her way to the library. I thought of calling to her. Telling her about the letter. It might help to speak of it. But Miss Always was a writer and therefore prone to hysteria. Horatio Banks's warning would be fuel to the fire. No, I would say nothing.

Rain thundered down on the roof of the great hall. I stood at the top of the stairs and listened. The storm clouds outside had bled daylight from the vast room – it was a patchwork of shadows. A gloomy chamber, more night than day. I closed my eyes, just for a moment.

It took no time at all for it to happen.

I felt someone approaching on the landing behind me. I heard no footsteps. Perhaps they were drowned out by the rumbling sky. But someone was there. I could feel it.

I heard footsteps in the hall below.

I looked down.

There was no one there. Then I remembered – behind me. Someone coming up behind me. I was about to turn around . . .

But my feet were no longer beneath me. I was lurching forward. Stumbling. A bird without wings. Dropping ... tumbling ... thumping.

Screams, but not my own. Then light. Bright light. Everywhere.

The floor rushed to meet me.

Chapter 10

There was no pain.

That was the first thing.

I wasn't dead.

That was the second.

I can't say exactly what position I landed in. All I know is that when Rebecca and Miss Frost found me at the foot of the stairs, my arm was twisted behind my back. I remember Miss Frost gently rolling me on my side and pulling my arm free.

'Are you hurt?' she said.

'Terribly,' was my reply. But when I was finally alert enough to really take a moment and *feel*, I was amazed. Despite the fact that I had apparently tumbled down the enormous staircase, I wasn't hurt at all. Well, apart from a slight headache. Nor was I bleeding. As Rebecca helped me to sit up, my mind flew back. Back to when I was standing at the top of the stairs. Back to footsteps in the hall below. Back to feeling someone come up behind me. Back to falling.

Had I been pushed? Surely not! Yet I couldn't deny that *someone* was up there.

'How is your arm?' said Rebecca urgently. 'And your head, Ivy, how is your head? Oh, Miss Frost, it's too awful!'

I saw Miss Frost's face harden. 'Yes it is,' she said coldly. 'Awful and unnecessary. But what's done is done. Your legs, Miss Pocket – can you move them?'

'They're broken, I'm sure,' I said gravely. To be honest I was rather disappointed in myself. How can a girl tumble down a great staircase and come out of it unscathed? It was a scandal!

Miss Frost felt both my legs. Had me bend my knees. Wriggle my toes and whatnot. 'You are perfectly fine,' she announced.

'No injuries at all?' said Rebecca, gently pushing a strand of hair from my face.

'None,' said Miss Frost.

'What happened, Ivy?' said Rebecca. 'Can you remember?'

I shook my head. 'Not completely. But I think perhaps I was pushed.'

Rebecca gasped. 'Surely not!'

Miss Frost scowled. 'I hate to disappoint you, Miss Pocket,' she said, getting to her feet, 'but I was passing by when you fell and there was no one near you on the landing.'

The governess swept from the hall to inform Lady Amelia and Lady Elizabeth of the incident. She promised to come back with a damp cloth for my head. Rebecca checked me over several times. She was *very* preoccupied with my injuries. Or rather, my lack of injuries.

When Miss Frost returned with a flock of onlookers (including a near hysterical Lady Amelia), Rebecca said the most remarkable thing. Or rather, she whispered it. 'If they ask,' she said, as Miss Frost and the others crossed the great hall and walked towards us, 'say that you slipped on the last few stairs and fell only a short way.'

I looked up at the girl in confusion. 'Why on earth should I say that?'

'Please, Ivy,' said the girl, her eyes dark and anxious, 'I cannot explain. Just please do this for me. It is most important.'

I sighed. 'Don't pop a button, dear. If it matters that much to you, I'll do as you ask.'

'Oh, Ivy, are you all right?' cried Lady Amelia. 'You poor, poor girl!'

'What happened?' asked Miss Always, who had come running out from the library. 'Ivy, where does it hurt?'

Rebecca informed the gathering that I was uninjured and that I had only slipped near the bottom of the stairs. As such, no harm was done.

'You might have been killed,' said Miss Always (that sweet creature!).

'Yes, dear, you are right,' I said bravely. 'I suppose I shall have to be pushed around in a wheelchair until I recover. Lifted into chairs and carried about the place by a footman.'

'Claptrap,' snapped Lady Elizabeth, waving her cane at me. 'I see your ridiculous imagination has not been injured either.'

'I will send for Dr Longfellow,' fretted Lady Amelia.

'There's no need,' said Miss Frost. 'She is perfectly unharmed.'

Rebecca and Miss Always helped me to my feet. Regrettably, I didn't faint.

'The poor girl *must* be examined,' continued Lady Amelia.

'Pocket's neck didn't break,' said Matilda coldly (she had been standing by the banister watching the proceedings). 'You are worrying about nothing, Mother.'

Miss Frost quickly agreed. I had tumbled down the stairs. Was apparently unhurt. And there was nothing more to it. So the matter was settled. For them.

But not for me.

The crowd of onlookers disbanded and I was left to rest in the conservatory until supper. However, I was in no mood for that.

After all, I felt perfectly fine. In body, at least. My mind was another matter. As the rain had ceased, I went for a walk in the woodlands. A torrent of thoughts crashed around me. I remembered standing at the top of the stairs. I felt someone there. I heard my name called. Yet Miss Frost had seen everything. She claimed I was alone up there. Was she telling the truth? And if she wasn't, why would she lie?

I wanted to scream. So I did. Several times. There was no harm in it. While the woodlands afforded a perfect view of the summer house and the wild-flower meadow, they were far enough away to ensure privacy. It was a mess. All of it – a mess.

The afternoon sun filtered through the canopy of maple and oaks crowding the woodlands. It filled the forest with a rose-coloured shimmer that was something like dawn. I took a deep breath. Steadied myself. Through a clearing I saw Rebecca and Matilda emerge from the summer house followed by Miss Frost. They appeared to be studying the wild flowers. Or bees. Something of that kind. Miss Frost pointed to several blooms and was talking a great deal.

'They are so different,' came a voice.

I turned. A woman stood behind me. She was tall. Blonde hair sweeping her shoulders. Her delicate hands clutched together. She was looking at Matilda and Rebecca. And she was smiling.

'I'm sorry?' I said.

'The girls,' said the woman, and her voice was like honey. 'They are very different. Matilda has all the answers. Rebecca all the questions. Who is the wiser, do you think?'

I shrugged. 'If it's a contest, I would win. I'm monstrously wise. Everybody says so.'

The lady laughed softly. There was something odd about her. And also rather wonderful.

'Do you know the Butterfields?' I said.

'Once upon a time.'

I looked at her carefully. She had a pretty face. Round. Soft. Her eyes caught my attention – one was green, the other blue. She said, 'I haven't seen you here before.'

'I'm just visiting,' I said. 'On frightfully important business.'

'I see.' Her eyes drifted back to the clearing where Rebecca and Matilda were now pressing wild flowers into a book. 'They have so much to learn.'

'You know Matilda and Rebecca?' I said.

'Oh yes. Once upon a time.'

Suddenly I understood. I knew who this strange, beautiful creature was. Miss Rochester – the vanishing governess! She had come back to check on her pupils. How violently interesting!

I looked at Miss Rochester. Then back at the girls. 'Why

don't you come and say hello?' I said, watching as Matilda stomped on a cluster of daisies. 'I'm sure they'd be thrilled to see you.'

'Don't lose heart, Miss Pocket.'

I turned. Baffled at how she knew my name.

'How did you know – ?'

But the governess had disappeared.

She found me before I found her. Rebecca's face was a cloud of anguish when she spotted me walking out of the woodlands and hurried over. 'Have you seen Miss Always?'

'Not recently,' I answered, rather surprised by the question. 'Is something the matter, dear?'

The girl shook her head. 'No. Yes. Oh, Ivy, you must be terribly confused about why I asked you to lie about falling down the stairs. There is so much you don't –'

'I've seen her!' I declared triumphantly, unable to hold it in a moment longer.

'Who?' Rebecca looked alarmed, poor dear. 'Who did you see?'

'Miss Rochester,' I said excitedly. 'The missing governess!'

Rebecca frowned. 'You have seen Miss Rochester?'

'I'm utterly positive,' I said with pride. 'Of course, most people wouldn't have a clue, they would just think her a passing stranger. But I knew it was your tragic governess – for I have all the natural instincts of a junior Sherlock Holmes. Trust me, Rebecca, Miss Rochester has returned!'

A faint smile washed the frown from Rebecca's face. She said, 'Ivy, are you sure it was her?'

'Positive! At least, I *think* it was her. I can't be completely sure, since I have never laid eyes on the woman. Have you a picture of her?'

'No,' said Rebecca glumly. Then she brightened a little. 'But you could tell me what she looked like.'

'That is easy,' I said, 'for her face is fixed in my mind. Lovely blonde hair. Face like a cherub. And her eyes. They were remarkable – one blue, one green. I never saw such thing.'

Rebecca made no reply. But the poor creature was trembling. In fact, she looked positively stricken. My brilliant description had floored her. Miss Rochester had returned!

'It's true,' whispered Rebecca. There were tears welling in her eyes. Then she lunged at me. Hugged me like a madwoman. She pulled back. Hugged me again.

Her eyes roamed my face. 'Have you told anyone else – about the lady?'

I told her I hadn't. 'You are the first.'

'It would be better if you said nothing about her to anyone else,' said Rebecca. 'Just for now.'

'Why shouldn't we tell everyone about Miss Rochester? Her return is a good thing, isn't it?'

It was as if a great wave of grief or happiness washed over the girl. She sobbed. Wiped her eyes. Sobbed again. The girl wept like a fountain. I did my best to calm her. Patted her head two or three times. Smiled kindly.

'Please, Ivy, I know I have asked a great deal of you,' she said, her words tumbling out in a flurry, 'but it isn't without reason. There are things ... things that make no sense. Yet they are true. Impossibly true! Please, just do as I ask.'

I sighed. 'As you wish. But I have to say, dear, in my professional opinion – you're barking mad.'

She hugged me again, kissed me on the cheek, then ran off towards the house.

Rebecca didn't come to dinner. And I hardly saw her at all the next morning. The house was a hive of activity – which was no great surprise, as the ball was tomorrow night. I spent much of the morning with Miss Always in the library. She was still busy working on Matilda's speech, but she always had time for me.

There was so much I wished to tell her about the events of the last few days, but I had made promises to Rebecca and I was a girl of my word. Instead, I told Miss Always about the letter from Horatio Banks – his grim warnings and that he would be calling on me at Butterfield Park tomorrow.

Miss Always was terribly interested. She threw a dozen questions at me. Asked me what train the lawyer was coming on. Expressed a strong interest in seeing the letter.

The poor creature looked rather anxious. Jumpy, even. She explained that her nerves were still afire following my monstrous fall the day before. She said her heart was in her throat when she saw me at the bottom of the stairs. She expressed amazement that I hadn't broken my neck.

Miss Always loved me like a sister!

'It is very good news that Mr Banks is coming,' she said as we walked out into the rose garden for morning tea (there was to be cheesecake, so I was violently excited). 'From his letter it sounds like he has new information about the Clock Diamond. Perhaps now we will learn its great secrets!'

We found Lady Elizabeth snoozing in the arbour, the cat on her lap. Lady Amelia was fussing over the teapot. She looked terribly agitated. It was all on account of Rebecca.

'She won't be joining us,' she said gravely. 'I *do* wish she wouldn't hide herself away day and night.'

'I refuse to pry. It's the height of bad manners,' I said, sitting down in a wicker chair, 'but tell me this, Lady Amelia – what does Rebecca have hidden in that room of hers?'

The poor woman paled. 'It is difficult to explain, Ivy.'

'She should be locked up,' said Matilda brightly. 'She'll go mad one day and kill us all.'

I smiled warmly at Matilda. 'Not all of us, dear. I'm certain Rebecca would lose interest once she finished you off.'

The dear girl unleashed a passionate response – all in French. I'm certain she was complimenting my silky hair. And possibly my chin. It's difficult to be sure.

'Have you seen Miss Frost?'

We all turned as Rebecca came quickly towards us. She looked a ball of nervous excitement. 'Have you seen her?' she asked again.

'No, dear,' I said, 'perhaps she is in the summer house.'

'Miss Frost is a devil,' declared Matilda. 'All she ever does is *teach*. It's not normal.'

'Miss Frost is good and brave and noble!' shouted Rebecca. It was quite an outburst and caught everyone's attention. Even Lady Elizabeth stirred from her nap.

'She dresses like an undertaker and her accent hurts my ears,' said Matilda, folding her arms. 'And everyone knows she has the complexion and manners of an orang-utan.'

'You take that back, Matilda!' yelled Rebecca. 'Take it back!'

'I won't!' snapped Matilda.

I had high hopes that things might get violent, but Miss Always calmed things down by alerting us to the governess, who was stalking towards us across the rose garden.

I cut a slice of cheesecake and sat down again.

'Rebecca, would you join me in the schoolhouse?' said Miss Frost, stopping a short distance from our tea party. She did not offer a greeting to anyone else.

'But Miss Frost, surely Rebecca has finished with her lessons for the morning?' protested Lady Amelia.

'It's just a small matter,' said Miss Frost crisply. 'It will not take long.'

'I don't mind, Aunt,' said Rebecca quickly, walking over to join the governess. 'I asked Miss Frost to help me with my penmanship.'

'I should think so,' barked Lady Elizabeth, opening her eyes, 'you write like an infant!'

Miss Frost and Rebecca made a hasty retreat to the summer house. They were deep in conversation almost immediately. Which was violently interesting.

'Goodness, Grandmother,' cried Matilda, peering at Old Walnut Head, 'how long have you been out here in the hot sun?'

Lady Elizabeth huffed. 'No idea. One hour is much the same as the next when you get to my age.'

In truth, the beastly fossil had been sleeping in the arbour since breakfast, but the maids were too scared to wake her. And now her face was as red as a tomato. While Lady Amelia was at the table fetching a glass of lemonade for the old woman, I made my move. Crouching down before Lady Elizabeth, I examined her face.

'The news isn't good, dear,' I said gravely. 'You have the complexion of a boiled lobster. Your skin is practically crying out for moisture. Fear not, I have just the remedy.'

'Don't you touch me!' she bellowed, and the cat jumped from her lap into Matilda's.

Lady Elizabeth reached for her cane. I had to act quickly.

'I don't wish to alarm you, Lady Elizabeth,' I said, scouring the table for something suitable, 'but this is a skin emergency.'

The old woman tried to get up (possibly to hug me), but I pushed her back down. It only took a second for me to reach across the table, picking up the plate of cheesecake and a spoon.

'Ivy, what are you doing?' said Lady Amelia urgently. 'Are you sure you know – ?'

'Very sure, dear!'

'Stop her, Mother!' cried Matilda. 'She's dangerous!'

'Stay away!' shrieked Lady Elizabeth.

Which was ridiculous. I scooped up a large helping of cheesecake and splattered it on the old bat's face. Then another blob. Then another. She was making strange noises by that point – not unlike an injured piglet – which I put down to the soothing qualities of the cheesecake. I put aside the spoon and proceeded to smear the healing balm all over her face, leaving only her eyes. It took just a moment or two for her red skin to be fully covered by the dessert.

'The treatment must stay on for at least an hour, Lady Elizabeth,' I said, cleaning my hands on a napkin. 'You may attract flies, so I suggest you go indoors.'

She cursed me with gratitude and leapt up, waving her cane! That's when things went slightly bonkers.

Lady Elizabeth's cane went swishing through the air and hit a maid on the buttocks. She shrieked – which was understandable – and in the process, tipped the jug of lemonade into Matilda's lap. She and the cat were soaked. As such, Matilda jumped up suddenly (crying like a madwoman) and the cat went flying into the air. Alarmingly high.

I had to think quickly. It would be necessary to break the cat's fall. I grabbed the closest thing – Lady Amelia.

'Prepare yourself, dear!' I cried, spinning her around and pushing her on to the table. Her generous bosom and wobbly stomach would make an ideal landing pad.

'Prepare for what?' cried the poor creature.

The whole thing was over in no time. The cat came down right on Lady Amelia's magnificent torso. It landed with a bounce and flew across the table, crashing into Lady Elizabeth. The creature flew into her lap and almost immediately began licking the cheesecake on her face. Disaster averted!

There was much carry-on, of course. Matilda questioned my sanity. Lady Amelia fainted. Old Walnut Head called for me to be dropped down a well. Or at the very least tied to a tree and hit with sticks. I felt it best to excuse myself and retire to the house. But I must admit, I felt bitterly disappointed.

All that effort, and not even a thank you!

I went up to my room with the intention of finishing Lady Amelia's book before lunch. The house was eerily quiet. Matilda was having a final fitting for her birthday dress. Lady Amelia was on hand to tell the brat how pretty she looked. Lady Elizabeth was taking a bath to remove the cheesecake. It was a perfect moment to read and rest.

But as I sat on my bed, all I could think about was the Clock Diamond – just lying there hidden amongst a cluster of costume jewels. Just waiting for me to hold it in my hands and look within it. Just waiting to show me what I yearned to see. It was a hunger so urgent and painful that it made my teeth chatter.

Which would explain why I found myself kneeling on the floor amongst a pile of dusty trunks, staring into the stone. Praying that it would show me another vision. I gasped as heavy snow churned inside the diamond. A winter forest began to emerge. The woman in the yellow bonnet was no longer holding me. I was walking beside her. Not walking. Being dragged along. Somehow I knew we had been trudging through that forest for hours. Then a dark blur passed in the trees behind us. It was a farmer, head bowed against the snow, pulling a horse laden with logs.

I turned. Spotted him. In an instant I pulled free from the woman's grip and was running, my legs vanishing beneath the thick blanket of frost. I was calling out – though I couldn't hear the words. The farmer stopped. Looked hard into the heavy snowfall. I called out again, but a hand flew over my mouth. The woman in the yellow bonnet pulled me back. We cowered behind a tree, my mouth muzzled. I struggled to free myself, but her grip was too tight.

The farmer waited a moment. Then he whipped his horse and moved away.

Only when he was out of sight did the woman release her hold on my mouth. She shook the snow from her bonnet and grabbed me again. With my hand locked inside hers, she pulled me deeper into the white woods.

The snow fell harder until the diamond was a radiant white. Then a dark mist churned, swallowing the light. The vision ended. I stayed there staring at the stone for the longest time. Willing it to come back and show me more. To tell me what happened next.

But of course, it didn't.

Chapter 11

It was already afternoon when I finally came down from the attic. I had just turned into the hallway that led to the landing above the main stairs – it was a vast corridor, littered with hideous urns and dull paintings of hunters and hounds. I was in rather a hurry to get to the kitchen and see if Cook could spare a few raw potatoes. Perhaps a cabbage or two. I was famished, but all thoughts of food flew from my mind when I glanced down that dim hallway. What I saw at the other end stopped me cold. A small figure in a dark cassock.

His face was shrouded by a hood, but I felt quite certain he was staring at me.

My first instinct was to look about the vast corridor in search of a weapon. But there wasn't time. For at that exact moment, Miss Always swept around the corner and as she did the little villain seemed to vanish. As if into the very folds of her dress. It was most remarkable!

'You look as if you had seen a ghost,' said Miss Always when she reached me. She was frowning now. 'Are you unwell?'

I told my bosom friend what I had just witnessed. The poor creature was stunned.

'Ivy, what a remarkable story,' she said gravely. 'You say this little gentleman vanished as I came around the corner? But you know such things are impossible. You *do* know that, don't you?'

'Of course I do, dear,' I said, trying to sound bright. 'But I tell you, he looked just like the villains who attacked me in London. And if such things are impossible, what on earth did I just see?'

Miss Always' eyes travelled over my face. She pursed her lips. Murmured every so often. Then said, 'Trauma. That is the only explanation.'

'Is it?'

'I believe so. It is perfectly understandable that you might imagine those awful thieves from London had followed you here to Butterfield Park. In fact, I would be shocked if you *weren't* seeing things.'

But it had looked so *real*. Was I to doubt my own eyes? Yet Miss Always sounded very sure and what reason would she have to lie? She must be right. It was just trauma. From the robbery. Nothing more. Which was a great relief.

Miss Always insisted on taking me to the kitchen for a pot of strong tea. We passed Miss Frost on the main stairs. For some reason Miss Always seemed keen to hurry me along, but when Miss Frost showed a passing interest in why I looked so pale, I informed her that I was deeply traumatised.

The governess seemed less interested in my trauma and more interested in the hooded villain I had hallucinated in the hallway. Remarkably, she didn't think I had *imagined* him at all. And that wasn't the only shock. 'I should think,' she declared with astounding certainty, 'that Miss Always might be *just* the person to ask about such creatures.'

'I'm sure I don't know what you mean,' said Miss Always quickly. 'Come along, Ivy, let us –'

'But are you not writing a book on myths and legends?' said Miss Frost with a faint smile. Before my friend could answer, the governess continued, 'I seem to recall reading about a band of tiny hooded monks, just as Miss Pocket described. Let me think, it was *so* long ago that I studied mythology.' The governess tapped her chin. 'Ah, now I remember! They are called Locks.'

'Locks?' I said.

Miss Always laughed rather too loudly. 'What nonsense, I never heard of such –'

'From what I remember,' interrupted Miss Frost (she seemed to be enjoying herself enormously), 'Locks are hooded creatures who wear dark robes. They are small, usually travel in packs, and are fast and highly dangerous.'

I gasped. (It seemed the right moment.) 'That has to be them!'

'I seem to recall they serve a particularly hateful mistress,' Miss Frost went on. 'A cold-blooded hag of misery and death – though I cannot remember her name. Can you, Miss Always?'

'I cannot,' came the firm reply. 'And Ivy is much too clever to be carried away by the ravings of a second-rate governess.'

Miss Frost glared at my bosom friend. 'I would have thought it was entirely reasonable, given what has befallen Miss Pocket of late. I am shocked, Miss Always, that you haven't heard of Locks.' She folded her arms. 'In fact, I would think it quite impossible.'

'Yes, well ...' Miss Always adjusted her glasses. 'I *may* have read of such creatures – just in passing. And from what I remember, Locks are not at all as you have described, Miss Frost. They are a band of merry monks. Agents of peace, not violence.'

'You're wrong, dear,' I declared. 'They're nasty little things.'

Miss Frost walked off looking rather pleased with herself. Miss Always and I continued down the stairs and through the entrance hall. It would hardly be worth noting, if not for the fact that Miss Always stumbled rather suddenly and fell to the floor. Tripped, apparently. Which was odd, as there wasn't so much as a speck of dust upon the polished floor. The poor dear landed with a thump and when I helped her up, I saw her wrist was beginning to swell.

'I am a clumsy fool,' said Miss Always, looking at her injury.

'I'm afraid so, dear,' I said helpfully.

Miss Always began to frown. Said her wrist was feeling numb. Apparently that was a bad sign. As she was holding her red and swollen wrist in front of my face, I felt it only proper to reach out and gently lay my hand upon it. I said, 'Can you feel that, dear?'

'I . . . I can indeed,' came the reply. Her eyes fluttered shut. Just as quickly they sprung open. Then she pulled her arm away, covering her wrist with the sleeve of her dress. 'I'm sure it's fine, Ivy. Nothing to worry about.'

Which was most peculiar.

'I hope you do not take Miss Frost to heart, Ivy,' said Miss Always as we made our way into the kitchen for a cup of tea. 'I think it is very cruel, the way she delights in unsettling you – filling your mind with mischief and folly.'

I frowned. 'Is that what she's doing?'

'Well, what other explanation is there?' said Miss Always. 'Whatever you saw or think you saw, I am certain the explanation is simple. A smart girl like yourself would never actually *believe* that a band of mythical Locks had come to Butterfield Park to steal the Clock Diamond.' She poured steaming tea into a cup and pushed it towards me. 'But Miss Frost hopes that you will. It would amuse her greatly.'

It confirmed my own fears about the devious governess.

'Beastly woman!' I said, reaching for the sugar bowl.

I would have thought no more about Miss Always' injured wrist, if not for a strange incident on my way down to dinner that evening. I had been looking for Rebecca, keen to find out more about her odd behaviour over Miss Rochester. She was not in the garden, nor the summer house, so I decided to check the conservatory. I was hurrying past the morning room when I stopped suddenly. How could I not – when from behind the closed door, I heard Miss Always utter my name?

With all the natural instincts of a Russian spy, I pressed my ear to the door. Miss Always was speaking with some urgency.

'She is different from all the rest . . . that much is clear.' Then her voice dropped and all I could pick up were fragments. 'My wrist . . . Ivy . . . hand upon it . . . healed . . . my plan is –'

Then silence. Hurried footsteps. Before I could retreat, the door swung open and Miss Always was eyeing me with suspicion. With staggering subtlety I peered over the writer's shoulder. The room appeared to be unoccupied.

'Ivy, what are you doing?' said Miss Always rather sternly.

'Just eavesdropping, dear. It seemed like the right thing to do, as I heard you mention my name. Which is rather odd, as you appear to be alone.'

Her hard gaze gave way to a giggle. 'You must think me unhinged!'

'The thought had occurred to me, dear.'

My friend raced to a writing table by the window and grabbed her bonnet. Then, putting her arm through mine, she walked with me towards the entrance hall.

'I was composing a letter to my mother,' she explained, 'and it is a habit of mine to speak the words aloud before I write them down.' She blushed. 'I'm afraid you heard me singing your praises, Ivy. Mummy delights in reading about the wonderful things you say and do.'

That explained a great deal. But not everything.

'Forgive me, dear,' I said, 'but I rather thought you said something about me *healing* your wrist. You know, after you fell and hurt yourself earlier. Now that I think of it, you did react rather strangely when I put my hand upon your injury.'

Miss Always roared with laughter. Put a sisterly head on my shoulder. 'Oh, Ivy, you do beat all! What I said was that you *held* my wrist. You see, I was very touched that when I was hurt you showed such loving kindness – and I wanted to share that in my letter.'

Which made perfect sense. And yet . . .

'May I see it, Miss Always?'

My friend stopped in her tracks. Her brow buckled. I believe she gulped. 'See it?'

'Yes, dear – your wrist.'

'That seems rather unnecessary, Ivy.' She smiled tightly. 'But if you insist. After all, I have nothing to hide.'

Slowly, she pulled up the sleeve of her dress. Her wrist looked slender and pale. There was no redness or swelling at all. In fact, it appeared to be completely healed. In a single afternoon.

I was stunned.

'It is still terribly painful, though it doesn't look it.' Miss Always was speaking quickly. 'As for the swelling, well, the sprain was very minor. Also, I am a remarkably fast healer and these things always fix themselves, don't they? So it's no great surprise.' Then she looked at me with a mixture of pity and mild amusement. 'Ivy, you don't *seriously* think – ?'

'Heavens no!' I said, slapping her shoulder. 'Are you mad?'

I only hoped she believed me.

When we reached the entrance hall, Miss Always put on her bonnet and announced she was heading out for the evening. Didn't say where she was going – just that she had an errand to run. Something that couldn't wait. And that she wouldn't be joining us for dinner.

I saw her to the door, then decided to continue my search for Rebecca before the supper gong sounded.

The conservatory was deserted. As was the music room. When I tried the drawing room, I didn't find Rebecca, but I *did* find Lady Elizabeth and Lady Amelia. They were dressed grandly for dinner. Lady Amelia was doing some embroidery and the old bat was reading a book. She hissed at me as I entered the room.

'You're a public menace!' she barked. 'It took three baths to get the cheesecake from my skin!'

'No need to thank me, dear,' I said humbly. 'The glorious glow on your haggard face is reward enough.'

'Hideous child!' she growled.

I was making a hasty retreat when Lady Amelia pricked her thumb with the needle. She cried out as it began to bleed.

Naturally, I was delighted.

'Let me have a look, dear,' I said, hurrying towards her.

Lady Amelia was making the sort of idiotic noises you would expect from a simpleton of high birth. Threatening to faint at the sight of her own blood. Wondering if the doctor should be called for and whatnot.

'Bunkum!' snapped Lady Elizabeth. 'You're barely bleeding, you foolish woman! I shot off a toe during a fox hunt and didn't even stop for a bandage.'

I crouched down before Lady Amelia and looked at the wound. It was a great disappointment. Barely a drop or two of blood.

'Do you think I should have it bandaged?' she asked me fretfully.

'No need, unfortunately.'

Lady Elizabeth peered at me. 'You sound disappointed, Miss Pocket.'

'I won't lie, it *is* a great shame.' Then I had a glorious idea. 'Lady Amelia, would you be a dear and let me slam your fingers in the door?'

'I beg your pardon?' came the stunned reply.

'What did she say?' barked Lady Elizabeth, cupping her ear with a bony hand.

'I only ask in the interests of science. You see, I am testing a theory.' I was explaining myself beautifully. 'But I require a slightly more serious injury. It would be a *great* help, dear.'

Lady Amelia gasped and paled. 'Heavens, Ivy.'

Before Lady Amelia had a chance to leap up and run away, I grabbed her hand and quickly wrapped my fingers around her bleeding thumb.

'Slap her silly!' hollered Lady Elizabeth, swinging her cane at me (but missing by a mile). 'She's a dangerous lunatic!' The crazed fossil was squinting furiously at us. 'What's she doing, Amelia?'

'I have no idea,' said Lady Amelia, trying to yank her hand away.

'Trust me, dear,' I told her, holding on tightly, 'you will be amazed. Astounded. Stupefied.'

I recalled that with Miss Always, I had only touched her injured wrist for a moment. But just to be certain, I held the bleeding thumb for a full minute. I may have even closed my eyes and made the odd *mmm* sound. It seemed appropriate.

Then I slowly uncurled my fingers and, filled with hope, looked down at Lady Amelia's thumb. It looked perfect. No sign of bleeding at all. I was about to call the entire household together and declare myself a mystical healer. And I would have, if not for the hideous sight of blood oozing up from the pinprick and pooling on Lady Amelia's thumb. The wound was not even *slightly* healed. Which was violently inconvenient.

I got up. Patted Lady Amelia on the head like a puppy. Wished her well with her injury. And made a swift exit from the drawing room.

Lady Elizabeth may have shouted at me as I left – something about me being a homicidal fruitcake – but I was walking so quickly, I didn't hear a word of it.

To my relief, I found Rebecca in the library. She was slumped in an armchair tucked away in a far corner of the darkened room, her hand dangling from the armrest. She looked dead. Fortunately, I saw the rise and fall of her chest. Just asleep. Then I noticed something else. Well, two things, to be exact. The first was a small red book in her lap – her hand was wrapped around it, her finger acting as a kind of bookmark. And it wasn't just any book. It was *the* book. The one I saw Miss Frost force upon her. The same book Rebecca was clutching when she had her midnight meeting with Miss Frost. That's when I noticed the *second* thing. Something was tied on a ribbon around her wrist. The key. The key to her room.

It seemed that fate was giving me a choice. I could read the book. Or take the key. My decision was an easy one.

With tremendous care – for I have all the natural instincts of a safe-cracker – I put a hand under her wrist. Then with the other hand, I pulled gently on the pale blue ribbon. It unfurled and the key dropped silently into my waiting palm.

At last!

I flew up the stairs and in no time was standing outside Rebecca's bedroom door. I looked up and down the hall. No one was about. I slipped the key into the lock. Turned. It clicked crisply. The anticipation was delicious as I opened the door and stepped inside.

'Heavens . . .'

I looked about, bug-eyed, my gaze passing quickly over the wondrous bedchamber. What had I expected to find? Something shocking? Something sinister? Perhaps. But not *this*. Not a room crowded with, covered in, blanketed by – clocks. Clocks of every conceivable kind. Cuckoo clocks. Chiming clocks. Bracket clocks. Travel clocks. Chimney clocks. Lantern clocks. Mantel clocks. Big and small clocks. Clocks in black marble and green. Clocks in brass and silver and gold. Figurine clocks. Wooden clocks. Porcelain clocks. Gold clocks. Silver clocks. There were hundreds of them. Thousands, perhaps. Clocks covering every tabletop, every chest of drawers, every side table, every shelf. Clocks covering every part of the wall. Clocks crowding the floor. A path had been carved between the floor clocks, leading from the bed to the door, with smaller tracks leading to each table, desk or cabinet.

And that was not the most shocking thing.

No. What gave me chills was the moment I realised that every single clock in that bedroom was perfectly synchronised. All ticking in unison. Each collective tick practically shook the room. *Tick. Tick. Tick.* Like a heartbeat. This was the sound I had heard coming from her room. As I stood there I was certain it would drive me bonkers. Perhaps that was what had happened to Rebecca.

Suddenly her peculiar behaviour made more sense. Her secret package on the train. Matilda listening to the box. Yet it made no sense at all.

I wandered about the room, looking at that museum of time. It had a strange beauty and I got slightly lost in it, I suppose. Which might explain why I didn't hear Rebecca slip into the room behind me. She didn't yell. Didn't throw me out. Didn't even ask how I got the key. She simply said, 'It's not what you think.'

'And what do I think, dear?' I said.

'That I'm mad,' she said. 'That the clocks mean something bad.'

I sat down on the bed. 'Wouldn't it be better for you to explain it for yourself?'

The girl followed the path between her collection of clocks and sat down beside me on the bed. 'When my mother got sick they gave her a year. That's what all the doctors from London said. She had one year to live. When I heard the news, I decided to work out *exactly* how much time my mother had. It mattered, don't you see? If she only had a year then every day and every hour and every minute mattered. It was all that mattered.'

She looked at me and her eyes were pleading. Asking me if I understood. I can't say that I did – not completely – but I nodded. 'Go on,' I whispered.

'It started with one clock,' she said, looking about the room, 'then two. I figured out that Mother had eight thousand, seven hundred and sixty hours left. One year. That's five hundred and twenty-five thousand, six hundred minutes. I suppose I thought if I knew how long, *exactly* how long, and I marked the minutes and the hours . . . I suppose I thought I could hold on to it.'

'To time?'

Rebecca nodded. 'If I could watch the seconds and the minutes and the hours I could somehow master it. That I could somehow get her more. More time.' She smiled sadly. 'It's foolish, isn't it?'

'Monstrously stupid,' I said, slipping my hand over hers. 'But it's also rather beautiful. Did your mother know about the clocks?'

'No.' She took a shaky breath. 'You see, the doctors were wrong. They lied. She didn't have a year at all. She died on the fourth day of the ninth month. She only had two hundred and forty-six days.' Rebecca looked at me, tears tracking down her face. She wasn't sad. She was furious. 'You understand, don't you? We lost one hundred and nineteen days. That's two thousand, eight hundred and fifty-six hours. All stolen from us – each and every minute.'

I nodded. 'But the clocks, Rebecca, why do you keep them now that your mother is gone?'

'It makes me feel close to her, I suppose.' Rebecca smiled sadly. 'I can't stop collecting them. I *have* tried, but I can't let them go. Do you think I'm mad?'

'Definitely,' I said. 'But we are all a little bonkers. And what you're doing here isn't crazy. I think I would just call it sorrow and leave it at that.'

The girl seemed to like my diagnosis. We talked for an age. About clocks. And days. And minutes. About her mother. When Rebecca had spoken of her on the train, her voice had been full of sadness and regret. But something had changed. Now she seemed remarkably . . . hopeful. Yes, that was it.

She took me on a tour of her collection.

By the time we were finished, I would gladly have never looked at another clock again. But I am a kind-hearted creature – so I pretended to find them all fascinating. Whilst Rebecca was babbling on about a silver clock she had bought from a travelling salesman in Bristol which she had smuggled into the house under her dress, I wandered around the room, nodding at regular intervals. I stopped before a crowded bookcase by the window and let my eyes wander over its ticking treasures. There were perhaps fifty clocks upon the shelves. And something else too. It was pushed back behind a walnut travelling clock and a fob watch on a rusted stand. The fact that it wasn't a clock caught my eye. It was a miniature portrait in an ugly gold frame. I was curious to have a look. So I moved the clocks and reached for the picture. As I pulled it out, I saw that it was of a woman.

Rebecca had suddenly stopped talking. I heard hurried footsteps. Then she was by my side, snatching the portrait from my hand. 'That is nothing,' she said quickly.

But it was too late. I had already seen her. Flowing blonde hair. Cherub face. Even her eyes, blue and green, were captured in the miniature painting. 'That is Miss Rochester!' I cried. 'But you said you had no picture of her.'

Rebecca made no reply. She looked lost. Uncertain. Her eyes looked everywhere but at me. Something was wrong.

'The woman in the portrait,' I said, trying to swallow the dread rising in my throat, 'the one I saw in the woodlands – she is your old governess, is she not?'

No answer.

Tick. Tick. Tick. Tick.

I reached for the picture but Rebecca pulled it away.

'Rebecca, who is she?' I was shocked to hear the anger in my voice. 'Tell me!'

It worked. Rebecca looked at me.

'She is my mother,' said the girl.

Chapter 12

I could speak to the dead. I never *used* to be able to. In fact, I'd gone twelve long years without ever once chatting to a ghost. But that was days ago. Before the Clock Diamond. Before Butterfield Park. Now it was something I did a great deal. Murdered duchesses. Dead mothers. I spoke to them all.

It turns out, I'm rather good at it.

'This can't be,' I said, pacing back and forth along the paths carved between the oceans of clocks. 'It's impossible. While it's true that as far as girls go, I'm rather extraordinary, *this* is something else.'

'I've heard of such things before,' said Rebecca quietly. 'There's a lady in the village who will pass on a message from the spirit world for five shillings.'

'That is different,' I said, turning and walking the length of the room again. 'Women like that have crystal balls and warts on their noses and whatnot.'

Rebecca poured me a glass of water and placed it gently in

my hands. 'Is it really such a bad thing, Ivy?' she said. 'What you can do – it's amazing.'

'It's bonkers!' I snapped.

The girl sat down on the bed. She didn't seem entirely surprised about my new talent – which I put down to the fact that she was barking mad herself.

'If I could talk to my mother the way you did . . . well, I would be the happiest girl in England.' Rebecca looked up at me. 'Did she have a message for me? Did she say anything about me?'

I sighed. 'I have a feeling she watches you from afar quite often.' If it made me feel any better to offer Rebecca some words of comfort about her dead mother, that notion quickly faded (which I put down to the fact that I was in shock and therefore slightly cold-blooded). 'Your mother knew my name. How is such a thing possible?'

'I don't know,' said Rebecca. 'Perhaps you have always had this gift.'

'Stuff and nonsense,' I said.

'In time it might make more sense,' said Rebecca carefully. And her words curled their way into my ear like a worm. She knew something. Something that I didn't.

'You knew, didn't you, Rebecca?' I stopped right in front of her. 'You knew that the lady I met in the woodlands was your mother. Yet you let me think it was Miss Rochester.'

The girl paled. 'I didn't want to scare you, that's all.'

'But why weren't *you* scared?' I replied quickly. 'After all, you had just learned that I'd had a lovely chat with your late mother. Now that I think of it, it was as if . . . as if you were not entirely surprised.'

'Of course I was,' said Rebecca, clearing her throat. 'It was as much a surprise to me as it was to you.'

But I didn't believe her. 'Where did you go?'

Rebecca looked startled. 'When?'

'Right after I told you about the lady in the woods you ran off. In fact, you were in a terrible hurry. Where did you go? Or should I ask, to *whom* did you go?'

'I . . . I went to my room. I was overwhelmed after what you told me and –'

'It was Miss Frost, wasn't it?' I said, interrupting. 'You went to tell Miss Frost.'

The girl's head dropped. Her lips began to tremble. She didn't have to answer me.

'Why were you so keen to share the news with your governess?' I said next. 'Some secret business is going on between you and Miss Frost. She has caught you in her web. Made you an accomplice. What is going on, Rebecca?'

'She is trying to help!' cried the girl, jumping to her feet. 'She has important work to do. Horribly important. She cannot be everywhere. She cannot keep an eye on you and Miss –' She shook her head. 'She needs my help and I give it gladly.'

'What sort of help?' I said urgently. 'Rebecca, what is so important that she needed to meet with you under cover of darkness in the schoolhouse? I demand you tell me!'

'Miss Frost . . .' Her voice was faint and the sigh she made was that of defeat. 'She wished to show me the picture you drew the other day – the one of the gardener tending the roses.'

I recalled the picture. And I recalled Miss Frost asking to keep it. 'Whatever for?'

'It was of Wickam.' Rebecca said this mournfully.

'Who?'

'Don't you remember, I told you about him the day you arrived at Butterfield Park?' She looked at me with something like sorrow. 'Wickam died last winter.'

Which was rather unsettling. But not *completely* surprising. Ghosts seemed rather fond of me. 'Why did Miss Frost wish to show you that I had drawn a picture of a dead gardener?'

Rebecca paused. She looked agitated. Fidgety. 'Don't you think it strange, Ivy, all that has happened since you took possession of the Clock Diamond?'

'It's slightly odd, I suppose. But a lady's maid must be prepared for a certain amount of nonsense when she's surrounded by a pack of aristocratic oddballs.'

Rebecca shook her head. 'These strange events *must* be connected to the stone.' She was breathless now. Frowning. 'You do see how everything began with that necklace . . . you do see that, don't you, Ivy?'

'Well of course I do, dear. But the peculiar events that have occurred since the Duchess of Trinity gave me the stone are no great mystery. Not to me.'

The girl looked positively puzzled. 'They're not?'

'Heavens no. In Paris, the Duchess warned me that dark forces were after the Clock Diamond. It's clear I'm dealing with a band of wicked thieves. As I said, no great mystery.'

'But how do you explain the ghosts,' Rebecca demanded to know, 'and the Locks who attacked you in London?'

'Who told you about the Locks?' I huffed. 'Let me guess, Miss Frost?'

Rebecca ignored the question. 'How do you explain these strange occurrences, Ivy?'

I shrugged. 'I'm sure a grim old house like Butterfield has *scores* of ghosts lurking about – I just happen to have met one or two. As for the Locks, well, they are nothing more than pint-sized fortune hunters – probably from the jungles of Budatta where the diamond was first discovered, or perhaps a disreputable circus. But they don't frighten me. I bashed them silly.'

'But the book says –' Rebecca stopped suddenly. 'What I mean is, these Locks don't sound as if they are from …' Her voice dropped to a whisper. '… *our* world.'

I snorted. Daintily. 'Our world? How many worlds do you imagine there are, dear?'

'Two,' she answered with grim certainty. 'I believe there might be two.'

I stood up and said, 'You are a cherished friend, Rebecca, so I'd normally only say this kind of thing behind your back – but as your family already thinks you're nuttier than an almond cake, I urge you not to go around talking of other worlds. It's frightfully bonkers.'

'You must listen to me, Ivy,' said the girl, her face furrowed and pale. 'Miss Frost is terribly worried about the birthday ball. She believes you will be in grave danger.'

'Calm yourself, dear. It's a scientific fact that hysteria causes freckles, and in that regard you've suffered enough. As for Miss Frost, she has warped your mind with her silly stories. Leave her to me.'

Rebecca fell into stony silence, her eyes glazed and anxious. I retreated from the ticking bedroom, but Rebecca's voice stopped me in the doorway. 'I'm sorry about everything, Ivy. I hope one day you will understand and forgive me.'

I didn't see her again all evening.

With supper over, Cook had retired to her quarters. As such, I had slipped into the pantry and was finishing up a small snack. A few raw potatoes. Half a cabbage. My cravings were a slight concern, but I was certain there was a perfectly reasonable explanation. After all, I still loved cake. Only now I preferred to eat it by the pound. But I was still thin as a whippet, so no harm done.

When my belly was full, I was keen to vacate the pantry before the scullery maids returned with the dinner plates. I was hurrying across the cavernous kitchen when I heard raised voices coming towards me. Fearing discovery, I leapt back into the pantry. I had just taken up a crouching position behind a sack of raw sugar when Miss Frost and Miss Always strode into the kitchen. Miss Always was still wearing her bonnet and gloves.

Neither one looked especially jolly.

'Do you want her to put the pieces of this puzzle together?' hissed Miss Always, stopping before the chopping block and taking off her hat. 'She would tell the world.'

'And you would be exposed,' said Miss Frost coldly.

'*We* would be exposed.'

'Do not compare us,' declared the governess. 'We are not the same.'

'But we want the same thing.' Miss Always stepped awfully close to Miss Frost. Which was thrilling!

Miss Frost laughed harshly. 'You are deluded.'

'I am right!'

The governess reached out and seized Miss Always' arm. 'I know what you are thinking, Miss Always, and I tell you this – if you try anything tomorrow night, I will stop you.'

My bosom friend hissed like a rattlesnake. 'Unhand me!'

'Leave the girl in peace.'

In a flash my bosom friend had reached for a carving knife lying beside a bowl of peaches. She lifted the blade and waved it rather freely before Miss Frost. Which was highly unexpected.

The grim spinsters were staring daggers at each other.

'Fortune favours the brave, Miss Frost,' said my friend. 'We shall see who wins the day.'

That was entirely the wrong moment to sneeze. Yet sneeze I did. Quietly – having all the natural instincts of a cloistered nun. Miss Frost and Miss Always did not hear a thing. I was sure of it. Miss Always *did* glance towards the pantry. But only for a moment. Then Miss Frost gave a slight nod of her head. Miss Always lowered the knife – which was a heartbreaking disappointment – and reached for a peach, beginning to slice it.

When she spoke again her voice was considerably louder. She said, 'It would ruin the surprise if Ivy knew I was planning a special celebration for her after the ball. The poor girl deserves it after all she had been through. I know you find such things silly, Miss Frost, but you mustn't tell Ivy what I am planning.'

Miss Frost smiled tightly. 'I won't – for now.'

Dear Miss Always! Not a nefarious, knife-wielding lunatic. Just a dear friend planning a surprise party. I was seized by another sneezing fit. The pantry was violently dusty. As such, I had little choice but to show myself. Miss Frost did not look terribly surprised when I stepped out. But poor Miss Always was positively stunned.

'Oh, Ivy,' she said nervously, 'I *do* hope you didn't hear me talking to Miss Frost.'

'About my surprise party? No, dear, not a word.'

Miss Frost cleared her throat. 'I have a letter to write, if you will excuse me.'

A great well of anger bubbled up inside me as I watched the prim and proper Miss Frost walk from the kitchen. Which was why I said, 'I hope you will stop filling Rebecca's head with any more nonsense about hidden worlds, Miss Frost. The girl is confused enough as it is.'

The governess stopped. Turned around. 'My job is to educate her.'

'About places that do not exist?'

'The universe is a confounding place, Miss Pocket. Some believe there is another world sitting beside our own. A world hidden by the thinnest of veils. My job is to teach Rebecca not just what is, but what may be.' Miss Frost regarded me coolly. 'As a girl who sees dead people, I should think you would be more open-minded.'

I sighed. 'Yes, yes, that silly drawing I did. Honestly, dear, is seeing the occasional dead gardener really so peculiar?'

'Actually, Miss Pocket, it is,' came the governess's crisp reply.

'I know of a castle in Scotland that has over sixty different ghosts,' said Miss Always. 'I don't think there is anything remarkable about what Ivy has seen. Nothing at all.'

I wanted to kiss the dreary bookworm! Instead, I turned to her and said, 'And what is your view on hidden worlds, Miss Always?'

'Complete nonsense,' came the reply.

God bless her!

The governess folded her arms. 'We are surrounded by a universe which the naked eye cannot see – and yet it is there.'

I shook my head. 'Unlikely, dear. Mrs Crabapple, the head housekeeper at Midwinter Hall, was a keen student of cosmology and tea leaves and whatnot. She had it on very good authority that the world is actually floating inside a frightfully large glass ball – rather like a snow globe.'

'I see.' I could tell by the slight flare of her nostrils that Miss Frost wasn't at all pleased. 'How does your Mrs Crabapple explain the planets one can view through a telescope?'

'Stray balloons, dear. From birthday parties and such.'

Miss Frost's mouth twitched. She glared. 'That is the most *ridiculous* thing I have ever heard. You cannot be this idiotic, Miss Pocket. I refuse to believe it.'

Then she stalked from the kitchen.

Miss Always looked mightily pleased when the governess had departed. She sat down at the table, urging me to sit beside her – which I did – then offered me a slice of peach.

'She is no match for you, Ivy,' she said, smiling madly. 'What a clever girl you are!'

The dead woman came just before dawn. I woke up with a start from a rather troublesome dream. She was there. At the end of the bed. Her enormous body rippled and glowed like a lantern on a lake, her ghostly blubber spilling over the sides of the tiny bed frame. She was grinning faintly. Smoke coiling from her mouth. I didn't gasp or tremble, despite the fact that she had flown at me in a murderous rage the last time we met.

'They don't like each other,' she sang at me.

'Who, dear?'

The ghost groaned. 'Miss Frost and Miss Always. They do not like each other.'

'Miss Frost is a horrible creature. She is full of mischief and skulduggery.'

'And Miss Always?' asked the ghost.

'She is my friend,' I said. 'My bosom friend.'

That seemed to delight the Duchess. She laughed and as she did starlight leapt from her hair.

I sighed. Felt rather cross. 'You're dead, so I assume you know a great deal more about what is happening in this house than I do.' I lit the candle beside my bed. 'These Locks Miss Frost told me about – I am certain it is nonsense just as Miss Always says – but what do you think? Are these strange little creatures real?'

The ghost closed her eyes. 'Did the attack in Belgravia feel *real* to you, child?'

'Well of course it did, you ghoulish fatso!'

'Then you have your answer.'

'What are Locks? Who do they work for? And why am I seeing ghosts? Everywhere I turn there is mystery and secrets! What is happening, Duchess?'

The ghost huffed. 'I am a ghost, *not* an oracle.' The light pouring from her flesh seemed to dim. Just for a moment.

'You are right about one thing – there are people in this house who are determined to get their hands on the Clock Diamond. Miss Frost is one of them, but there are others. They will try to stop you giving Matilda the stone. They want it for themselves.'

'What should I do?'

'Be on your guard,' sang the ghost. 'Do not become distracted by intrigue and shadows. Remember why you came to Butterfield Park.'

'Do the Locks work for Miss Frost?' I asked again. 'Is she –?'

'Have you forgotten your promise to me?' hissed the dead woman. 'That is why you are here, *that* is all that matters. Keep the necklace well hidden until the ball and then hang it around Matilda's neck. The rest is of no concern to either of us.' The ghost was at the other end of the bed, yet her voice seemed to whisper into my ear. 'Remember the five hundred pounds, child. Your future is a bright one, so long as you do as I have asked.'

Despite the fact that she was dead and had recently tried to devour me – she made a great deal of sense. All that mattered was fulfilling my mission. And collecting the reward.

And starting afresh.

'She thinks you are a menace,' said the ghost. She licked her lips and I noticed that her tongue was black. Which was revolting. 'She does not like you at all.'

'Miss Frost?'

'Lady Elizabeth.' The Duchess fixed her eyes – two dark pools – upon me. 'You have tried so hard to win her favour – but nothing works, does it, child?'

I shrugged, but I confess the situation bothered me. 'The old bat is frightfully prickly.'

'I believe she would warm to you if *only* there were some way you could win her favour. It would please me to see you two becoming friends. Have you any ideas?'

'Perhaps I could read to her – old people love that. Or I could fix her hair or file her bunions. I'm certain she has monstrous bunions.'

The ghost appeared deep in thought. She said, 'It must be something simple. Lady Elizabeth must not suspect you are trying to impress her.' She sighed. 'When we were girls and we would quarrel, I used to know *just* how to make amends. But no, you will think it too silly.'

I tried not to appear eager. 'I'm sure it's terribly stupid, but just out of interest – what was it?'

'Iced tea,' said the ghoul. 'Iced tea with a few drops of vanilla and a squeeze of lime. There is no surer way to Lady Elizabeth's heart than that. It will remind her of better days. She will be moved beyond words.'

Then the ghost grew restless, and without so much as a

goodbye, dissolved into the bed coverings like a morning fog. After she was gone, and I was once again alone, her voice lingered in the crisp air. 'Remember, child,' it sang, 'iced tea with vanilla and a squeeze of lime.'

I pulled back the covers and jumped from the bed.

Chapter 13

The day of the ball had arrived. Before I ventured downstairs for breakfast I checked the Clock Diamond. It was right where it should be – lost amongst a cluster of worthless costume jewellery. I held it up to the light. In truth, I wasn't looking at it simply to marvel at its mystical beauty. It was about what the stone had shown me the last time. The girl being pulled through the snow. *Me.* But the diamond glowed like a sunrise over Butterfield Park and nothing more.

The disappointment stung. If the stone was a riddle, then I hoped it might also be the solution. With a sigh, I replaced the necklace and covered it with a few dusty frock coats. Then I closed the lid of the trunk and placed a sad-looking boar spear and a few homemade crossbows on top for good measure.

The great hall was a hive of activity as I came down the main stairs. Maids of all shapes and sizes scurrying about. Footmen moving furniture. Butlers polishing doorknobs.

Matilda's birthday cake was already in position. It had been baked in London by someone monstrously important and had been brought overnight by stagecoach. It stood on a round oak table in the middle of the hall beneath the massive chandelier. The cake was five tiers tall. One layer yellow. The next blue. It looked utterly delicious.

The ghost's words rang in my ears as I headed for the library. About the sinister Miss Frost. About the Locks. About everything strange that had happened since I took possession of the Clock Diamond. Then I thought of Mr Banks – what monstrous news would he bring me? I checked the time. He was due on the morning train. It embarrassed me to admit how eager I was to see him.

'I am utterly confused!' I groaned aloud. I might have said more – something about what a horrible mess I was in and what a wonderfully plucky girl I was. But I didn't. Because by that time I had entered the library. And there he was!

Horatio Banks, in his dark suit and top hat, stood before me.

'But I thought your train would not be here for at least another hour?' I said, rushing over.

'Well, I am here now,' he said sternly, fixing his steely green eyes upon me. 'Miss Pocket, there is a great deal I need to speak with you about.'

'Goodness, this room is awfully cold.'

'Miss Pocket, let us begin,' said Horatio Banks. 'I haven't much time. Not much time at all.'

'Yes, dear, immediately,' I said, offering the grim-faced lawyer a seat on the couch. He declined. It was then that I noticed the cut on his forehead. Just below the line of his hat.

'Mr Banks, you are hurt,' I said, pulling out my handkerchief.

'It is nothing,' he said briskly, waving me away. 'As I wrote in my letter, I have conducted a great deal of research into the Clock Diamond since last I saw you. I have a contact – a master criminal, Miss Pocket – who had business with the Duchess around the time the stone came into her possession. This *gentleman* had fallen on hard times. As such, he was willing to tell me something of the diamond's lineage for a few hundred pounds. And tell me he did – a very great deal. I must tell you, the day after our meeting in Liverpool the man was found with a dagger in his heart.'

I gasped. 'You think he was killed for talking to you?'

'I am certain of it. I believe the people who have been hunting the stone were following me.' He looked off into the distance. 'I led them right to the wretched man.'

'This is a beastly business,' I said, shaking my head. I felt the need to walk about. And talk. So I did both. 'I don't mind telling you, Mr Banks, that I feel terribly ill-used. The Duchess of Trinity made me a perfectly simple offer. Take a stupid diamond back to England and give it to Matilda Butterfield on her twelfth birthday. What could go wrong?' I turned back and glared at the lawyer. 'Plenty, that's what. I've been haunted by ghosts, strapped into my bed, I've fallen into a fire, been thrown against a wall and pushed down the stairs, seen baffling visions in the Clock Diamond, talked to dead people – and that's just in the past week!'

If my tirade shocked the ageing lawyer, he gave no sign of it.

Mr Banks stood utterly still. He stared at me and for the first time I saw a kind of sorrow in his eyes. The wound on his head began to weep – a trail of blood tracking slowly down his face.

'It is all connected,' he said, each word slow and thick with meaning. 'Those creatures who attacked you in Belgravia and the Duchess's murder before that. *Nothing* is by chance.' He shook his head slowly. 'Why did you put on that necklace, Miss Pocket?'

'What do you mean, Mr Banks? Spit it out!'

'I mean this: you may have come upon the Duchess and her diamond by chance, but I am afraid there was also something else at work.' He looked at me with such sadness. 'Something like fate, Miss Pocket.'

'At last we are getting somewhere,' I said, trying to sound unruffled. 'Now be a dear and tell me *exactly* what you mean.'

'To begin with, you must not let Matilda Butterfield have the –'

'There you are, Ivy!' It was Lady Amelia. She sounded flustered.

I turned just as she hurried towards us, waving her hands about like she was hailing a carriage. 'I do hope I'm not interrupting anything important?'

'I'm afraid you are, dear. We are just in the middle of a most important conversation.'

She appeared not to hear me.

'Lady Elizabeth has a dreadful headache,' she said breathlessly. 'And on the day of Matilda's birthday ball, of all days! There is so much to do.' Lady Amelia stopped in front of me and put a hand on my shoulder. 'Can you help her, Ivy?'

'Of course I can,' I said proudly. I would have said more about my many talents had I not remembered Mr Banks. 'How rude of me. Lady Amelia, allow me to introduce you to a very old friend of mine, Mr Horatio Banks.'

Lady Amelia looked baffled as she peered over my shoulder. She didn't offer Mr Banks a greeting, which I thought was monstrously rude. I turned to introduce the lawyer to Lady Amelia – he at least would say hello. But he had gone. Utterly vanished. I understood immediately – he wished to keep his presence at the house a secret.

'Yes … well, Ivy,' said Lady Amelia, 'if you could come with me now and attend to Lady Elizabeth I would be very grateful. I only ask that you limit your remedy to onions and lavender. Lady Elizabeth is afraid you might attack her again with a cheesecake.'

'I saved that old bat's skin,' I protested.

'Yes, of course you did. Come, Ivy, we must hurry!'

Lady Amelia practically ran from the room. I followed after her but paused at the library door. When I glanced back Mr Banks had returned. He was standing by the large windows which looked out over the garden.

'I'll be back in a moment,' I told him. 'You make yourself comfortable, dear.'

'I haven't much time, Miss Pocket,' he said.

'Ivy?' called Lady Amelia from the hallway. 'Ivy, are you coming?'

'Yes, dear, but first I must stop by the kitchen.'

I waved to the lawyer and hurried away.

Lady Elizabeth did a great deal of groaning. And a tremendous amount of moaning. In just a few minutes there were two sprigs of lavender wedged in her nose and she had settled. When I offered her a glass of delicious iced tea, she looked thoroughly unimpressed. When I told her I had made it myself, she looked positively stunned.

'What's this about?' she barked.

'I thought you might like it, dear,' I said brightly. 'The recipe is one that I got from –'

No point bringing up the Duchess. Better to claim all the credit myself.

'It is a Pocket family recipe,' I said rather grandly.

Lady Elizabeth took the glass from my hand. 'What's in it?'

'The ingredients are a closely guarded secret,' I said. 'But when you taste it, I am certain you'll sob like a lost child who has found its mother. Now shut your trap and drink.'

With a huff, Old Walnut Head did as she was instructed. She took several large gulps. Smacked her lips. Frowned. 'It's not *completely* revolting.'

'It's delicious and you know it,' I said, feeling rather triumphant. 'Drink up, dear.'

'Open those doors,' barked Lady Elizabeth. 'It's like a furnace in here.'

Which was odd, as it was really rather cold. I was so pre-occupied with the French doors that I didn't even hear the glass drop. But when I turned I saw that Lady Elizabeth was slumped on the couch like a sack of potatoes, the glass upon the floor.

I raced across the room and knelt beside her. That's when I saw that her face was puffing up – inflating like a horribly wrinkled balloon. Her tongue swelled inside her mouth, pushing its way out (she looked like a thirsty pack mule). Her eyes were swollen shut.

She was groaning. Her skin felt monstrously hot.

Lady Amelia had come into the room by then. I know, because I heard her scream when she saw Lady Elizabeth – who by now resembled a seal, her entire body magnificently bloated.

'What on earth happened?' she cried, after sending one of the maids to fetch the doctor.

I explained that Lady Elizabeth was perfectly fine only moments before. Happily drinking her iced tea. That made Lady Amelia frown and say, 'What was in it, Ivy?'

'Just the usual ingredients, dear,' I said. 'Ice, tea, a few drops of vanilla.'

That seemed to relieve Lady Amelia.

'And a squeeze of lime juice,' I added.

She gasped. 'Lady Elizabeth is allergic to lime! Oh, Ivy . . .'

Which was terribly unfortunate.

We applied wet towels to the inflated monstrosity that was Lady Elizabeth Butterfield and waited until the doctor arrived. Dr Longfellow was not available, so Dr Grace from the next village came instead. He looked her over. Opened his bag and pulled out various instruments of torture. Took her pulse and whatnot. Then he announced that it was a simple allergic reaction. The old bat should be fine in a few hours. Six under-butlers carried Lady Elizabeth up to her room to rest and deflate before the party.

I felt awful. Lady Amelia assured me it wasn't my fault. Which was true enough. I knew *exactly* where the fault lay. The Duchess of Trinity! But I would deal with her later. For now, I was keen to get back to Mr Banks. He had insisted that he did not have much time, so naturally I didn't want to keep him waiting (for I am devastatingly considerate).

'I cannot find Rebecca anywhere!' barked Matilda, as Lady Amelia and I entered the great hall. 'She is the only one who can fix my hair just how I like it.' She looked about the hall like a hungry lion. 'She's hiding from me, I can tell. When I find her I'll pinch her arm till it bleeds!'

'Don't do that, dear,' I said, 'or I'll have to hang you from the pot rack and pummel you with carrots. Which wouldn't look at all fetching for your grand ball.'

The girl glared at me. I'm sure she wanted to scratch my face. Or at the very least poke an eyeball. 'Why are you still here, Pocket?' she hissed. 'Today's my birthday so hand over the diamond and get lost!'

'Never,' I hissed. I hadn't meant to. What I meant to say was *not yet* or *not until tonight*. But instead I had acted as if the diamond were mine. All mine. And I would never part with it. Not until it showed me another vision. Of the girl in the snow. And the woman in the yellow bonnet. Not until my story had an ending.

'What did you say?' snapped Matilda.

I coughed daintily – for I have all the natural instincts of a geisha. Then I said, 'You'll get the necklace at the ball. That was the Duchess of Trinity's dying wish.'

'Blast!' Matilda flicked her hair, brushed past me and went off in search of her cousin.

I had never seen the great hall so crowded. It seemed as if every servant in Butterfield Park were gathered there, polishing and sweeping and arranging flowers. So it was a perfect moment for me to slip away. Lady Amelia was fussing over the cake and I had nearly passed out of the great hall when I heard a carriage pull up before the main doors.

Hurried footsteps filled the hall. Then a voice. A young man.

'Ivy Pocket?' He stopped to catch his breath. 'Is Ivy Pocket about?'

Lady Amelia was pointing to me as I walked back into the great hall. The man's name was Fergus Green and he ran errands for Dr Longfellow in the village.

'You Ivy Pocket?'

'I am. What's this about?'

He gulped. 'You know a Mr Horatio Banks of London?'

I was flooded with relief. 'Of course I do. He is in the library this very moment, you foolish fathead.'

Fergus looked at me with a most peculiar expression. Like I had just introduced myself as the Queen of England. He said, 'There's been an accident, miss. Dr Longfellow was called to the scene.'

Lady Amelia gasped. 'An accident? What sort of accident?'

'The train, my lady,' he said. 'Went off the drawbridge and into the river. Seems someone tampered with the signal. It's an awful mess. Six dead.'

'Good heavens!' Lady Amelia made the sign of the cross.

The young man reached into his pocket and pulled out a crumpled envelope. He looked down at it. Turned it over in his hand. Then he passed it to me. The envelope was smeared with blood. My name written on the front.

'Dr Longfellow found this in Mr Banks's coat pocket,' said Fergus. 'It's addressed to you, so we thought you should have it.'

I was baffled. It was all so sad. So silly. Now I understood the wound on Mr Banks's head – but he'd made no mention of an accident. Typical!

I looked down at the envelope. 'I don't think it was right for you to go rifling through Mr Banks's coat,' I said firmly. 'And I won't open this letter. I will return it to Mr Banks and he can decide what to do with it.'

The young man took off his cap. He looked at Lady Amelia, then back at me. Then he said, 'He won't be needing that letter. Not where he is.'

'Whatever are you talking about?' I snapped. 'Mr Banks is in the library.'

'That can't be, miss,' said the boy gravely. 'The old man died in the accident.'

Chapter 14

'Why won't she speak?'

'It's the shock, I suppose.'

'Should we send for the doctor?'

'Let her rest, Rebecca. Miss Pocket will come back to us in her own time.'

They were all there. Miss Always. Rebecca. Miss Frost. Even Matilda.

The ghost had been generous. One thousand pounds. That was my bounty. It was more money than I had ever seen in my entire life. All thanks to Mr Banks. The *late* Horatio Banks. The envelope was addressed to me. The one found in his frock coat. The one stained with blood and now resting on my bedside table. The envelope contained money. My payment from the Duchess. One thousand pounds. But that wasn't right, was it? The sum was *five* hundred pounds. Yet the lawyer had put in double that amount. And I knew why. He wanted me to have enough money to get away. To escape this tangle. He was coming to rescue me.

But he never made it.

'What on earth happened?' It was Miss Always. She sounded horrified. 'I heard Lady Amelia say the train plunged into the river.'

'There are reports the drawbridge signal had been tampered with,' said Miss Frost calmly. 'The driver believed the bridge was down when in fact it was up.'

A gasp. Rebecca. 'How could such a thing happen?'

'Sabotage, I should think,' was Miss Frost's reply. 'You went out last night, didn't you, Miss Always? Do you recall seeing anything suspicious on your travels?'

'I went into town to speak with Reverend Moore,' said Miss Always, looking tenderly at me. 'I asked him to pray for a friend of mine who is troubled. But I saw nothing untoward.'

'How unfortunate,' said the governess.

I was surrounded by ghosts. Four at last count. A devilish duchess. An angelic mother. An ancient gardener. A crotchety lawyer. All dead.

I had gone looking for him. After I heard about the train, I ran like a lunatic back to the library. I was sure he would be there – right where I had left him. But he wasn't. I suppose it was just as Miss Always had explained. Mr Banks was not an earthbound ghost. He had only a short time to visit before crossing over. And he would not be back.

'Would you like a drink of water, Ivy?' said Rebecca. She was sitting on the side of the bed, stroking my hair. 'Are you hungry?'

I shook my head.

'I'm awfully sorry about your friend, Ivy,' said Miss Always. 'I wish there was something I could do to make you feel better. When terrible accidents like this happen we are at a loss to understand them. But we must put our faith in God.'

'Mr Banks came to see me,' I said.

Rebecca gasped again. 'His ghost?'

I nodded. 'He was wounded. He wanted to speak with me urgently but I was so busy talking nonsense that he hardly had the chance.'

'And what did he tell you, Miss Pocket?' said Miss Frost casually.

Here was my chance. To say out loud all that I was thinking. To tell them what I'd been told. They would think I had lost my mind. Or worse – they might believe every word. 'I can't remember,' I said.

'Perhaps it was a dream, Ivy,' said Miss Always, walking over to the little window and drawing back the curtains. 'You've suffered a great trauma so we shouldn't be surprised. Yes, just a dream. Nothing more serious than that.'

'You must be joking,' said Miss Frost coldly. 'Did you not write a book about ghosts?'

Miss Always and the governess glared at each other with shocking intensity. Was it hatred? I was sure more was being said in that silence than a thousand words could express. Then Miss Always said, 'If Mr Banks *did* make a ghostly visit, then perhaps he did so to let Ivy know that he was all right. That death was not the end. Yes, I am sure that's all it was.'

'Pocket's disturbed,' said Matilda helpfully. 'What sort of girl has dead people coming to visit her? It's outrageous! If she's not throwing herself down the stairs, she's attacking poor Grandmother with cheesecake and iced tea or making up fanciful stories. I can't be the only one who thinks she's demented.'

'How can you be so cruel?' said Miss Always, her voice trembling.

Matilda smiled darkly.

'Your party is in just a few hours,' said Miss Frost, putting a hand behind Matilda's back and walking her towards the door. 'I'm sure you have more pressing things to do than stay up here and be horrible.' The governess glanced at me briefly. 'Besides, Miss Pocket needs her rest.'

'Yes, that is very true,' said Miss Always, who kissed my cheek and quickly departed.

But Matilda couldn't leave without slinging one final arrow. She paused at the door and said, 'I'm sure my cousin will take excellent care of you, Pocket.' She smiled sweetly. '*Tick tock.*'

Miss Frost pulled the evil nitwit away.

'Ignore her,' I told Rebecca, as the sound of footsteps in the narrow hall outside began to fade. 'She doesn't mean half the awful things she says.'

'Yes she does,' said Rebecca.

I smiled faintly. 'True. But I have to believe that one day Matilda will wake up and realise what a horrible, fatheaded, nitwitted, black-hearted lump of horse poop she really is.'

Rebecca smiled, but it soon slipped from her face. She sat down on the bed again. 'I'm sorry about Mr Banks.'

'So am I,' I said.

'Ivy ... how old were you when you first went to the orphanage?'

I hadn't expected such a question. In fact, I'd never told Rebecca that I had grown up in the Harrington Home for Unwanted Children. Yet clearly she knew about it. I thought about launching into a fantastical story – but I didn't have the heart for it.

'Five,' I said.

'And before that?' said Rebecca.

'I lived with my parents, of course,' I said quickly.

But Rebecca didn't look at all convinced. 'What can you remember of those years, Ivy?'

'Everything,' I lied. 'Wonderful memories.'

'I don't believe you,' said the girl gently. 'Please, Ivy, can you tell me the truth? It's very important.'

I sighed. I hated the truth as a general rule. But I decided to give it a try. 'I don't remember much before the orphanage.'

'You have no memories of your parents at all?'

'Not really. But I was taken from them,' I said softly. 'I always suspected as much – after all, who would give up a child as heartbreakingly adorable as me? And then I saw a vision in the Clock Diamond and I knew it was true. I was stolen.'

If Rebecca was shocked or confused by this reference to the stone she didn't show it. 'What did you see, Ivy?' she said.

'Someone taking me from a house and leading me through the woods. A woman – wearing a long coat and a yellow bonnet. She was taking me from my parents. Stealing me away.'

Which is when Rebecca started to cry. The poor dear wept buckets. 'I'm sorry, Ivy.'

I shrugged. 'It's not your fault, dear.'

'Everything that's happened,' she sobbed, 'Mr Banks's train . . . and the stairs . . . it's horrible!'

The girl's complete misery forced me to find the silver lining.

'Who knows why the train crashed? Perhaps it was just an accident,' I said, patting Rebecca on the head (which is always a great comfort). 'And as for the stairs, well, I'm sure I was so busy daydreaming I didn't look where I was going.'

Rebecca's eyes locked on to mine. 'You were pushed.'

I gasped. Like a damsel in distress. Which was embarrassing. 'Are you *sure*?'

She nodded. Tears streaming down her face. The girl leaked like a burst pipe.

'I'm sure,' she said.

My next question came out of me in a rush. 'Who did it, Rebecca? Who pushed me?'

'I did,' whispered the girl.

She wouldn't say why. That was the worst part. No, the worst part was that Rebecca Butterfield – my dear *friend* – had confessed to pushing me down the stairs. Trying to kill me, one would assume. As news went, it was grim.

'You hate me,' said Rebecca.

I was standing by the window now. She was sitting on the bed looking washed out and broken. For the tenth or eleventh time I said, 'I don't understand any of this.'

'It's not what you think, Ivy,' she said faintly.

'Were you angry at me? Did I *do* something?'

'No, nothing.' She looked up at me and her eyes were pleading that I might understand.

'Help me, Rebecca,' I said, 'because right at this moment the voice in my head is shouting that you're a murderous maniac.'

'I didn't want to hurt you,' she sobbed.

'Well I have news for you, dear,' I said swiftly, 'if you didn't want to hurt me you shouldn't have pushed me down a flight of stairs. Over my short career as a maid a great many people have threatened to kill me, but none have actually tried.'

'No,' said Rebecca, 'it's not that. It's the opposite.'

I glared at her as if she were bonkers. 'The opposite of what?'

Rebecca stood up. Rushed towards me. Naturally, I thought she might push me out of the window. So I backed up. Which made her cry. Again.

'Oh, Ivy, there are things you don't know.'

'Then tell me!'

She was shaking her head. 'Miss Frost says I mustn't.'

'Why not?' I asked. It seemed a reasonable question.

But Rebecca wouldn't say any more, apart from repeating that she had never meant to hurt me. Which was ridiculous. But I was more interested in Miss Frost and her role in twisting Rebecca's mind.

'You pushed me down the stairs for her?' I said. 'For Miss Frost?'

'No. Not really. What I mean is . . . I did it because . . . Oh, what's the use, Ivy? You wouldn't believe me anyway and I don't blame you.'

A knock at the door.

'Excuse me, Miss Rebecca.' It was Daisy, one of the maids. 'Miss Matilda would like you to come and attend to her hair.'

'Tell her I'll be right there,' said Rebecca flatly.

The maid departed.

'I'm sorry, Ivy,' whispered the girl.

'Yes, you've said that already.'

Then I turned my back and stared out of the window.

'Come this instant, you wicked windbag. You blubbery beast!'

I put my hands on my hips (which felt enormously satisfying) and bellowed into thin air. Waiting impatiently for the Duchess of Trinity to appear before me. She didn't.

But I wasn't going to give up without a fight.

'Show yourself, Duchess, or our deal is off!' I declared this with heartbreaking conviction. 'You can have your money back and I will bury the Clock Diamond in the woodlands – Matilda will never get to wear it!'

She came from the water jug. Which was slightly unusual. I heard a clanking sound and when I looked over, the jug atop the dresser had lifted from the basin and was rising into the air. It stopped, hovering before me. Then the jug tilted as if by an unseen hand, and water poured from the spout. A great deal of water. And instead of pooling on the floor in a giant puddle, the liquid moulded itself into the shape of the dead Duchess.

She looked rather beautiful, a great tower of rippling water.

Then her luminous flesh began to absorb the water like a sponge. In just moments the ghost was a familiar glowing nightmare, her bloodied nightdress hovering above the ground.

The jug seemed content to float above her head.

'You seem upset, child,' she purred.

'You tricked me,' I snapped. 'You tricked me into giving Lady Elizabeth the iced tea with lime juice. That old bat is allergic! Monstrously allergic!'

The ghost gasped. 'I do hope she wasn't hurt?'

'Hurt? The poor cow puffed up like a balloon! Her tongue swelled like a pork sausage!' I narrowed my gaze. 'Why would you want to hurt Lady Elizabeth if you sent me here to make peace with her? What is going on here, Duchess?'

I don't know how I thought the ghost would react. But what I hadn't expected was that she would begin to cry. Nor did I imagine that her tears would be an inky black. But she did and they were. She sobbed into her fat hands, a valley of tears streaking darkly down her luminous face.

'Death, child,' she cried, 'it scrambles the brain. Muddles the mind. Instead of telling you Lady Elizabeth's favourite refreshment, my frazzled memory offered up the one drink in the world that could injure my old friend. I'll never forgive myself. My shame will be eternal.'

Which was rather surprising. She looked violently sorry.

'Can you forgive a lonely old ghost?' she sobbed.

I shrugged. 'Unlikely, dear. I have a talent for grudges. I once carried one for an entire winter. The back pain was monstrous.'

She growled faintly, then said, 'You won't break our agreement, I trust? You will deliver the Clock Diamond as promised?'

'I suppose so.' I sighed and looked earnestly at the ghost. 'Everywhere I turn there is mystery and calamity, Duchess. Mr Banks is dead – I suppose you know that already?'

The Duchess nodded her head.

'He came to visit me, just as you do. Only with less growling and overturned furniture. Have you seen him? Because I'd very much like to pass on a message.'

The ghost huffed. 'Mr Banks was my lawyer, not my friend. What reason would he have to seek me out?' Then the dead woman cackled. 'Besides, I am not an easy ghost to find.'

'Duchess . . . do you know why Rebecca pushed me down the stairs?'

The dead woman did not answer. Instead, she began to bleed. Not blood – water. It trickled from her flesh, a thousand little drops, until her whole ghostly being was lost to a tide of rippling liquid. This column of water rose as if through a blowhole, pouring back into the jug hovering above the ghost. When she was gone – every last drop – the jug moved quickly through the air, settling down in the basin with a faint splash.

Once again, I was alone.

Lady Elizabeth wouldn't see me. Said she wasn't foolish enough to invite an assassin into her bedchamber. Perfectly understandable. I waited until her maid had departed and slipped in anyway. The old bat was propped up in bed. She looked far less bloated than when I'd last seen her.

Before Lady Elizabeth could scream for help, I made a grovelling apology. Said I was a fool, although my intentions were pure. Offered to file her bunions. Rub her temples. Trim her whiskers. Reminded her that I would be gone from Butterfield Park tomorrow so there was really no need to have me arrested. Mentioned the one-of-a-kind diamond I would be presenting to Matilda at the ball tonight.

In reply she threw a clock at my head.

Which was enormously encouraging.

'See you at the party, dear,' I said, rushing out of the room just as a vase of tulips shattered against the door behind me. 'We will laugh about this little mishap in years to come!'

Despite what I had told the dead Duchess, I'm terrible at grudges. Forgiveness is in my nature – for I have all the natural instincts of a Buddhist monk. That's why I decided to find Rebecca and make peace with her. It's not that I understood why she had tried to kill me. But I knew two things for certain. One, Rebecca had a good heart. Two, she knew more about what was happening in this house than I did.

And I had to find out what it was.

Rebecca had hugged me. Rather savagely. Said we needed to talk. Which was encouraging. Then she ran off to finish Matilda's hair for the ball, promising to be back in no time at all.

Which was why I was standing in her bedroom, amongst her collection of clocks.

I heard footsteps approaching from the hall outside and turned, expecting to find that Rebecca had come back. Instead, I found Miss Frost standing in the doorway.

'Rebecca isn't here,' I said.

'I can see that.' She didn't attempt to come in. 'You had a great shock this morning. Are you feeling any better?'

'I'm stronger than I look, dear. Prettier too.'

Miss Frost smiled faintly.

'I know Rebecca pushed me down the stairs,' I said.

The governess didn't flinch. Which was infuriating!

'And I know you told her to do it,' I added.

'I did no such thing,' said Miss Frost calmly.

'But you were involved,' I snapped. 'Somehow you were involved.'

Miss Frost merely glared at me.

'Tell me, Miss Frost, why would Rebecca do such a thing?'

'Perhaps she was testing you.'

'What for?' I fumed. 'To see if I would *bounce*?'

The governess offered no reply. She seemed to like awkward silences.

'Shame on you for filling Rebecca's head with such horrors,' I said boldly. Then I narrowed my gaze. 'You seem to find me violently fascinating – surely I have a right to know why.'

Miss Frost put her hands behind her back. 'You are one of a kind, Miss Pocket.'

Which was very true – but what on earth did she mean? Miss Frost was silent as the grave. And I had a murderous desire to push the hideous woman into a shark tank. Or at the very least a bathtub full of electric eels. But instead, I decided to do a little fishing. 'What happened this morning with Mr Banks's train?' I said, locking on to her cold eyes. 'Was it an accident?'

'I very much doubt it.'

'Was it done to stop Mr Banks telling me what he had learned about the Clock Diamond?'

'Possibly. Probably.'

'Was it you?'

Miss Frost sighed. She seemed frustrated. 'You will have your answers tonight, Miss Pocket,' she said. 'I pray you are ready for what you find out.'

'What is so special about tonight? I insist you tell me!'

Miss Frost took a deep breath. 'You are entangled in something rather diabolical, Miss Pocket. It is not your fault, but there it is. If you are smart, you will give me the stone and leave this place before nightfall. I will take care of the rest.'

Did she really think I would simply hand the diamond over? After *all* that had happened? I shook my head. 'I don't think so, dear.'

Remarkably, Miss Frost did not look at all upset. She said, 'As you wish.'

I found myself staring at her for the longest time. Finally I said, 'You're no ordinary governess, are you, Miss Frost?'

She smiled darkly. 'And you are no ordinary maid, Miss Pocket.'

Chapter 15

Miss Always had a plan. It was breathtakingly simple and utterly perfect. And it had all started with my hair. Miss Always had come to fix it for the ball. I thought it looked perfectly lovely already – having all the natural silkiness of a prized stallion. Or at the very least a well-bred donkey.

'It won't do for such a grand party,' said Miss Always, holding a lock of my hair.

I looked at my friend – in her dull brown dress, her pale face scrubbed clean, her brown hair pulled back from her face. Was *this* dreary creature going to transform me? Apparently so. She sat me down in the middle of the tiny bedroom and got to work. With a few clips, some cleverly placed combs and a blue ribbon, she had my hair looking glorious in no time.

'We should go,' she declared with breathtaking simplicity.

'Go?' I glanced up at her through the mirror. 'Go where, dear?'

'Away from this place,' said Miss Always, pulling a chair from against the wall and setting it down in front of me. 'Now that you have the payment from Mr Banks, why should we stay here a moment longer?'

I was stunned. And terribly excited. 'You would go with me?'

'Are we not bosom friends?' said Miss Always, as if the idea of abandoning me were an impossibility. 'We could head south and visit my mother. Her cottage is small but we would make do. I know she would be delighted to have you.'

I blushed with embarrassment. It seemed like the right thing to do. 'Are you sure, dear?'

'Of course I'm sure!' She was grinning madly. 'I have thought about nothing else for the last few days. This house isn't good for you, Ivy. What with your bad dreams and poor Mr Banks's accident and your mishap on the stairs. I'm sure it's all a terrible coincidence . . . but I cannot help but think it would be safer for you to get away from here tonight.'

I gasped. 'Tonight?'

'Why not?' said Miss Always. 'I have finished working on Matilda's birthday speech and you owe them nothing beyond the Clock Diamond. Naturally, you will have to hand it over before we leave – but why should you wait until the ball?'

I knew it would mean breaking my promise to the Duchess, but the thought of doing just as Miss Always suggested thrilled me and terrified me in equal measure. Which struck me as odd.

The stone wasn't mine. I was merely the delivery girl. Better to give Matilda the diamond now and get out of Butterfield Park.

'I agree, Miss Always,' I said. 'How soon can we leave?'

My friend clapped with delight. 'No time like the present! We just need to pack our things.' She got up, looking intently at me. 'Then we can retrieve the Clock Diamond from its hiding place and give it to Matilda. Perhaps we should go and fetch it now. After all, it's getting late and we will have to hurry to catch the last train out.'

I felt elated. Thrilled. Above all, hopeful. I could just leave everything behind. The ghosts. The clock-obsessed girl trying to kill me. The sinister governess. Which was why I said, 'Excellent idea. I will go next door and –'

I stopped. Never finished the sentence. It would have been easy to say, but I was learning with each passing hour that the Clock Diamond had a strange effect upon me. Better for me to retrieve the stone by myself – once I had packed my carpet bag.

I said as much to Miss Always.

She frowned, putting her hand on mine. 'Is there something you're not telling me, Ivy?'

'A great many things, dear. My head is positively bursting with *somethings*. The terrible part is, the more I learn the less I understand.'

'Which is why we are going,' said Miss Always, her smile returning. 'I have great plans for you, Ivy. There is a fine school in my mother's village. You will get a proper education and I will finish my book. We will be awfully content.'

I didn't cry. I wasn't the type. But I wanted to. For Miss Always had just seen into my soul. Naturally, I couldn't say it aloud, so I simply hugged my friend and said, 'Thank you, dear.'

Miss Always reminded me of the time, then hurried off to pack.

We had a plan. One hour. Then we would leave Butterfield Park forever.

My carpet bag was packed in no time. As I waited for Miss Always, I wandered aimlessly around the little bedroom. Which was how I arrived at the window. I looked out. Saw Rebecca and Miss Frost coming out of the summer house. Rebecca was wearing a pretty lavender gown (no doubt dressed for the ball) but Miss Frost was typically grim in her black frock. They walked along the garden path, talking eagerly the whole time. How dearly I would have loved to eavesdrop on that conversation!

I was so busy spying that I didn't hear it. Not right away. The piano. Each wretched note ringing through the attic, all at once close by and far away. The tune was unmistakable. 'Row, Row, Row Your Boat'. I knew she would be there before I turned around.

Yet it didn't terrify me any less. For I knew why she had come.

The Duchess of Trinity's enormous bed blocked the door. Her fabulous blubber spilled out on all sides, swelling beneath her blood-soaked nightdress. Her skin still glowed like winter – a frosted blue – and the dark smoke still puffed from her nostrils.

'Going somewhere?' she sang at me.

I didn't bother to explain. Probably because I knew that she knew. So instead I said, 'You're here about the necklace. Well, fear not, I'm giving the stone to Matilda before I leave.'

'The birthday ball,' she purred. 'That was our agreement, child.'

'What does it matter?' I snapped. 'You wanted Matilda to have the stone on her birthday and I will make sure she gets it. Whether it's now or tonight, what difference does it make?'

She shook her head. 'The ball, child. You will give it to her at the ball.'

'Why? Why must it be at the ball?'

'Because that is what I wish,' said the ghost with a ravenous smile.

'I know it's not a nice thing to say, but you're a beastly old bat.' I took two tallow candles from the bedside table and packed them in my carpet bag. 'And don't think of following me where I am going. I'm starting a new life. A wonderful life. And *you're* not invited.'

'You really think it is that simple?' said the Duchess with a ghostly cackle. 'You think you can simply *go*? That you can betray me like this and not suffer? Child, there is no way out. Besides, if you leave now you'll miss the best part.'

'I am going,' I declared, pointing in triumph at my bag, 'and you can't stop me!'

'You looked into the stone and what did you see?' sang the dead woman. 'Little Ivy carried from a grim house. Little Ivy dragged through the woods. But you have not seen how the story ends.' She smiled wickedly. 'I know you want to.'

'You are wrong,' I lied.

My plan was rather simple. I would turn my back on the dead woman and look out of the window until she vanished. And I would have done it too. If not for the snow. The snow falling in the attic like a winter frost. It didn't start with a few flakes drifting gently down from the rafters. No, it began all at once. A great deluge of snowfall, billowing and churning about the tiny room, covering everything in a blanket of frost and sleet.

I could no longer see the Duchess through the snowfall. I looked down and saw footprints crunching into the frost, one after the other – they formed a terrifying and unmistakable path from the ghost's bed straight to me.

The Duchess was nowhere.

Until she was.

She came up out of the frost like a phoenix rising from the ice. Her skin crisp and slippery and frozen. I tried to move, but my feet were fixed in the snow.

'You will never be free of me,' she hissed. Her plump finger uncurled, creaking and snapping like an icicle, and stroked my cheek. 'I will haunt you to the grave, child. To the grave and beyond. Do you really want such a fate? Stay for the ball – deliver the stone just as you promised. Do as I have asked and I will leave you in peace. You have my word.' The ghost pressed close to me, her frosted lips brushing my ear. 'And one more thing. Miss Always has plans for you. Be on your guard.'

She collapsed like an avalanche, falling suddenly into a large pile of snow and icicles at my feet. Just like that.

'Ivy?'

I looked up. Miss Always was standing at the door, bag in hand. She had her travelling bonnet on. Her smile was full of warmth and sisterly love. Did that beastly ghost *really* think I would doubt my bosom friend? Of course Miss Always had plans for me. To begin a new life together. There was nothing sinister about it.

'Ivy, you look so pale!' said Miss Always. She put down her bag and stepped into the bedroom. Surprisingly she did not trip over the six inches of frost. Because it was gone.

'I had a slight headache,' I managed to say, 'but happily it has passed.'

'I have been thinking, Ivy,' said Miss Always. 'It would be better for me to be there when you give Matilda the Clock Diamond. For legal reasons, you understand. What do you think?'

'About what, dear?'

'About the diamond,' said Miss Always eagerly. 'I suggest we go and get it immediately. Your wonderfully clever hiding place need no longer be a secret. Let's fetch it right now and then be on our way.'

'I have changed my mind, dear.' I tried to look bright. 'The Duchess wished me to give the stone to Matilda in front of her guests, so it's only proper that I should. I'm a girl of my word and whatnot.'

'Oh. I see.' Miss Always walked to the window and looked out at the creeping dusk. 'Tonight is the half-moon – did you know that, Ivy?'

I recalled Miss Frost telling me the very same thing in the schoolhouse. 'Yes, dear.'

'Such a moon has a special kind of beauty, don't you agree?' Miss Always turned to face me and her eyes sparkled like gemstones. 'Shall we go and take a closer look, Ivy? I believe the stairs out in the hall lead up to the roof. You could fetch the necklace – to save you time later on – and we could sneak up and stargaze before the ball. We would be like two astronomers! Wouldn't that be glorious?'

'Gazing at the moon? Sounds frightful.' I opened the wardrobe and pulled out my favourite blue dress. 'Besides, now that we are staying, I have to get dressed for the party.'

Miss Always nodded, her hands knotted tightly together. 'As you wish, Ivy.'

The ball was stupendously glorious. The great hall glowed like a freshly cut orange under the dazzling chandelier. A grand mass of ladies in shimmering gowns filled the hall, wearing bucketloads of rubies, sapphires, diamonds, pearls and tiaras. There were furs and cloaks as far as the eye could see. Men in top hats and tails. Girls in silk dresses and gloves with flowers or precious stones threaded in their hair. Servants in their best livery, carrying silver trays laden with mouth-watering food and sparkling wines. A string quartet played softly at the back.

I wandered amongst Matilda's guests feeling better than I had in days. The Clock Diamond was still safely hidden away. The thought of carrying the stone around with so many strangers milling about had filled me with anxiety. The Duchess would haunt me until my dying day if I lost the necklace before Matilda's speech. Much better to keep it hidden away until the last moment.

Usually at such a fine ball I would be carrying food from the kitchen. Or collecting coats. But now I was one of *them*. A genuine guest at a genuine ball.

The cake looked like a five-storey monolith beneath the radiant chandelier. It was at the centre of the great hall. The star attraction. Well, apart from *her*.

Matilda stood by the fireplace holding court before a gaggle of girls. They seemed to hang on her every word. Even I had to admit the birthday girl looked very fetching in her dress of white embroidered silk with a yellow velvet trim – her dark hair piled atop her head like a crown. I spotted Rebecca. She was standing by the grand staircase, looking about nervously.

Miss Always was nowhere to be seen. I hadn't laid eyes on her since we agreed to delay our departure. No doubt she was busy preparing my surprise party. I did spot Miss Frost,

248

hurrying up the main stairs. Instinctively I looked for Rebecca. The girl was gone.

'Do not imagine you are fooling any of my granddaughter's guests, Miss Pocket. A maid cannot pass for a princess, despite what you read in novels.'

Lady Elizabeth was leaning on her cane, resplendent in a glittering black gown. Her face was still slightly bloated, which was a blessing. She eyed me with suspicion. 'Why are you smiling at me? Stop it this instant!'

For some reason I thought of Matilda's story about her grandmother's first husband. And I couldn't resist. 'I was just trying to picture you as a young woman,' I said brightly. 'I'm sure you were pretty in an uninteresting kind of way. Did you have a great love? Something tells me you did. But his heart belonged to another. Didn't end well, I shouldn't think. Nothing says heartbreak like a bolt of lightning. Or so they say.'

It was cruel. But then, so was she.

Lady Elizabeth looked at me as a vulture does its prey. 'Who told you?' she hissed.

I smiled innocently. 'Told me what, dear?'

'The Clock Diamond has given you a lot of power, hasn't it, Miss Pocket?' The old crow's withered face bristled with rage. 'You have enjoyed living above your station, keeping my granddaughter waiting these past days. But that time is at an end. The cake is soon to be cut and Matilda will be giving her speech. Have the diamond ready to present to her in fifteen minutes.'

I patted her head (it seemed the right moment). 'Excellent idea.'

I climbed the stairs, leaving the hum of voices and the sweet melody of the string quartet behind. The time had come to part with the stone. There would be no more visions. I would never learn the end of my story. And that thought filled me with crushing sorrow.

By the time I reached the attic room, I felt as if I might burst into tears. Which was shameful! Pale moonlight pressed through the narrow gaps in the sloping roof. I didn't bother lighting a candle. No need. I would only be there a moment. I stopped before the trunk. Moved the boar spear and crossbows from the top, opened it, and dived down to the cluster of worthless jewels below. The cleverness of my hiding place still thrilled me. I pulled apart the tangled mess of imitation necklaces looking for the Clock Diamond. Even in the half-light, it didn't take long for the truth to dawn. Great strings of imitation stones were webbed between my fingers. I checked. Checked again.

The horror hit me like a punch.

The stone was gone.

I struck a match. Lit the candle. Churned to the very bottom of the trunk hoping against hope that the diamond had somehow come loose from the cluster and slipped beneath a hat or a bonnet. It hadn't. My heart thumped madly.

I closed the trunk. Sat on the lid. Took a deep breath. The Duchess would *kill* me!

Who had stolen it? Miss Frost? Yes, that devious governess was just the type to steal the Clock Diamond! Was she not unnaturally preoccupied by it? Had she not demanded I hand it over just hours ago? I would hunt her down. Expose her as a villain!

I would have too. If it hadn't been for the creak of the floorboards from a darkened corner of the room. Ever so faint, but undeniable. I stopped dead. Listened. *Snap.* This time from the other end of the attic. The faint shuffle of feet.

'Hello?' I said boldly. 'Miss Frost? Show yourself, you nefarious nitwit!' I reached over and picked up the boar spear. 'I have a weapon and I shall use it with deadly force!'

The candle trembled in my other hand. I set it down on the trunk and stepped into the centre of the room. Footsteps. Rapid footsteps. They moved in unison – emerging from the shadows like ghouls. Four hooded Locks. One from each corner. I thrust the boar spear out in front of me, turning in a clockwise direction. 'Give yourselves up and hand back the stone!' I shouted. 'Because let me be very clear, I am a fierce sort of girl and won't hesitate to skewer the lot of you!'

The Locks moved again in unison at great speed. Rushing to the centre of the room. Swarming me in seconds. I felt icy talons grip my arms and snake around my ankles. I saw the stone sparkle in the candlelight, twisted around one of their bony fingers. Then the spear flew out of my hand. Next I was spinning. Then my feet were swept from under me. I landed on the floor with an almighty thump. Groaned. Managed to pull myself up. Looked about.

I was alone.

My attackers had fled with the Clock Diamond.

I ran like the wind. Tore down the rickety back stairs. Barrelled along the hallway towards the landing. I saw a flash of dark cloak at the far end of the corridor. My chest burned, but I didn't stop. I charged like a bull down the vast corridor, willing my feet to move faster to catch those hideous little villains! Then another glimpse. A Lock rushed into the mouth of the hallway. He turned sharply and vanished through a door. The door to Rebecca's bedroom.

Fear flared inside me.

'Rebecca!' I shouted.

I gave chase, skidding to a stop before her door. It was open. I raced in at full speed, knocking a dozen clocks to the floor. Frantically, I looked around. No sign of the thieving blackguard. I bent down and checked under the bed. Nothing. The closet. Empty. Without warning the door slammed shut. I ran over and tried the handle. It was locked.

'Blast!' I thundered, pounding on the door.

'Ivy?'

I gave a startled cry. Spun around. Miss Always was standing in a dim corner of the room. Her dark brown dress seemed to meld with the shadows. Had she been there all along? She walked towards me, carefully navigating Rebecca's multitude of clocks.

'Miss Always,' I said, catching my breath, 'you startled me.'

'I'm sorry,' she said, 'you burst into the room in such a hurry I suppose I was dumbstruck. Whatever's the matter?'

'The diamond,' I said, 'it's been taken. I was chasing the Locks who stole it!'

Miss Always walked past me, stopping before a small table. A teapot lay upon it. Two cups. A single spoon. A bowl of sugar. 'You are not yourself, Ivy,' said Miss Always slowly. 'The fall.

The shock of your friend, Mr Banks. Miss Frost's silly stories. It has taken a terrible toll on your nerves.'

With great care my friend poured a cup of tea. A cloud of steam curled up into the air. She put the cup on a saucer and held it out to me. She said, 'Drink this. It will make you feel better.'

'Miss Always, now is not the time for a cup of tea,' I declared. 'If I am making this up, who locked the door? Was *that* my nerves?' Then a new thought troubled me. 'What are you doing in Rebecca's bedroom, anyway?'

'I thought I heard a noise,' said Miss Always.

'Then you *must* believe me!' I said. 'What you heard was those nefarious Locks.'

Miss Always smiled thinly. 'But you can see, there is no one here but you and me.'

'Look, dear, I haven't the time to convince you that I am telling the truth,' I said, trying again to open the door. 'They are getting away. We are running out of time!'

The heavy *tick tick tick* of Rebecca's clocks was like a hammer in my head. It's amazing that in moments of such monstrous crisis my most brilliant ideas are born – for I have all the natural instincts of a trapped miner.

Without hesitation I leapt over the painstakingly arranged clocks. Jumped on to the bed. Stepped across to the window ledge. Pulled up the window. It would take great skill, but I was confident I could crawl along the ledge and get to the window next door (which was Lady Amelia's bedroom). The risks were huge, but nothing else mattered to me except getting that stone back. My very life depended upon it.

'I will come back for you, dear!' I yelled.

I was halfway out of the window when I felt a hand grip my arm. Yanking me back inside. Those villainous Locks had returned. I twisted my head, trying to pull my arm free. But I did not see a Lock. Instead, there was Miss Always with the strength of Hercules, heaving me through the window.

'Ivy, don't do it,' she cried, gritting her teeth. 'You will fall to your death!'

'Stuff and nonsense!' I barked, pulling away. Miss Always' grip slipped – slightly. I put one foot on the ledge and steadied myself. 'I know what I'm doing, dear! Let me go!'

I gave a final heroic yank. My hand pulled free. Miss Always stumbled back. I steadied my footing and prepared to step beyond the ledge. Then I heard her cry out like some sort of monstrous crow. I stopped. Looked through the window. Miss Always was glaring at me. Her face ghostly white. Her eyes fierce. The room seemed to tremble. The window shook. Clocks rattled and fell. From behind her – almost from the folds of her dress – they came. A dozen hooded Locks in dark cassocks.

They flew out like a flock of rabid wolves. Two at a time. Cloaks billowing. Arms outstretched.

I was stunned. Horrified. The hideous little scoundrels moved as one. Their bony fingers grasped my arms like shackles. Then my ankles. Pulling me as if I were a rag doll. I flew through the open window and tumbled to the floor of the bedroom.

Miss Always cried out in horror. 'It can't be real!'

One of the devilish monks hovered over me. I looked up. Glimpsed its face. Bronzed skin. Eyes like two dark moons. Pale lips. And something else. This creature's chest was heaving but I heard no breaths. Instead, there was an unmistakable ticking sound. I lifted my leg and kicked the nasty inhuman beast as hard as I could. He flew back and crashed to the ground. Miss Always shrieked and fell on the bed. 'Ivy, be careful!' she called.

I looked about. Five or six Locks were edging steadily towards me. Closing in like a noose around my throat. What I needed was a weapon. I looked about. There was nothing. Nothing but . . .

That was it!

I spun around and picked up two large clocks. One gold. One silver. I took aim and threw the first. It struck the Lock square in the face. Then the second, which landed perfectly in another's chest. The little monsters stumbled. Hissed. Then dropped to the floor. The remaining villains rushed at me. But

I was fast. I kicked one in the stomach, then grabbed two more clocks. Repeated my assault – thumped a pair of them on their heads. They fell in a heap. Only one remained. He lunged at me, his hood flying back. It was a beastly sight. No hair. Teeth like glass. Eyes black as ink. Skin flaring like a lantern. Talons reaching for my throat. I picked up a marble clock in both hands and brought it down upon the villain's monstrous skull.

The hissing fathead dropped like a brick. And something else. As he fell the Clock Diamond tumbled from inside his cassock. I lunged. Scooped it up. Raced to the open window. Climbed out at speed. I slipped the stone into my pocket and jumped on to the ledge. Carefully, but quickly, I edged along the side of the great house. Beneath me, the torches lit for the arriving carriages illuminated the two-storey drop in gloomy detail. I was terrified. But also terribly brave. Stupendously anxious. But heartbreakingly intrepid.

Miss Always stuck her head out of the window.

'Ivy, come back!' she shouted. 'You will kill yourself!'

I prayed she was wrong.

Chapter 16

I didn't look down. I barely breathed. All that mattered was the window of Lady Amelia's bedroom chamber. My feet moved swiftly, taking small sideways steps. My hands dug into the grooves of the stonework. I no longer heard Miss Always. It felt as if I had been traversing the narrow ledge for days, until I reached out and felt the cold glass of the window against my hand. I had made it!

'Please be unlocked,' I said.

I took a breath and pulled. It opened! With one hand on the window frame, I climbed into Lady Amelia's bedroom. A lamp was lit on a table by her bed. The room was silent. Empty as far as I could tell. My frenzied mind had space for just a single thought. The Clock Diamond. I felt for it inside my pocket. Thank heavens it had not fallen out.

I ran towards the bedroom door – but never reached it. For I heard the unmistakable squeak of the handle being turned. Someone was coming in! In a flash – for I have all the nimble quickness of a startled rabbit – I threw open the lid of a trunk at the foot of Lady Amelia's bed and jumped inside. As I silently closed the lid, I saw the bedroom door swing open. Then heard the shuffle of feet. It was them.

I heard doors opening and closing. Drawers being pulled out. Windows being raised. I managed to pull a blanket over myself. Inside the trunk, I was locked in utter darkness. It felt like a coffin. The Locks made little sound – just the loud ticking from deep within their hideous little bodies. I held my breath. Prayed they wouldn't find me.

Next, I heard one of them walking close by. Then stopping. I closed my eyes tightly. Said a prayer. Then heard movement again. The rapid shuffle of little feet fading away.

They were leaving!

I didn't dare open the lid. Not yet. Not until I was sure it wasn't some kind of trick. But at least I felt calm enough to open my eyes. To my surprise the darkness inside the trunk had given way to a kind of half-light. Not strong, but enough to illuminate the wooden box. It was the Clock Diamond. Shimmering like moonlight in my pocket. I pulled it out.

A wave of pure delight washed over me.

I might have even squealed, had it not been for the snow. It began to fall inside the stone, just as before. Snow. Then a forest. A track of footprints. Two people. A woman in a yellow bonnet and a girl. A girl who was me.

The woman and I had been walking all day. I simply knew that we had. And as we trudged along the scene began to shift. The woods melted away, sinking into the snow. In their place, buildings began to rise up from the ice. Town houses and factories. Banks and bakers. Cobblestones sleek with frost. Streets and lanes. Horses, carriages and barrows crowded the scene.

We were in London.

The woman pulled me through the crowded streets, her face still concealed by the yellow bonnet. She dragged me by the hand until we came to a stop before a red-brick building. It was narrow and high. White windows. Blue door. A faded brass plaque was fixed below the doorbell. I didn't need to read it, for I already knew *exactly* where we were. The Harrington Home for Unwanted Children. The door swung open. And even though I was too young to yet read the plaque, I understood where I was. And what it meant.

The wind roared and churned. I pulled from the woman's grasp and ran down the steps. But not far. My feet slipped on the icy cobblestones and I fell. The woman was upon me in moments. She reached down to yank me to my feet. Just then a gust of wind howled around us – blowing the yellow bonnet from her head. The woman's red hair flared like a torch in the snowstorm.

The woman was Miss Frost!

She pulled me up and dragged me back up the steps to the orphanage. We vanished inside, the door slamming shut behind us. *No, not yet!* I wanted to cry out. A dark mist whirled inside the stone, devouring the light.

The vision was over.

It was her. That wicked creature! She took me from my parents. Ripped me from the life I had before. The life I couldn't remember. It was Miss Frost. It was *all* Miss Frost. But why would she have stolen me away? And why had she come to Butterfield Park? And why was Rebecca helping in her evil scheme?

I needed answers and I would get them. The truth about this whole beastly business. I pushed open the trunk and climbed out. My heart hammered as before, but no longer in fear. It was rage that coursed through my veins. Rage that propelled me as I ran from Lady Amelia's bedroom. Rage that glistened in my dark eyes. I was going to end this once and for all.

I was going to find the evil governess.

The hallway was empty, but Miss Frost had to be close by. I had seen her climbing the stairs earlier. And it made sense that she was overseeing the work of those beastly Locks.

I took off towards the back stairs, breaking into a spirited run. I bolted like a steed. The hallway flew by in a blur. Which is why I didn't see the two Locks hiding in the doorway on either side of me. They shot out like arrows. Before I even felt them latch on to my arms, I was off my feet, flying backwards. Their grip was deathlike. I landed on my back with an almighty thump.

But I recovered quickly, kicking the nearest one in the stomach. The vile ghoul landed in a tangle halfway down the corridor. I jumped to my feet as the second one came at me. He was awfully quick. I was thrown against the wall. His talons flew to my throat, thrusting my head against the wall. I could feel the air being squeezed out of me. My vision began to blur. My throat was afire. The Lock's grip tightened. He was going to kill me.

In a flash I sank my teeth into the villain's arm, biting with gusto. I have wonderful teeth. Slightly large. Not in a camel kind of way. But big. Useful. The Lock hissed. His black eyes rippled. His grip slackened. On a stand nearby was a ghastly gold and purple urn. I hooked the lip of it with my finger. It fell. Landed in my hand. Next I was bringing it down on his hideous little head. It smashed brilliantly. The Lock fell to the floor in a heap. His arm was wonderfully red and full of teeth marks. A clear liquid oozed from the wound. If it was blood, it was unlike any I had seen before.

Then I remembered. Miss Frost. I thundered on down the hallway, my eyes fixed on the end of the corridor. They came around the corner. Four of them. Charging towards me at great speed, their cassocks fluttering around them like capes. Was there an endless supply of these wretched creatures? I skidded to a stop. Turned and took off the way I had come.

I sprinted out of the hallway and on to the landing which overlooked the great hall (where the ball was taking place). To my left, two Locks were guarding the main stairs, blocking my escape. Across the landing, a dozen more came swarming out of the hallway like a pack of hungry jackals. I looked back. The Locks chasing me had stopped.

I was surrounded on all sides.

There was no escape.

One of the monks by the stairs lifted a clawed hand towards me, his talons unfurling. The others followed in unison. They never spoke, but I knew perfectly well what they were saying. *Hand over the Clock Diamond or die.*

As one they began to move. Like a caged animal, I looked desperately about. There was no way out. Well, apart from jumping over the banister, which would break my neck. Or at the very least, a leg or two. By now, the Locks were nearly within reach. Which might explain why I started running. Right at the banister. It's certainly why I leapt into the air. My feet hit the railing. I pushed off. Jumped higher. I didn't look down at the great hall below. I just flew through the air towards salvation. I would either reach it . . . or die trying.

The chandelier rushed at me. My arms flailed about. I could feel myself beginning to drop. In desperation, I stretched out my fingers. Hooked an iron branch between the row of glowing candles. I grunted. My arms strained. My knuckles were white. The chandelier swayed violently. A scattering of crystals fell to the great hall below, hitting the Earl of Vickers and his wife on the head. Naturally, they looked up. As did others around them.

That's when the screaming began.

'Good lord, what is that?' cried one stupid woman.

'A child!' screamed another. 'It's a child!'

'Help her. Somebody help her!' hollered a girl.

'I'm perfectly fine!' I shouted. 'Please, go on with the ball! Pretend I'm not here!'

But I wasn't fine at all. My fingers were slipping, unable to keep a grip on the chandelier. I was dropping before I knew it. I heard thunderous screams. Shut my eyes. Waited for the crunch of my bones on the hard floor.

Instead I hit with a splatter.

As if I had landed in a pile of mud.

Or a five-storey birthday cake.

Great chunks of cream and icing and vanilla cake arced through the air like a water fountain – a mighty shower of deliciousness raining upon the aristocrats of Suffolk, hitting foreheads and hats and eyeballs and gowns with thrilling accuracy.

My eyes flew open. I was wedged in Matilda's cake. My back hurt, but nothing appeared to be broken. Two of the servants rushed to lift me from the landing site.

Dismounting from the cake proved rather humiliating. The entire room was gathered around by that point. I felt an explanation was in order. Something that would satisfy their curiosity, but conceal the true horror of what was happening upstairs.

'It's actually a *very* funny story,' I said, wiping large chunks of chocolate cake from my dress. 'It involves a slippery floor, a jar of marmalade and my tragic past as a violently unreliable trapeze artist.'

'You've ruined my cake!'

It was Matilda. Naturally.

'I never wanted you at my party! I never wanted you in my house! What a spectacle you have made of yourself, hanging from the ceiling like a monkey. Are you really so desperate for attention? I almost feel bad for you, Pocket. It's no wonder you're an orphan. Your parents probably died of shame.' She looked over at her friends, the shock a mask upon their faces.

'Don't feel bad for the little maid. She does this sort of thing all the time. Where is the diamond, Pocket? Give it to me and get out of this house!'

My mind was elsewhere. Miss Frost. The Locks. I didn't have time for this. Well, perhaps just a moment or two.

I smiled at Matilda. 'You seem upset, dear. Have some cake.'

My hand was behind her head in a flash. Her face flew towards the battered birthday cake and landed with a glorious splutter. A large piece of cream sailed through the air and planted on Lady Elizabeth's nose. Matilda shrieked like an angry parrot. Lady Elizabeth called for my public execution. All around the guests were gasping and sniggering in shock. I believe I even glimpsed Lady Amelia stifling a giggle.

But I didn't stay around to enjoy the moment. For I had spotted Miss Frost racing at great speed across the landing above, a look of thunder upon her face. I licked a blob of butter frosting from my finger and bounded up the stairs after her.

Miss Frost had vanished down the east wing, though I wasn't at all sure why – if she knew I had the Clock Diamond, why had she not come after me? My head flicked from side to side as I charged along the hallway, eagerly glancing into each open door.

No sign of Miss Frost. Or her devilish Locks. Even the door to Rebecca's room was wide open again – I was relieved that Miss Always had managed to escape. At the end of the corridor, I mounted the stairs to the attic. My bedroom sat silent and still. But in the old storeroom – where I had hidden the necklace – there was a great racket coming from behind the closed door.

I grabbed the poker from my bedroom hearth. Then I hurried out into the corridor and threw the door open, fully prepared for battle.

Here is what I saw: Miss Frost clutching a sword. She was panting rapidly. Around her were a dozen hooded cassocks in piles upon the bare floor. White smoke rose from the garments like the embers of a dying fire.

Miss Frost fixed her eyes upon me. She lowered her sword. 'Miss Pocket, I have been searching for you all night.'

In that instant my mind flew to the vision in the Clock Diamond.

I lifted the poker and pointed it at the governess. 'I know everything!' I shouted.

'Lower your weapon,' said Miss Frost coolly.

'I won't!' I thundered, stepping towards her.

Miss Frost lifted her sword and we began to circle each other.

'Where is the Clock Diamond?' said the governess.

'Where you can't find it, you villain!'

'Calm yourself, Miss Pocket. I am sure you are full of questions about the events of tonight. But right now I am trying my best to keep you safe. Miss Always believes that her time has come and she will do whatever it takes to –'

'Stop blaming Miss Always!' I hissed. 'I know you took me! I saw it in the stone. You stole me from my home. From my family. You dragged me to that beastly orphanage!'

Anger boiled within me. It felt like a tempest in my chest. I lunged, thrusting the poker at the governess. With ease she used her sword to sweep it aside.

Miss Frost sighed as if in defeat. 'Hunting for the Clock Diamond has led me to many dark places, Miss Pocket. It was in such a place that I found you.'

Hearing the truth at last was rather shocking. There were so many thoughts and questions, I didn't know which one to grab first. 'The house I saw in the stone,' I said, finally, 'the one you took me from – did I grow up there?'

Miss Frost shook her head. 'The house was full of vagrants, criminals and other undesirables. It was a forsaken place, Miss Pocket. A place of last resort.'

'A poorhouse?' I heard myself ask.

'Worse' was the answer. 'I was there following a lead concerning the Clock Diamond. I found you and your mother in a back room. You were sleeping in her lap – curled up like a kitten.'

I squealed. A wave of joy rushed through me. My mother!

But Miss Frost was frowning. 'She was dead, Miss Pocket. Quite dead.'

The governess stepped towards me, but I backed away.

'You were sound asleep and so I took you. What else was I supposed to do? Leave you there? Yes, you tried to run away and yes, I stopped you.' Miss Frost cleared her throat. 'For reasons of my own I didn't wish to be seen, so I left on foot, cutting across the woods. You woke up, told me your name and . . . and asked for your mother. When we got to the orphanage, you threw a fit. Hit your head on a desk. I came the next day and you didn't recognise me. The doctor said you had no memory of the previous day. Or of your mother. I was relieved.'

'Who was she?' I said next. 'Who was my mother?'

Miss Frost's eyes shifted about. Just for a moment. She said, 'I do not know. Your mother had no possessions. Her clothes were threadbare. She wore no jewellery. Perhaps her family had turned her out on the street. Who can say?'

'But what about my father?' My voice rang with bitterness. 'I must have one, mustn't I? Why didn't you try and find him? Anything would have been better than sending me to that awful place.'

'Miss Pocket, judging from where I found you, I suspect your father is either dead or unaware you exist.' The governess bowed her head to meet my gaze. 'Life had abandoned you both, Miss Pocket. Your mother wore no wedding ring. Do you understand?'

Of course I did.

My eyes locked on to Miss Frost. 'You've been lying to me this whole time. Lying and plotting and scheming behind my back.'

A shadow passed across Miss Frost's face, though she made no reply.

'Does Rebecca know?' I demanded. 'Is that what you two have been conspiring about in the shadows? Is that the big secret? Tell me, Miss Frost – I have a right to know!'

'This isn't the time.'

She was wrong. Now was *exactly* the time. I wanted answers and I would have them. 'Did you come to Butterfield Park for the Clock Diamond or for me?' I barked.

'The simple answer is – both.'

'I suppose you killed Rebecca's old governess to take her place?'

Miss Frost gave me a disapproving glare. 'I paid Miss Rochester two hundred pounds to leave Suffolk and spend the summer in Italy.'

Which was hugely disappointing.

'The stone, Miss Pocket,' she said with icy calm, 'where is it?'

I lunged for a second time. Miss Frost stepped back and with a flick of her wrist, she had her sword at my throat. I looked at her, the hatred crackling in my eyes. 'You are a bad person, Miss Frost.'

'Perhaps.'

A scream broke the spell. It came from the hall outside. It was unmistakably Rebecca. I turned towards the door.

'Rebecca?' I shouted. 'What have you done to her, Miss Frost?'

Silence.

When I turned back, the governess had vanished.

I charged down the rickety back stairs, around the corner and into the hallway. Rebecca was at the far end, being set upon by a gaggle of Locks. They had her in their grasp and were dragging her away. Not if I could help it!

'I'm coming, dear!' I cried.

Gripping the poker tightly in my sweaty hand, I took off at speed. Rebecca was being pulled into a doorway near the landing. She clung to the sides of the door frame, trying desperately to hold on. As I raced past Matilda's bedroom a Lock flew at me. I didn't even stop. Just swung the poker, knocking the bronzed fathead right in the stomach. He doubled over and dropped.

'Hurry, Ivy!' shrieked Rebecca.

I was upon them now. Two of them rushed at me, claws out. I thumped one on the head. The other seized my wrist and began to squeeze it like a vice. In a flash I was burying my teeth in his hand.

Inspired by my brilliant fighting skills – for I have all the natural instincts of a warlord – Rebecca stomped on another Lock's foot. She followed up valiantly with a kick to the shins, but slipped and fell herself (she lacked my gift for combat). The evil pygmy fled like a startled rabbit. I went to work on the other two, bashing one on the head and the other in the chest. I was marvellous! I scanned the corridor expecting to see a fresh supply of the tiny monsters charging from either end of the hallway. But there were none . . . at least for now. I grabbed Rebecca by the hand and pulled her up.

A wasteland of Locks lay upon the floor around us.

'Are you hurt?' I asked Rebecca.

The poor girl tried to catch her breath. She held out her arm. Three scars were seared across her wrist. 'I'll be fine,' she said. 'Ivy –'

Hurried footsteps echoed in the hallway behind us. And screams. Blood-curdling screams. I twisted around. Miss Always flew past, followed swiftly by three Locks. Then I heard an awful thump. Next, Miss Always' wretched cry. What I saw next, passing at the end of the hall, chilled my blood. The villains, dragging Miss Always along the ground like she was a bag of grain. Her legs kicking, her nails clawing at the floor in a useless attempt to stop them. Then she was pulled from view towards the back stairs.

'Fear not, Miss Always, I will save you!' I shouted.

'Ivy, what you just saw is a trick,' said Rebecca, grabbing my arm. 'Miss Always is not the great friend you think she is. This whole time she has been using you terribly. Promise me you will not follow her up on to the roof.'

The roof? So that was where Miss Frost was conducting her wicked scheme!

'You poor, deluded halfwit,' I said gently. 'If Miss Always wanted the stone she could have grabbed it on the boat. But she did not wish to even *look* at it.'

'That is only because she thinks you might be of some use to her,' came the beastly reply. The girl tightened her grip on my arm. 'You told Miss Always that you had tried on the Clock Diamond, didn't you, Ivy?'

What did *that* have to do with anything? 'Yes, I suppose I did.'

The girl nodded her head and muttered, 'She believed that it was proof.'

'Proof of what?'

'Everything.' Her voice was trembling. 'Oh, Ivy, Miss Always has a black heart.'

'And Miss Frost is a saint?' I snapped. 'She took me, Rebecca. She dragged me to the orphanage and left me there to rot.'

'What if she had no choice?'

I was stunned. Rebecca *knew* about Miss Frost's treachery? And still she defended her? There was only one explanation. 'You are suffering a brain fever, dear,' I said. 'Stick your head in the nearest bowl of fruit punch – it is an excellent remedy.'

I hurried down the hallway, bound for the roof.

'Ivy, let me help you!' shouted Rebecca.

'No need,' I said, not looking back. 'I will see to Miss Frost.'

'But Ivy, you don't understand! Please don't go up on the roof. It is a trick!'

Rebecca was calling after me, talking a great deal, but her words quickly died away.

For I was already gone.

Chapter 17

The trapdoor was open. I glimpsed a twinkling of stars in the sky above. I could hear the clashing of metal against metal. Grunts and gasps. I put my foot on the first step of the rickety little staircase. Stopped.

The Clock Diamond.

Something told me it would be a grave mistake to bring it up on to the roof. So I hurried into my bedroom. Looked about for a suitable hiding spot.

I raced to the dresser, pulled the stone from my pocket, and dropped it into the water jug. It landed with a satisfying plop and quickly sank to the bottom. Perfect!

I crawled through the trapdoor and stepped on to the roof (which wasn't easy, carrying a large fire poker). The house had a pitched roof over the east and west wing and a flat one capping the great hall. Which is where I stood. The sharp clash of metal hitting metal charged the air. There in the distance – Miss Always and Miss Frost. Around them were piles of smouldering cassocks. Miss Frost and Miss Always stood not three or

four feet apart. There was a dagger on the ground at Miss Always' feet. And a sword at her throat.

My first instinct was to cry out. To yell something devastatingly useful like – 'Don't do it!' or 'Lower your sword, you diabolical fathead!' But I did neither. Instead, I sneaked up on the pair. Miss Frost had her back to me. Miss Always was remarkably brave. Her eyes were not pierced in terror. In fact, she didn't look frightened at all. I crept over, stepping carefully between the joists in the slate roof. I noticed Miss Always glancing my way. But just for a flash. She was a smart one, Miss Always. She knew I had come to rescue her but she didn't give the game away.

'Why are you doing this, Miss Frost?' she cried suddenly. 'I do not understand!'

This seemed to confuse Miss Frost. She said, 'What game are you playing now?'

'I do not have the Clock Diamond,' said Miss Always frantically. 'I cannot give you what I do not have. Please don't kill me!'

'Kill you I must,' came the cold reply. 'Though why you are acting like a damsel in distress, I cannot imagine.'

I was upon them now. Poised to strike. Just at that moment, Miss Frost seemed to sense my presence on the roof. She swung around. But too late. I brought the poker down upon her hand. The sword dropped from her grasp. In a flash, brave Miss

Always had scooped up the dagger at her feet and was bearing down on Miss Frost.

'Well done, Ivy!' she said.

Miss Frost raised her arms in surrender and began to back away.

'Don't be a fool, Miss Pocket,' said the governess. 'See what is right in front of your face. Your friend is not what she seems.'

'Watch her, Ivy,' said Miss Always, waving the dagger at Miss Frost, 'she is a cunning beast. An assassin who wants the Clock Diamond for herself. She will do anything, kill anyone, to get it.'

'Miss Always is twisting the truth,' said Miss Frost. 'It is she who would do anything to get the stone. I wish to guard it. She wishes to control it.'

The governess continued taking careful steps back, retreating from the dagger until she hit the stone parapet that ran around the edge of the roof. Miss Always lunged at her, the blade of the dagger pressing into the governess's pale neck.

I fell in beside Miss Always – my poker pointed at the governess. 'Those hideous Locks work for *her*, don't they?'

Miss Always didn't answer. But Miss Frost did.

'The Locks do the bidding of the Gatekeeper.'

'Is . . . is that what you are?' I said.

She shook her head. 'That is what Miss Always is.'

'Lies!' hissed Miss Always. 'There is only one way to end her reign of terror and that is death.'

I gasped. 'You . . . you want to kill her?'

'It must be done,' said Miss Always.

'After she kills me, she has plans for you, Miss Pocket,' said the governess. 'Horrid plans.'

My head was spinning. What was I to believe? Naturally, I trusted Miss Always. But I had never seen her like this. The woman I knew would faint at the sight of a wasp. Now she was eager to cut Miss Frost's throat? It was baffling. Yet how could I trust Miss Frost? She was a villain.

'All these years, I thought it was my mother who put me in that awful place,' I said faintly. 'But it was *you*, Miss Frost. You put me there.'

'The orphanage was clean and reputable,' said Miss Frost crisply. 'I knew you would not be beaten or starved. That you would have shelter and food in your stomach.'

'It was beastly,' I whispered.

'It was an orphanage, Miss Pocket,' came the stiff reply. 'I kept something of an eye on you over the years – always from a distance – paid for your clothes and certain privileges. Tried to ensure you got on in the world. Why do you suppose the Midwinters took you on as a maid?'

I gasped. 'That was your doing?'

'I felt such a position would give you a decent future. I never imagined that you would find your way to Paris and end up with the Clock Diamond. If I could have stopped it, I would have – but by the time I traced the stone to France the Duchess was dead and you were sailing for England.'

'What a remarkable coincidence,' said Miss Always with a mocking grin. 'You *happened* upon Ivy and her mother whilst hunting the stone. Then Ivy *happened* upon the diamond in Paris. It would make a sensational work of fiction, though I doubt anyone would believe it.'

'It does sound rather unlikely,' I told Miss Frost.

'And yet it is the truth,' she replied coolly.

'I believe your mother is alive, Ivy,' declared Miss Always. I was stunned! 'She is probably still looking for you. We can find her together, you and I. We will travel all over England if we have to. Leave no stone unturned. Do not be fooled by Miss Frost. She is a kidnapper and a killer. Who do you think tampered with the drawbridge signal, killing Mr Banks? And who do you think plunged a dagger into the Duchess of Trinity's heart? It was all *her*.'

Now, normally I am brilliant in a crisis. But I confess to a certain amount of confusion. Fortunately, a thought occurred to me. I turned to my friend. 'How do you know so much about my mother?'

She didn't answer. Not right away. At last she said, 'I have been conducting some research into Miss Frost and her evil deeds … the information I gathered has been most shocking … this woman is from a faraway place … I didn't want to tell you about it until I was sure, Ivy.'

'Her research is very hands-on,' said Miss Frost with a dry laugh. 'She commits the crimes, then blames them on me.'

I needed to think. But there wasn't time, for Miss Frost made her move. She pushed the dagger from her throat and ripped the poker from my hand in an instant. She spun around, swiping Miss Always' hand, clipping the dagger. It twirled through the air. Now it was Miss Always who had her back to the wall.

I was about to charge at the governess (it seemed like the heroic thing to do), but she looked at me and said, 'Think, Miss Pocket. If all I wanted was the Clock Diamond, why would I encourage you to hide it? Would it not have been easier for me to overpower you and steal it days ago? Tracking the Clock Diamond is my job, murder is not.'

'She tore you from a loving home, Ivy,' said Miss Always, her eyes moving between Miss Frost's weapon and me. 'She destroyed your one chance at happiness. Haven't I cared for you and tried to keep you safe? Ivy, can you really trust the word of a kidnapper over your bosom friend?'

It was suddenly so clear. I thought about all that had happened since I first met Miss Always. All that we had shared. All that we had spoken of. And for the first time I saw the whole picture. All the pieces that I had been unwilling to put together. And it was monstrous. I looked at my friend and said, 'Now that I think of it, you were fixated on the Clock Diamond from the very first. You were always asking me about it on the ship. And when we docked you were *terribly* interested in where I would be staying in London. The only person who knew I would be at the house in Belgravia was *you*, Miss Always. And the night of the break-in, there was a woman in the shadows.'

'Miss Frost!' she shouted. 'It was Miss Frost!'

I shook my head. 'I saw you on the ship – your publisher never had a long-lost son, did he? You were conspiring with one of your Locks. And tonight I saw those hideous creatures emerge from your dress. As such, I have no choice but to assume you are a diabolical, diamond-hunting, Lock-loving lunatic. Which is violently disappointing.'

'Well done, Miss Pocket,' said the governess, her eyes fierce with pride. 'It took some time, but you got there in the end.'

Miss Always didn't take it at all well. In fact, she was rather upset. She threw back her head and let out a murderous cry. The skin on her face began to ripple. Her eyes turned an inky black. Her neck puffed out like a lizard. Then a dozen villainous

Locks flew out from the folds of her dress. It was terrifying and spectacular all at once. They swarmed around Miss Frost like a tempest, clawing at her with icy talons. The poker flew from her hand. She fell back against the parapet. Miss Always raced across the roof and picked up her dagger.

Miss Frost began kicking and punching like a madwoman. She bent down, collected the poker and ruthlessly drove the sharp end into the heart of each and every one of the Locks. They seemed to crumble before my eyes, their flesh collapsing in a pile of smouldering ash. All that remained were their cassocks.

I looked across the roof for Miss Always. She wasn't there.

'Ivy, watch out!' cried Miss Frost.

But too late.

Miss Always spun me around and pushed me against the parapet. A dagger pointed at my heart. 'Where is the Clock Diamond, Ivy?' she said softly.

'Somewhere you'll never find it,' I hissed. 'You were my friend, Miss Always. You said we were like sisters.'

'I already have a sister,' said the villain coldly. 'Pushed her down a well when she was nine. Unfortunately, she lived.'

'You killed the Duchess, didn't you?'

A mad kind of pride glistened in her dark eyes.

'How could you be so cruel?' I said. 'I believed you, Miss Always. I believed in you.'

She smiled thinly. With one hand she pushed the dagger against my chest. With the other she searched the pockets of my dress. 'I apologise for lying to you, Ivy,' she said brightly. 'Believe it or not, I fully intended to tell you the truth right before I killed you on the ship. But then I discovered you had tried on the necklace.'

'What has that to do with anything?' I snapped.

'Only *everything*.' Miss Always said this with wicked delight. 'You became far more interesting after that.'

Miss Frost had retrieved her sword. She charged towards Miss Always, her weapon extended. But Miss Always stopped her cold. 'One more step and I will pierce her heart.'

'You *can't* kill her and you know it,' said Miss Frost evenly, inching closer. 'Besides, without Miss Pocket and the stone, you have nothing.'

I felt the blade pierce my flesh. I didn't cry out. But I wanted to.

'It is a half-moon, Ivy,' said my villainous friend. 'Do you know what that means?'

'Haven't a clue, dear.'

'It means I can go home. And you shall come with me.'

'That will not happen,' declared Miss Frost fiercely. 'The girl would not survive it.'

'Survive what?' I asked, rather anxiously.

'Do you remember the story I told you the other day, Ivy?' Miss Always' voice hissed like a rattlesnake. 'The lost myth about the Dual?'

Yes, I remembered. Hidden world. Beastly plague. Millions dead. And a silly story about a girl who can pass freely between two worlds. A girl who will heal the plague, ascend the throne and whatnot. I sighed. 'What about it?'

She glared at me. 'Can't you guess?'

'Miss Always thinks you are the Dual,' said Miss Frost, her voice thick with doubt. 'She is wrong, horribly wrong, but that won't stop her trying to prove it.'

I looked at Miss Always. Of all the questions swirling through my head, I could think of only one. 'Why would you think such a thing?'

The villain looked at Miss Frost and laughed. 'Shall *you* tell her or will I?'

The governess was frowning. 'The evidence is slight at best.'

'You are still here, Ivy,' said Miss Always, her eyes blazing. 'That has never happened before in the entire history of the Clock Diamond. Is that not peculiar? Is it not thrilling?'

I had no idea what the halfwit was talking about!

'And it is written that the Dual will have healing powers,' Miss Always continued breathlessly. 'Wondrous healing powers.

Ivy, you held my wrist when it was sprained. Your touch healed it in mere seconds. I believed that it would, and it did!'

'It was wishful thinking and nothing more,' snapped the governess.

'I'm afraid Miss Frost is right, dear,' I said, looking pitifully at my lunatic friend. 'After I heard you talking in the morning room, I tested my healing powers on Lady Amelia. I'm afraid I couldn't even mend her pricked finger. So you see – I'm not even slightly miraculous.'

Miss Always was smiling. Didn't look at all bothered. 'The Dual has no power in this world,' she said gleefully. 'She is a girl just like every other. It is only my people, from *my* world, that the Dual can heal. And heal me you did.' The bug-eyed fruitcake looked up at the moon. 'We can cross tonight, Ivy. The process is easy enough. Come with me. Come and fulfil your destiny.'

It was bonkers. The whole thing. And yet . . . if *any* of it were even a tiny bit true, it might be rather lovely to cure a plague and rule a kingdom and whatnot. It's not like I had anything better to do.

The governess was now only a few feet from where Miss Always held me at knifepoint. She said, 'You are tempted, are you not, Miss Pocket? Miss Always makes it sound rather thrilling. And why shouldn't she – after all, what has she to lose? If you *are* the Dual, she would seek to use you as an instrument for power and control. You would be her puppet. And if, as I suspect, it turns out you are *not* the Dual . . .'

'What then?' I asked.

'I would bring you back,' promised Miss Always hastily. 'I would bring you back to England, safe and sound.'

'She couldn't, Miss Pocket,' declared the governess, 'for there would be nothing left of you. The journey between worlds would destroy an ordinary child. You would be torn limb from limb.'

Which was monstrously unpleasant.

Before I could decline Miss Always' generous offer, Miss Frost swooped. Her sword sliced the air, came down with a spark upon Miss Always' dagger. But it did not drop. Miss Always spun around in a blur, swinging the dagger right at Miss Frost's neck. But the governess ducked. Brought down her blade. Cutting Miss Always' hand as if it were butter.

Before the wound had even begun to bleed, Miss Frost had knocked the dagger from Miss Always' hand and had her cornered. A sword under her chin.

'You are trapped, Miss Always,' she said, panting. 'You cannot take the girl *and* get the stone *and* make your escape. There isn't time. You will die on this roof – I will see to it.'

'We cannot have that, now can we?' said Miss Always. She

turned her head towards me, her eyes ablaze. 'Believe it or not, I have enjoyed our time together – but we shall have to postpone our journey. For now. But not forever.'

It happened quickly. Miss Always kicked Miss Frost rather expertly in the shin, pushed her over and leapt on to the parapet. She glanced back at me. Her smile was wicked. Then she stretched out her arms and jumped.

I screamed. Ran to the edge of the roof. Miss Frost got up and fell in beside me. The moonlight cast the ground below in a silvery haze. I expected to see Miss Always tumble to her death. But she did not. Her skirt billowed around her, her arms outstretched. She landed on the gravelled driveway in a crouch, then rose to her feet with ease. She took off, running at speed towards a dark carriage waiting by the wild-flower meadow. The door flew open as she approached. She jumped in. The driver whipped the four horses and they took off, vanishing into the woodlands.

Miss Frost grabbed my shoulders and held them tightly. 'Miss Pocket, listen to me. Do not give Matilda the necklace. It can do great harm. Keep the stone, Miss Pocket. Keep the stone and go from this place. I will find you.'

'Find me? Find me where?'

'Do you trust me, Miss Pocket?'

'Of course not,' I snapped. 'I have no idea what just happened.

I have no idea who *any* of you really are. How did Miss Always jump from the roof and not break her neck? Where is this other world you keep talking about? What is happening?'

'The moment you put on that necklace you entered a war, Miss Pocket. Now do as I say – take the stone and leave this place.'

She let go of me and jumped on to the parapet, concealing the sword in a sheath fixed to her waist.

'Where are you going?' I shouted.

'To kill your friend.'

Then she jumped. I watched her fly through the air, graceful as a swooping eagle. Her hair came loose and fluttered in the wind like scarlet ribbons. She landed lightly and took off towards the stables. Moments later a horse bolted out, Miss Frost atop it. She galloped into the woodlands and was quickly lost from view.

'Wait!' I hollered. 'You know more than you are saying! Who was my mother? Tell me who I am!'

But my words died in the cold night air.

The guests were gone by the time I came down from the roof. All traces of the Locks had vanished. I heard two maids gossiping on the landing – apparently the ball hadn't recovered after the business with the cake. The birthday girl had run up to her bedroom and locked the door, only coming out with the promise of a new horse.

The servants were clearing the great hall of food platters and half-empty glasses as I came down the stairs. A few of them gave me devious looks. As if the disastrous ball were all *my* fault. Perhaps it was. But I was past caring about any of it. My mother was dead. And if the world wouldn't give answers about who she was, then I would stop asking. Stop caring.

I had the Clock Diamond to fetch and a job to do.

And I intended to finish it.

The family was gathered in the library. All except for Rebecca. Lady Elizabeth was stroking Matilda's cake-crusted hair, whispering in her ear about how one day she would be mistress of Butterfield Hall. *Then* she would have the last laugh. Lady Amelia was pacing about looking anxious. They all glanced up when I entered the room.

'I hate you, Pocket!' hissed Matilda. 'I hate you and I wish you were dead!'

'Of course you do,' I said flatly. 'Normally that would be a huge blow – but not tonight. I'm sorry for shoving your face in your birthday cake, Matilda.'

'I should think so!' snapped Lady Elizabeth.

'Didn't I tell you, Matilda?' said Lady Amelia. 'Didn't I say

Miss Pocket would be terribly sorry?'

'I'm sorry I didn't do it days ago,' I said. 'Matilda, you're a stupendously awful girl. You treat Rebecca with monstrous contempt. You browbeat and bully your mother. You bark at the servants. The one person you treat with any regard is Lady Elizabeth and that's only because she's going to drop dead any moment, and you want to make sure she leaves this ghastly estate to you.'

'Have her flogged!' cried Matilda. 'Somebody fetch me a horsewhip!'

Lady Elizabeth used her cane to thump the table. Her beady eyes glowered at me. 'Wicked girl! Pack your bags and get –'

'Don't worry, I'm going,' I said. 'But first, there's something I have to do.'

I reached into my dress and pulled out the Clock Diamond. It glowed in the palm of my hand – a twinkling of stars, a half-moon. Matilda eyed it greedily. Lady Amelia gasped in wonder. Lady Elizabeth licked her thin, shrivelled lips.

'Someone told me tonight that I must keep the stone,' I said. 'That I wasn't to give it away. But as far as I can tell, it has brought me nothing but trouble.'

'Give it to me, Pocket,' ordered Matilda. 'Hand it to me now!'

I held the necklace out. It throbbed in my hand. Like a heartbeat.

'Take it,' I said.

I had my back to the library door, so I didn't see Rebecca slip quietly into the room. She had a gift for moving about unnoticed. Which was how she managed to get so close to me. So close to the diamond.

Matilda grabbed the stone from my hand. It felt like a blow to be parted from it. But I did not let it show. Matilda held it up, her eyes swelling with wonder and pride.

'Oh, before I forget,' I said, 'the Duchess of Trinity had a message that went with her gift. She wanted me to tell you that the Clock Diamond came with the kind regards of –'

I didn't see her move. But she must have. Rebecca ran at Matilda, snatching the Clock Diamond from her hand. Matilda screamed. Demanded the immediate return of *her* necklace. But Rebecca wasn't listening. She ran up the spiral staircase to the landing above.

'I have to do this,' she called, her voice shaking. 'I have to try it on just once.'

'What has come over you, Rebecca?' cried Lady Amelia.

'Give it back, you nutter!' hollered Matilda.

Perhaps I was still numb to what was really happening. The pieces of the puzzle were there. Yet I had not put them together.

But Lady Elizabeth was starting to. She gazed not at Rebecca, but at me. 'The Duchess's message – what was it, Miss Pocket? What did she wish you to say?'

In the confusion my mind went blank.

'Come down this instant!' shouted Matilda, stomping her foot. 'It's *my* diamond, not yours!'

'I can't,' said Rebecca softly. She unclasped the silver chain, gathering each end at the back of her neck. 'It's the only way, do you see? It's the only chance I have.'

'The only chance for what?' I said.

'The message,' cried Lady Elizabeth, thumping the table with her cane, 'what was the Duchess's message, you impossible girl?'

My gaze shifted from Rebecca to Old Walnut Head. The answer she was seeking was somewhere in the fog of my mind. 'She told me to say the Clock Diamond came with the kind regards of . . . of . . .' Then it came to me. '*Winifred Farris*. With the kind regards of Winifred Farris.'

Lady Elizabeth gasped. 'No . . . not *Farris*. Dear God!'

I looked up at Rebecca. She was looking back at me. Only at me. 'I have to see her again,' she said. 'I have to see her and speak with her, just like you did, Ivy. Tell Miss Frost I'm sorry.'

She threaded either end of the clasp together. Then let go. The necklace caught around her neck, the Clock Diamond coming to rest on the girl's chest. It glowed darkly. Then, a faint buzzing. A familiar buzzing. Charging and rippling through the air.

'Rebecca, *no!*' cried Lady Elizabeth. 'It is a trick. Stop her!'

The stone's black glow was smothered by a scarlet light. A pulsing scarlet light. Then yellow. Then red again. Rebecca stumbled. Reached out for the railing.

The buzzing was like a wasp in my ear.

'What on earth is going on?' snapped Matilda. 'Cousin, give me that necklace *now*.'

'Take it off, Rebecca!' shrieked Lady Elizabeth. 'Please, take it off!'

Now a bright mist churned and filled the stone. It was beautifully white, radiating from the diamond like a searchlight. An endless, perfect light.

Rebecca let out a piercing cry.

I was already running up the stairs by then. Calling Rebecca's name again and again. By the time I reached the landing she had fallen. The library was suddenly quiet. The buzzing began to fade. The two women and the girl below were utterly silent. I dropped to my knees. Looked at her. Rebecca's body had withered to a husk, as if her very life force had been pulled from her. Her face was a hollow shell. Her skin, bone dry. Her cheeks, monstrously sunken. Her arms, little more than drooping flesh hanging from bones. Her eyes, a milky white. Her hair, brittle as straw. Her lips yellow and curled into a grin.

It struck me as heartbreakingly cruel – the sound I heard in the deathly silence of that library. The mantle clock ticking above the fireplace. Each solemn tick counting the seconds and minutes since Rebecca Butterfield had run out of time.

Chapter 18

Vengeance had come to Butterfield Park. And it had a name. Winifred Farris.

The body had been taken away. Dr Longfellow could not explain what had happened to Rebecca. Some sort of rare blood disease, he supposed. We were still gathered in the library as the sun came up. It was as if no one had the heart to leave.

A few questions were asked about where Miss Frost and Miss Always had got to. I said Miss Always received bad news about her mother's health and had rushed to her side. As for Miss Frost, well, who could say? No one seemed terribly bothered that she had vanished.

The Clock Diamond had been taken from around the dead girl's neck. It lay upon the table, shining pink like the dawn. Now wasn't the time for questions. Yet I had so many. Lady Elizabeth sat in her favourite chair before the window, her back to us all. She was the first to speak. She said, 'When I heard the Duchess's message – *from Winifred Farris* – the name the Duchess longed to have . . . I knew the necklace was not a peace offering, but revenge.'

The story was simple and rather sad.

'When we were girls the Duchess always won – no matter what it was, she won. Luck of the angels, they used to say. I suppose I resented it. She was engaged to Nathaniel Farris, the handsomest young man in the county. Everyone believed they would live happily ever after.' The old bat smiled bitterly. 'But he broke it off – married me instead. Then like a fool he changed his mind. He said I was cold and wicked and that I only married him so the Duchess couldn't have him.'

'Was he right?' I said.

She huffed. 'I suppose. He ran to her house in the dead of night, begging for forgiveness. God smiled on me and sent a bolt of lightning. The Duchess saw the whole thing from her bedroom window. She lost her mind after that. Fled England, never to return.'

'I don't understand any of it,' said Lady Amelia, her face a track of tears and sorrow. 'What happened to poor Rebecca?'

'She put on that wretched necklace,' said Lady Elizabeth coldly. 'To think that it was intended for Matilda.'

'You think the necklace killed her?' said Lady Amelia.

'I know it,' barked the old woman. 'That diamond is cursed. It must be.'

And of course it made sense. Rebecca put on the necklace and dropped dead. And yet . . .

'Forgive me, Lady Elizabeth,' I said, 'but while I was on the boat coming from France, I put on the necklace. I promised I wouldn't, but I did. And, well, it didn't kill me.'

'I wish that it had!' hissed Lady Elizabeth. She rose from her seat and her eyes blazed with life and fire and hatred. She pointed her cane at me. 'You did this! You visited this curse upon us. I won't forget, Miss Pocket. Take that wretched stone. Take it and go!'

Matilda rose to her feet, her eyes fixed upon the Clock Diamond. 'But Grandmother, the stone is much too valuable to give away to a *maid*. I wouldn't wear it, of course, but it would be a wonderful addition to my collection.'

Lady Elizabeth regarded her granddaughter with a mixture of admiration and disgust. She said, 'I sometimes wonder if you have a heart, Matilda.'

The girl said nothing but gazed darkly at the stone.

Lady Elizabeth used the end of her cane to hook the necklace and lift it from the table. It dangled from the stick, right in front of my face. 'You and this instrument of suffering deserve each other, Miss Pocket. Take it, pack your bag and get out of this house. You are not welcome here.'

'Of course, Lady Elizabeth,' I said. 'I'll go.'

And so I did.

Before I left Butterfield Park I took something from Rebecca's bedchamber. I passed by her door on my way downstairs. The room looked as if a tempest had swept through it. The floor was a battlefield of scattered clocks. They no longer ticked as one. The room had lost its heartbeat. I wondered what they would do with all those clocks – now that she was gone. Bury them, I thought. Or throw them away. So I took one. It was small. Silver. Badly dented and scratched. With a brass top. I slipped it into my carpet bag and walked out of the great house for the very last time.

It is possible I heard the Duchess's ghostly cackle as I closed the front door.

The rising sun dappled the tulips and roses, causing the petals to sparkle like starlight. I would take the train back to London. I would start over. I had one thousand pounds in my pocket. But what of my one thousand questions? They nipped at me like termites upon a log. Yes, I had *some* answers. I now understood the Duchess's role in this dark mystery. She used me from the very beginning to get revenge upon Lady

Elizabeth. All that mattered to the ghost was killing the old bat's pride and joy – Matilda. But instead, Rebecca had been the victim.

And my mother, dead and forsaken. Who was she? And how did we come to be in that awful house? And what did Miss Frost know that she wasn't telling me? And what of Miss Always and her belief that I was the Dual she had been searching for?

Yes, I had answers. But not enough. Not nearly enough.

Chapter 19

I had a ticket to London in my hand. The train wasn't due for thirty minutes so I sat down and waited.

'I trust you have the stone?'

Miss Frost was at the end of the platform. The sword had vanished from around her waist and her hair was pulled back in a familiar tight bun. A dark horse stood grazing beyond the station gate. The governess walked across the platform and sat down beside me. 'The Clock Diamond, Miss Pocket – do you have it?'

I nodded my head. 'It killed Rebecca. She shrivelled up like some sort of monstrous raisin.'

'That is what it does,' said Miss Frost crisply. If she was sorry to learn of Rebecca's death her face betrayed nothing. But then she said, 'Foolish girl! I *told* her not to put it on.'

'I wore the diamond,' I said. 'I put it on just like Rebecca.'

'I know,' said Miss Frost.

'Then why am I alive and she is dead?'

Miss Frost lifted the hem of her dress and pulled a small knife from her left boot. She grabbed my arm. Pushed up the sleeve of my dress. The knife hovered above my flesh. Naturally, I tried to pull away. But Miss Frost had an iron grip on me.

'What on earth are you doing, you mad cow?' I snapped.

Miss Frost pressed the sharp blade into my skin, slicing a straight line across my forearm. The cut wasn't terribly long, but it was most effective. When it was done and I was staring at the wound, I didn't cry out. Not when the cut drew no blood. Not even when in its place, grey smoke coiled up from the wound like a tiny chimney pot. In seconds the smoke faded to a mist. Then the wound healed over as if it were never there to begin with.

I simply said, 'Am I dead?'

'When the Clock Diamond is worn it is fatal,' said Miss Frost calmly. 'No one has ever survived it before. That is what makes you of such interest, Miss Pocket.'

So I was dead. Or something like it. It was a most peculiar feeling.

'Rebecca pushed you down the stairs to prove that you *could* be hurt,' explained the governess. 'To prove that what I told her about you wasn't true.'

My mind was seething with slippery questions. *Could* I die? Would I get any older or be forever twelve (which would be violently inconvenient)? Would I continue to see ghosts?

Would I always be so hungry? Would I develop a ghostly glow like the Duchess of Trinity?

Miss Frost seemed to read my mind. 'For some reason you have survived the stone. Why, I cannot say. Perhaps we will never know.'

'If Rebecca knew what the Clock Diamond could do, why did she put it on?' I asked.

'Rebecca believed the stone would lead her to the one person who really mattered – her mother. I tried to make her understand that your case was most unusual. That you only saw ghosts because you are, at least in part, a ghost yourself – but she would not listen.'

In the sky above a cloud passed over the sun, casting us in a kind of mournful shroud – more shadow than light. I said, 'Is Rebecca inside the stone? Is she trapped in there?'

'The Clock Diamond isn't a destination, it is a door.'

'A door to where?'

'Prospa. It is my home – and Miss Always' too.'

'If the stone is a door, why does it kill people? There must be a *reason*.'

'The Shadow,' said Miss Frost.

I frowned. 'That silly plague Miss Always told me about?'

'It haunts my homeland, killing all but the lucky few who are immune. Once infection sets in nothing can be done. There is no treatment. Nothing . . . except for one thing.'

'Nothing except for *what*, you monstrous creature?'

'Souls,' said Miss Frost faintly. 'Human souls.'

I was baffled. Befuddled. Dumbstruck. What on earth was she talking about?

'A very great woman by the name of Professor Peggotty Spring found a way to cross from my world into yours using the stone,' explained the governess. 'She planned to bring back medicine to help our people.'

'And did she?'

'Yes.' Miss Frost closed her eyes. 'But it did little good. The story is long and rather gruesome, but in the end the professor settled in England and began experimenting ... on people ... finally discovering that the very vehicle which allowed her to cross over – the Clock Diamond – was the answer to her prayers. If worn by a person from this world, their very life force would pass through the stone, creating a powerful healing force in mine. It is terribly complicated, but the facts are not – the one thing that could ease great suffering in my world would cause great suffering in yours.'

I gasped. 'So Rebecca is in Prospa! Can you bring her back?'

Miss Frost looked rather uncomfortable. Just for a moment. Then she said, 'She is dead, Miss Pocket – you saw that for yourself. Each time a soul is captured it enters my world as a powerful energy. This healing light passes through a Sun Diamond kept in Prospa – only a lucky few can be healed each time. As you might imagine, this makes the stone very valuable indeed.'

'It's a nasty business, this stealing of souls. Utterly fiendish!'

'You are right,' said Miss Frost with a frown.

'How on earth did the stone end up with the Duchess of Trinity?'

'I am told she spent years searching for it. The Duchess felt it was the perfect instrument for revenge against Lady Elizabeth. We lost the stone last century. Over the decades it has passed from hand to hand – people have put it on and perished. And the sick in my world have benefited.'

'Did you kill her?' I said. 'Miss Always, I mean.'

'Unfortunately not.' Miss Frost stared off into the distance. 'My sources tell me she returned to Prospa just hours after fleeing Butterfield Park.' She was frowning again. 'Under normal circumstances the Gatekeeper would *never* leave England without the stone – not without a very good reason.'

Now it was my turn to frown. 'You encouraged me to invite Miss Always to Butterfield Park. Didn't you know who she was?'

'Of course, Miss Pocket. Once I learned that you had tried on the stone and lived, I knew Miss Always would get foolish ideas about you. I suspected she would attempt to drag you into

Prospa on the night of the birthday ball. As such, I wanted her within my reach.'

'Miss Always believes that I am the Dual.' I said this casually. 'I'm sure it's all nonsense. But it *does* make me wonder why the stone didn't kill me, like it does everyone else.'

'It is curious, I admit.' Then Miss Frost arched her left eyebrow and glared at me doubtfully. 'You have a great many talents, Miss Pocket – self-delusion, bad manners, general insufferability – but as for you being the saviour of an entire kingdom? I think not. Besides, the legend goes that the Dual will be a girl of high birth. Which rather excludes a common maid, don't you think?'

I huffed. 'Hideous woman!'

Then my mind flew to yet another confounding question.

'So if Miss Always is a Gatekeeper, what are you?'

'I am Mistress of the Clock,' said the governess, smoothing down the folds of her dress. 'My vocation is to chronicle the Clock Diamond's history in my book, monitor its use and ensure its survival.'

Which was awfully troubling. 'If you wish to ensure the stone's survival, and you know that it kills the innocent,' I said, 'how are you any different to Miss Always?'

Miss Frost bristled. She may have even fumed. 'I seek to use the stone *ethically*, capturing souls that are nearing the end of their lives here in this world. Miss Always cares little who the necklace kills – young or old, healthy or ill. And she seeks to possess the diamond as a way of controlling the fate of Prospa. We are *nothing* alike, Miss Pocket!'

'Don't burst your girdle, dear,' I said with heartbreaking good taste, 'it was just a question.'

The governess stood up. 'Hand me the Clock Diamond.'

I wanted to protest (it was awfully tempting), but I didn't.

The governess took the necklace from my hand and hung it around my neck. 'Right now it seems you are the only person in the world this stone cannot hurt.' She slipped the diamond under the top of my dress. 'Tell no one about it. Let no one see it. Understand, Miss Pocket?'

I nodded.

Then Miss Frost pulled an envelope from her pocket and handed it to me. 'Go to this address the moment you arrive in London.'

I pursed my lips. 'And what will I find there?'

'What you have always wanted. A home. A family.'

I gasped. My mouth dropped open. 'A family? Who? Who are they?'

'Good people.' Miss Frost saw the curious look upon my face and sighed. 'They have always wanted a child and as it happens, I have one to spare.'

I gulped. Such a thing did not seem *possible*. 'You have told them all about me?'

Miss Frost frowned. 'Not everything.'

'This is monstrously unexpected,' I said rather meekly. 'Perhaps they should meet me first ... What I mean is, I am *certain* they will adore me – how could they not? – but perhaps they should at least see me before –'

'Just be yourself, Miss Pocket,' said the governess. 'The rest will take care of itself. Think of it as a new beginning. A fresh start.' Her eyes softened. 'Be happy, Miss Pocket.'

I nodded. Didn't speak. Couldn't really.

Miss Frost lifted her gaze, her eyes cool and sharp once more. 'When Miss Always returns, she will think I have spirited you far away. The last place she will think to look for you is in London – the daughter of a thoroughly respectable business-man and his charming wife.'

The word *daughter* thrilled me so.

'What is their business?' I said, rather excitedly. 'They build railways, don't they? Or perhaps they own hotels or banks or gold fields. Oh, it is sure to be gloriously important!'

Miss Frost allowed a faint smile. 'They make coffins, Miss Pocket.'

The train rolled into the station, great puffs of steam billowing around our feet. Miss Frost picked up my bag and placed it in my hand. 'You must not miss this train.'

The time had come to ask the only question that really mattered.

'Miss Frost, who was my mother?'

The governess did not hesitate. She said, 'Your mother is dead. Beyond that, I cannot help you.' She pointed at the train. 'Do hurry. It is about to depart.'

I walked solemnly to the first class carriage, where the stationmaster took my ticket. The carriage door was shutting behind me when I heard Miss Frost call my name.

She put a hand upon the window and said, 'You will not see me, but I will be about.'

I nodded. 'Yes, I thought you might.'

Then the carriage door closed and the whistle blew as the train moved out of the station. I quickly found my seat and looked out of the window. Miss Frost had not waited to see the train roll away. She was already on her horse, galloping to destinations unknown. And as shocking as it may seem, I missed her already.

Epilogue

Lulled by the train's jolting rhythm, my mind wandered to lost friends. Mr Banks. Rebecca. And in a strange way, Miss Always. For I had lost her too.

And my mother.

For so long I had harboured a fantasy that she would come and take me home. But that wasn't to be. It was foolish to pretend it didn't hurt. But if these new sorrows settled inside me like a morning fog, shrouding my hopes and making happiness difficult to find – well, I felt certain it would not last. Misery did not suit me. I wasn't the type. And while I still had questions about the Clock Diamond and why it hadn't killed me, I refused to fret over them. I was bound for London. A new life. A family of my very own. There were sure to be wonderful parties. And glorious dresses. And a great deal of cake (not to mention raw potatoes). I won't deny a few nerves as I thought about all that was to come. But despite my fears and my sorrows, one thing was perfectly clear – I would be the most adored (slightly) dead girl in all of London. Perhaps even England.

Which was really no great surprise – for I have all the natural instincts of a coffin-maker's daughter.

Acknowledgements

Thank yous are a revolting business. One is expected to gush and praise wildly. Make heartfelt declarations of appreciation and whatnot. It's monstrous! Why on earth must I acknowledge people, simply because their efforts were instrumental in getting this book into print? Yet, if I don't offer undying gratitude to the small army of people who helped bring Ivy Pocket lovingly to life, then there will be hell to pay. As such, I will be brief.

Madeleine Milburn is utterly dedicated, hugely effective and awfully loyal. As far as literary agents go, I suspect she is one of the very best. Her able assistant is Cara Lee Simpson. She is smart and astute and thoroughly pleasant.

On the publishing side, there is Ellen Holgate. She is an editor by trade. Ellen works for Bloomsbury UK. She is very clever and terribly well regarded. And she has the infuriating habit of being right a great deal of the time. Rebecca McNally is the very best publishing director a delusional twelve-year-old maid could ask for. Helen Vick did everything that a managing editor should do and was a pleasure to work with. As was Polly Whybrow. John Kelly is an illustrator who seems to have wit and whimsy pouring from his fingertips. He has taken my cast of eccentric oddballs and produced a set of illustrations that amuse and delight.

At Bloomsbury and many other publishers around the world, there are teams of people who have done terrifically important work in bringing this book to market. If *Anyone But Ivy Pocket* roars into the bestseller lists, I offer you all my heartfelt thanks and a thousand good thoughts. But if Miss Pocket finds herself in the discount bin six months from now, then I wish each and every one of you a lifetime of disappointment and regret. Which is rather harsh, but there you are.

Closer to home, there are parents. Mine are above average and I thank them. Paul printed whatever needed printing. Carol urged me to stop waffling and write the damn book. Various nephews and nieces feigned interest from time to time – especially Shannon and Kaelin. While another took the time to regularly ask me how I might feel should this book be a colossal failure – thank you, Dylan. Which brings this torturous grovelling to a close.

And if you happen to still be reading this, and you know what books can do – how they are a door to another world, how they are a refuge and a wonderland, how they thrill and comfort, how they break hearts and kindle hope – well, there is no need for me to thank you as well. For you already know that life is simply better with books.

And with that in mind, I would urge you to go out this instant and choose your next adventure.

C. Krisp, Esq.

BUTTERFIELD
PARK

Somebody Stop Ivy Pocket

A Preview of Sorts

By

The Author

My task here, dear Reader, is really very simple – I wish to tease and tempt you with a tantalising glimpse of what befalls our heroine in the next part of her remarkable adventure. I am going to assume that you have only just finished reading *Anyone But Ivy Pocket* – I will also assume that you are now so devoted to Ivy that the thought of waiting until the publication of the next book fills you with unspeakable misery and a strong desire to tear out your hair. Which is not nearly as much fun as it sounds. Much better to tear out somebody else's hair. Or better yet, read what follows …

I am about to reveal a great deal regarding the events chronicled in *Somebody Stop Ivy Pocket*. I shall describe in glorious and captivating detail exactly what befalls Ivy when she reaches London and begins a new life with the Snagsbys.

Get comfortable. Have a glass of lemonade at hand. Perhaps a cupcake. The odd bowl of popcorn. Your best pair of slippers and whatnot. For I am about to begin …

Oh but *where* to begin? *Somebody Stop Ivy Pocket* is positively bursting with mystery and adventure. With danger and treachery. I could describe how Ivy befriends a gorilla with a peg leg and a tragic secret, giving you a heart-stopping account of how they collect driftwood, bedsheets and abandoned puppies and use them to defeat an evil, fire-breathing milkmaid. Or I could make your blood run cold as I offer you a terrifying glimpse of the moment Ivy falls into a shallow puddle and isn't seen again for seven chapters.

The trouble is, none of these things actually happen. What *does* happen is monstrously unexpected and rather thrilling. And I would tell you all about it, if I wasn't so busy writing the infernal thing!

What I can say is that Ivy will find that her new life is not exactly as she imagined. The past casts a long shadow. London is a rather dangerous place. And friends are hard to find.

To say any more would spoil things, don't you think? I am almost certain it will be worth the wait. I advise you to put down this book and wait quietly on a park bench until the next part of Ivy's great adventure is ready.

Until then, farewell.

If you want to encounter this charming,
and only slightly demented, heiress:

Or this perfectly lovely (and possibly murderous) librarian:

Or even these two humpbacked horrors:

then you simply must read
SOMEBODY STOP IVY POCKET,
out May 2016